"Come see the kitchen. It's my favorite room..."

"I like the bar stools."

That amused Ben. "What about the rest?"

Ella turned back to him, her face glowing. "It's beautiful, Ben. I can't believe this is our old cottage."

"Well, it really isn't, Ella. That was torn down, remember? But I like to think it is in spirit, anyway."

"That's a lovely thought." She moved closer.

His heart swelled. "Ella, I—"

Her upturned face was shining with pleasure. He could barely hear what she was murmuring over the pounding in his chest.

"This isn't a good idea, Ben."

He closed his eyes. "Yeah. You're right. Guess we better head back."

He swallowed hard against the lump in his throat. She was leaving the next day and he had a sinking feeling that this might have been his last chance to prove they could go back in time.

Dear Reader,

The Christmas Promise is the second book in my Lighthouse Cove series about a tragic prank that brought long-lasting consequences to the teenage girls involved. The first book, *His Saving Grace*, is the story of one of the key figures in the prank.

But there were two victims of that prank—the youth who died and the girl who was blamed, Ella Jacobs. Ella's determination to expose the truth of that tragedy pits her against Ben Winters, her teenage crush, as well as the entire Winters family. Ben's instinct is to protect his family from public scrutiny and to hide his own secrets. His dilemma is that he's also determined to recapture his summer love with Ella, the girl he never forgot.

Can one be forgiven for a thoughtless act? Is love enough to withstand the guilt and shame of that act? These are some of the questions that led me to give life to Ella and Ben, to show their struggle to regain their love and trust in each other. As they eventually learn, happy-ever-after also depends on acceptance by a whole community.

Enjoy!

Janice Carter

HEARTWARMING

The Christmas Promise

Janice Carter

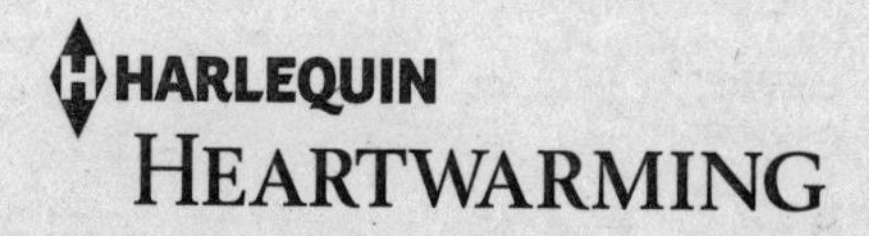

Recycling programs for this product may not exist in your area.

ISBN-13: 978-1-335-17971-5

The Christmas Promise

This edition published by arrangement with Harlequin Books S.A.

For questions and comments about the quality of this book, please contact us at CustomerService@Harlequin.com.

Harlequin Enterprises ULC
22 Adelaide St. West, 40th Floor
Toronto, Ontario M5H 4E3, Canada
www.Harlequin.com

Printed in U.S.A.

Writing has been a passion for **Janice Carter** since elementary school, but her second career (after teaching) began with the publication of a Harlequin Intrigue novel many years ago. Janice says she's been very lucky to be able to do what she enjoys most—writing about the connections between people, their families and the places where they live. And of course, love is always at the heart of those connections.

Books by Janice Carter

Harlequin Heartwarming

For Love of a Dog
Her Kind of Hero
His Saving Grace

Visit the Author Profile page at Harlequin.com for more titles.

For my family—Peter, Andrea, Kirk, Marina, Cheryl and, last but definitely not least, Sybil

CHAPTER ONE

BEN WINTERS OPENED the door to Novel Thinking, his sister's bookstore, simultaneously cursing and admiring Grace for her skillful manipulation. He was beginning to think he didn't know his little sister half as well as he thought. Either that, or some parallel-dimension version of Grace Winters had moved into Lighthouse Cove. Certainly, the unnerving events of the past five months were proof of that theory. After the shock of her upending the whole family clan with a revelation about the past, along with the news that she'd fallen in love with a man she'd only recently met, Ben no longer knew what to expect from her.

Yet here he was, waiting on Grace's behalf to greet a guest author invited for a book talk and signing. And not just any author, but *Ella Jacobs*. Ben supposed that if he read fiction rather than history, he might have discovered sooner that the girl who'd stolen his heart seventeen years ago was now a published author. A young adult fiction author, Grace clarified. Then she'd given him a definition of that term, which he hadn't paid the slightest attention to because all he'd heard was the sentence that she'd opened with—*Ella's coming to the Cove!*

Since his sister's announcement, Ben had browsed the internet for all references to Ella Jacobs or E. M. Jacobs, her writing name. Of course, he'd made a few Ella Jacobs internet searches since he'd last seen her, even throughout some of the four years of his marriage, but he hadn't done so since his return to the Cove, where reminders of Ella Jacobs were everywhere.

He'd already known that she'd graduated with a degree in journalism from NYU and was currently a reporter for the *Boston Globe.* In his latest search, he'd found a short Wikipedia bio that highlighted her recent debut as a fiction writer and mentioned articles she'd written for journals and magazines. Ben had stared long and hard at the single line referring to her marriage and divorce. She'd gone on with her life, just as he had with his.

He forced himself away from the what-if that instantly arose as it had so many times the past few years. He'd tried—half-heartedly, he had to admit—to persuade Grace to cancel the invite. *What can possibly be gained by this impulsive decision?* he'd asked her. He'd almost said *reckless* decision, because that's what it was. *There's no going back*, he'd pointed out. Then she'd gazed up at him with big dark eyes that were identical to his, and he had a flash of a young Gracie begging a favor from her big brother. He'd given in as he once used to, struggling to ignore the echo in his head—*this is not a good idea.*

He walked the length of the narrow store, flicking on lights as he went. The place could be gloomy, especially now in mid-December. What it needed was a makeover. Get rid of the dark wood paneling, put in a few skylights and ceiling pot lights, enlarge the front windows and substitute the oak door for a glass one. So far in her time as manager, Grace had refused to consider any kind of reno. She'd always been drawn to old things and seemed to like it just the way it was. Besides, the store barely eked out a living and Ben knew the family construction business was in no position to undertake a free renovation. The purchase of the bookstore had been an impulsive act by their father, Charles, who reasoned having some kind of employment would keep Grace in the Cove.

Well, that worked, Pop!

Now that she was engaged to the Coast Guard guy from Portland, Drew Spencer, there was no guarantee Grace would settle permanently in the Cove much less run the bookstore. However, the lighthouse restoration project she'd undertaken with Henry Jenkins and Spencer last summer would assure her presence for a while, at least until the memorial site for their cousin Brandon was completed. The whole family was still recovering from the shock of Grace's admission months ago about her role in the prank that had led to Brandon's drowning. Then Grace had dropped another bombshell. She'd invited Ella Jacobs to the Cove.

Why, Grace? What good could possibly come of this? he'd asked when she'd told him.

I have to do this, Ben. I can't ease my soul by confessing only to the family. What happened to Ella was unfair. She took the blame. I have to make things right between us.

The earnestness in her face had stopped Ben from saying that none of it could possibly be made right. Brandon was dead. No confessions and apologies could ever change that. And he was just as much to blame—something he'd hoped Ella Jacobs would never have to learn.

EXCEPT FOR THE sprawl of new housing extending west of the town on the other side of the highway to Portland, Lighthouse Cove hadn't changed quite as much as she had, Ella decided, parking in front of The Lighthouse Hotel. The idea that the Cove now had a subdivision was ironic enough to bring a half smile. A big reason she and her family spent every summer here had been to escape the Boston suburb where they lived.

She was tired after the two-hour drive but didn't rush to get out of the car. She'd had to get up early to meet with her publisher, pick up a box of books for tomorrow's presentation and swing by her office at the *Globe* to submit an article for the upcoming Saturday edition. Her boss and his boss had agreed to her request for a month's leave from her job as city reporter as long as she was willing to post an op-ed piece each Saturday.

Initially Ella had been reluctant to shift from a reporting job to a columnist's, but once she'd started, she'd liked the change. It gave her an opportunity to express her thoughts on any topic, and she found—to her surprise—that she had plenty of opinions. It also freed her up to devote time exclusively to her debut novel's promotion. The book was the result of almost a year of therapy. *You're still carrying around the baggage of a summer seventeen years ago*, her therapist had observed. *Perhaps you could write about it in some way.*

Ella had resisted the idea for months until one sleepless night, haunted by the recurring flashbacks she'd had off and on since that summer, she'd booted up her laptop and begun to write. Surprisingly, the first draft had been completed within three months, and a contact with a Boston agent had fast-tracked her submission to a publisher. The whole process had taken a bit more than a year. Yet even now, Ella wasn't at all certain if the work had successfully erased the still-vivid memory of that awful night.

In retrospect, her thrill at finding a note from Ben Winters tucked into the bag of books she'd received from his sister, Grace, that summer had definitely ruled out rational thought. The day before the end-of-summer beach bonfire, he'd told her he'd be packing for his drive to college at the end of the holiday weekend and couldn't make it to the annual event. Disappointed, she'd told Grace and Cassie Fielding, Grace's school friend, that she couldn't make it to the bonfire either. But when she found Ben's note—*Meet me at the path to the lighthouse about 8 tonight. I want to say goodbye—in private!*—all that changed. Forever, as it turned out.

So here she was, after all this time, in Lighthouse Cove, Maine—the vacation paradise that was ruined for her when she realized that life could be cruel. Worse, that *she* could be cruel. Ella unsnapped her seat belt and reached for her handbag. The card that Grace Winters had sent in care of her publisher fell out, and she picked it up, then read the message for the umpteenth time.

Dear Ella,

I was thrilled to learn about your debut

novel, which I have just finished reading. It's a wonderful book and I've purchased some copies for the bookstore I'm managing in the Cove. Maybe you remember the town's only bookstore, Novel Thinking? I came back to the Cove almost a year ago, after my father's heart surgery. When Henry Jenkins retired, Dad bought the bookstore and I agreed to run it. My brother, Ben, has also moved back home.

Anyway, I was wondering if you'd be interested in coming for a book signing and talk sometime in the next couple of weeks? I realize that the time frame is short, but I've been out of town. It would be lovely to see you again and catch up on the last seventeen years! You can email me at the address below. I'm hoping you'll be able to come.
Sincerely, Grace Winters

Ella had received the card only three weeks ago, but it had drawn her thoughts every single day since—not for what was written but for what was missing. No reference to the prank. No hint of an apology. Not one word of remorse. She'd been tempted many times to toss it into the recycling bin, but a single sentence held her back. *My brother, Ben, has also moved back home.* It was almost pathetic that those few words could override common sense, but they had. She impulsively emailed Grace to tell her she would come. Afterward, every instinct warned her she was making a mistake, yet here she was, parked in front of a hotel that had always enchanted her and where she'd booked a superior deluxe room for two nights. While her advance for *Always Be Mine* was modest, this felt like the perfect chance to splurge a little. Ella took a deep breath and stowed Grace's card in her purse.

Well, she told herself, *you've made a commitment, but if it all goes downhill from here—which is a real possibility—you can cancel that second night.* She reached into the back seat of her car for her tote bag and small suitcase, left the box of books in the trunk, and headed into the hotel. As soon as she entered the lobby, Ella realized that one's childhood memories can be deceiving. Sure, the enormous chandelier still dangled from the ceiling, but the luster of the wood paneling had dimmed. The assortment of chairs and love seats scattered in the center of the lobby were a curious mismatch of Victorian and modern—fake leather vying with faded velveteen for attention that neither achieved. She paused for a moment to take it all in, guessing that this would be only the first of her Cove childhood memories to be altered. She walked to reception, noticing a few stains and scuff marks here and there on the marble floor.

It took the young man on the other side of the wood counter several seconds to notice her presence. “Oh sorry. I didn’t see you coming in.”

“I have a reservation for two nights. E. M. Jacobs.”

He scanned the desktop computer in front of him and looked up to say, “Oh yes, here it is. A superior deluxe room.”

“With a waterfront view.”

“Right. A good choice.”

Trying in vain to calm the nervousness she felt already mounting inside, Ella drummed her fingertips on the counter while the man—his name badge read Rohan—checked her in.

When he handed back her credit card, Ella asked, “Does the rate include breakfast?”

"No, sorry. We don't have a restaurant, but there's a very nice café, Mabel's, just down the street. Here you are. Room 410, top floor. The elevator is down there—" he pointed left "—at the far corner of the lobby. Will there be anything else?"

"I'm good. Thanks." Ella slung her handbag over her shoulder, grabbed her tote and wheeled her suitcase toward the elevator. The fourth-floor hallway was deserted, and as Ella walked along, looking for 410, she saw that all of the doors were new—some kind of metal made to look like wood—with locks to accommodate the card key she'd been given. Upgrading of sorts was obviously happening in the hotel. But not yet inside the rooms, Ella amended as she pushed open the door. She stood on the threshold, wondering which superior deluxe room had been pictured on the hotel's website. *Definitely not this one.* She sighed, thinking one night might be it, after all, for her stay in the Cove.

Before unpacking, Ella pushed aside the heavy velvet drapes in the bay window across from the double bed. At least the waterfront view lived up to its hype. She'd never seen the town from this perspective and at this time of year. Given the passage of time as well as the wintry landscape, she needed a few seconds to identify familiar landmarks. The wooden boardwalk on the water side of Main Street seemed wider, now it was covered in snow, but the stairs connecting that upper level to the walkway below, running along the water's edge, were still there.

Ella's family had often strolled along that walkway, licking cones from Tina's Ice Cream Parlor and gawking at the collection of pleasure boats and fishing trawlers moored there. Back then, the marina had been full of boats. Today it was basically empty, though Ella assumed most boats had been hauled up on shore somewhere for the winter. She scanned the bay beyond the marina. The open water was dark and forbidding, not the deep sea-green of summer. Far out in the larger Casco Bay, she thought she saw blocks of floating ice or snow but decided they could also be whitecaps.

The business section of town looked the same, except for a line of snow-covered planters decorated for the holiday season with large red bows, and lampposts with hanging baskets of spruce or cedar boughs. The main road—Main Street—curved toward a residential area, which included summer cottages beyond. Ella squinted. She could barely see them, but the cupolas of the twin turrets of the Winters family home partially emerged from the bare branches of the trees around the upper story of the house. Was Grace still living there? Or Ben? No. Likely, they'd both found places of their own. Especially if they were married. *If Ben was married.* Ella firmly pushed aside that thought. What did it matter?

Her eyes strained against the sunlight reflecting off snow, trying to locate the cottage her family had rented each of the ten years they'd vacationed in the Cove. She remembered it had been on the land side of the last street before the beach, tucked into the hill leading up to Grace's house, so not visible from this vantage point. Farther east, where the paved road ended in gravel and the long arm of the cove began, was Cassie Fielding's house. Ella couldn't see it either, but every cell in her body sensed its presence. If she let her eyes follow the snowy beach and rocky peninsula farther along, there was the lighthouse. Ella dropped the curtain and turned away from the window.

An hour later she'd showered and unpacked the few things she'd brought—the tailored slacks and scarlet cowl-necked sweater for her talk, a backup black skirt and cream blouse, and a pair of jeans and a more casual turtleneck for anything else she might do in town. She shouldn't need more clothes—she doubted she'd be in the Cove for more than the two nights she'd booked. That would be plenty of time to accomplish what she'd planned.

When she finished blow-drying her hair, she changed into the black jeans and cobalt blue turtleneck for her meeting with Grace. She posed briefly in front of the long mirror hanging on the outside the bathroom door. She seldom thought much about her appearance—that side of her had disappeared long ago—but the possibility that she might encounter Ben somewhere in town had her nervously self-doubting every aspect of her mirror image.

Since her talk wasn't until the next day, Ella decided to leave her car in the parking space out front of the hotel and walk to the bookstore. The cool air would be invigorating and help calm her nerves. Grace had emailed directions, not that Ella had needed them, and less than fifteen minutes later she was standing on the sidewalk, reading the stenciled signs on the front door window—Novel Thinking and, below it, Henry Jenkins Prop. Grace had mentioned that Henry had retired. Frankly, Ella had been slightly surprised that he was still alive, since he'd seemed old seventeen years ago. But when she was sixteen, everyone over thirty verged on old age.

Every summer she and Grace had divided their wish list of books and shared them, until that last summer, when her interest in books had flagged whenever Ben Winters was around. Ella took a deep breath. *That's old history now, Jacobs. Get on with this.* She had no idea what she was going to say to Grace or how their meeting would go. Better to let Grace take the lead, since she'd sent the invite. And *she* was the one who would have to make the apology. That's what Ella had come for after all. Not really to speak to a handful of people about her book. No. She wanted to look Grace Winters right in the eye. She wanted to hear "I'm sorry" in person. Hopefully today, but definitely before she left the Cove for the very last time.

Ella counted to ten and pushed open the door. The bell above it tinkled, and a memory of the store's cool dark interior juxtaposed against hot summer days rushed at her, causing her to stop suddenly to catch her breath. She could see the faint yellow glow of a lamp ahead, but otherwise there was no sign of anyone.

"Hello?" Clearing her throat, Ella managed another "Hello" before walking toward the light. On the way, she passed a table set up with a poster that she knew her publisher had sent and some of her books, which Grace must have purchased. The adult Grace Winters seemed to be more organized than the teen one. But the store itself hadn't changed much except for a computer in place of the big cash register that had once perched on the central counter. The only thing missing was Henry himself, though considering the heavy stomp of footsteps coming up the stairs from below, Ella figured he just might magically appear. Unless Grace was wearing very big shoes.

The door behind the counter swung open

and a large masculine figure loomed at the top of the staircase. Not Henry. Definitely not Grace. *Ben.*

Ella tried, but failed, to speak.

He moved into the orbit of the lamplight, and Ella's first thought was, *Ben—yet not Ben. Not the one in my memory anyway.*

"Ella," he said, his voice deeper than she remembered. He was carrying a cardboard carton, which he set down on the counter as he moved toward her.

Her next thought was that he wasn't surprised to see her. Well, of course, Grace would have told him about her visit.

"Um, I trust you had a good trip here."

Small talk? After seventeen years? She'd have rallied to make some indignant retort, but her brain, chugging along in first gear, was trying to process this adult version of the Ben Winters she'd dreamed about daily the summer she was sixteen. The pitch-black curly hair that once had bordered on being a tad too long was now shorter. His neck and torso had broadened into the firm, muscular shape of a man who kept fit. But his face, even with its shadow of bristles, was the same. Thick eyebrows above inky black eyes and the Winters nose, more prominent now in manhood, that Ella remembered from his father's face. Lines around the eyes and the circles beneath them told another story about this grown-up version of Ben, and for one irrational second Ella wanted to reach out a hand to touch his face and learn that story. Of course, she stopped short of anything more than "Hello. I was expecting Grace."

"Sorry. Grace had to run some errands, but she asked me to hang around in case you arrived before she got back."

"If the store was closed, I'd have returned later." She noticed his slight wince and adjusted her tone. "I mean, she needn't have imposed on you."

He gave a half-hearted shrug. "Yeah, well... you know Gracie."

It was exactly the comment he might have made back then and for a moment Ella was mentally transported to Ben's bedroom, its poster-lined walls and desk cluttered with books—and her, sprawled next to him on the floor at the foot of his bed, their heads connected by earphones and bobbing silently in unison to the summer playlist. She shifted her attention to the display table, unable to look at him any longer, afraid of what she might say.

"She…uh…she should be here any second," he added.

Ella didn't dare look up. His flat voice told her he was as uncomfortable as she was. The quiet room closed in on her. She'd resolved to make her comeback to the Cove as the strong, confident woman she'd grown into, not the tongue-tied sixteen-year-old completely in love—or so she'd thought—with Grace's big brother. This wasn't a good start.

Then anger rose, choking any chance of normal conversation. Anger at herself, for reverting so instantly to that smitten teenager, and especially at Grace, who surely could have done her last-minute shopping later. Unless… No, she wouldn't have. *Would she?*

Ella sighed, yielding to the dark suspicion that once again, Grace had set her up.

CHAPTER TWO

BEN COULDN'T TAKE his eyes off her. The girl he'd developed a crush on when he was eighteen was definitely no longer a girl. The curves beneath her black jeans and short black down winter jacket were testament to the very obvious fact that Ella Jacobs was all grown up. But there were other signs of maturity, too, especially around the eyes; a gossamer web of lines at the corners and pale circles beneath that looked as though she'd tried to conceal them with makeup. Her shoulder-length hair was styled differently than he remembered, but her eyes were the same dazzling azure, and right then, they met his with an intensity that made him shift his attention to the display table behind her.

"Um, Grace has set up a table for your books and she thought you might be able to sign some now to save time tomorrow. She should be back soon." He peered at his watch to avert her steely eyed expression. "She went to pick up coffee and stuff for after your talk." He heard her give a loud sigh.

"Sure. Whatever. Guess I might as well."

She walked over to the table and set her tote bag on it, slung her shoulder bag on the back of a chair and then unzipped her jacket. When she turned around, Ben had to look away again, struck by the brilliance of the formfitting blue sweater against her pale ash-blond hair. Yeah, the girl was most definitely a woman now—a beautiful one.

He watched her unpack items from the tote bag, wishing he could think of something to say that wouldn't be inane or just plain foolish. There was a time when he and Ella didn't need small talk. For a few weeks that summer, they'd seemed to be able to read each other's minds and finish sentences for one another no matter the topic. But now the weight of knowing there was one subject he had to avoid at all costs pressed in on him. *If only Grace would come back.*

When she was settled with a pile of books in front of her and marker in hand, Ella looked up. "Feel free to finish whatever you were doing when I got here."

Her comment stung. This was how two people acted when they hadn't seen each other for seventeen years? He realized he'd deluded himself about the whole return-to-the-Cove scenario he'd been picturing ever since Grace had told him Ella was coming back.

"Sure," he said and began to unpack the carton Grace had asked him to bring up from the basement. Except for the scratching of Ella's marker as she signed books, silence filled the room while he took out paper cups, napkins and paper plates from the box. He'd just finished when he heard the doorbell tinkle, and relief worked its way up from the pit of his stomach. Grace was back.

Ben noticed right away that his sister was as nervous as he was, although someone who didn't know her might mistake her bubbly greeting for enthusiasm. "Good heavens, you're here! Welcome back to the Cove, Ella."

Grace placed two shopping bags on the cash counter and extended both arms as if to hug her, but Ella quickly grabbed Grace's right hand in a limp shake. Grace's beaming smile slipped a bit and Ben felt sorry for her.

"I hope Ben has been entertaining you in my absence."

Ella shot a bemused expression his way. "Hmm, have you, Ben?"

He felt Grace's eyes on him and knew she was correctly interpreting the heat in his face and his half-hearted shrug. This reunion was going downhill rapidly.

"I'm thrilled that you accepted my invitation, Ella," Grace went on to say. "People—especially teenage girls—have been coming into the store all week to ask about your presentation and buy your book."

Ella smiled for the first time. "That's wonderful. Thanks for inviting me, Grace."

"Are you staying at The Lighthouse Hotel?"

"Yes I am." She gave a small laugh. "I was always so enchanted by that place as a kid, but now I realize it's seen better days."

Grace glanced quickly at Ben. He guessed what she was thinking.

"That's true. Our cousin Suzanna is the owner now, and she's been struggling. The Cove has had some tough years since the lobster industry here collapsed, but you probably saw the new development on the highway as you drove in. That's Ben's pet project these days," Grace explained.

"Did you go into architecture, then?" She turned to him.

"I did, but since I've been working for my father, I've become more interested in the building part of it rather than the designing." Ben saw right away that she was thinking back to one of their favorite conversations that summer—*what to do when we grow up.* His dream had been to design world-class buildings all over the world, like those of I. M. Pei. He knew she was a reporter but wondered what had happened to her vow to become an investigative journalist—the kind who traveled the world to expose conspiracies or political scandals. In spite of this inauspicious meeting, Ben was curious to find out what had become of her own teenage aspirations.

"When you're finished here, would you like to have a walk around the town with me? See how it's changed?" he impulsively asked.

"Sure."

Not exactly an overwhelming reaction, Ben thought, but it was a first step. Toward what, he couldn't say. Reconciliation seemed unrealistic.

The doorbell sounded. "That'll be a customer. Would you mind putting this stuff away for me in the fridge in the storeroom, Ben?" Grace tilted her head toward the back of the store. "And, Ella, I was hoping to treat you to dinner tonight. How about I meet you in the hotel lobby at six?"

"Oh? Thanks, Grace." Ella pushed aside the books she'd signed. "That's probably enough for now. Do you have any idea how many people will show up tomorrow? My publisher sent me with a box of books, as well."

"I'm not sure," Grace said.

Ben caught a glimpse of her frown as he walked by her with the grocery bags. He wondered if she was put off by the lack of enthusiasm for the dinner invite. He stowed the cream, milk and baked goods in the fridge, and by the time he returned, Grace was talking to a customer and Ella was putting on her jacket.

"Do you want to have that walk now or would you prefer later in the afternoon?" he asked.

"Now is okay. Unless you have to get back to work or something."

"I have some time off." In fact he'd taken the whole day off. "But if you'd rather…?"

"Now is fine. I'd planned to walk around anyway."

"Great. I'll get my coat." He retrieved his jacket from the closet in the back room, and when he returned, she was waiting by the front door. Grace flashed a thumbs-up signal that he found irritating. He wondered if the whole book-signing invite had been engineered to arrange this reunion. As much as he loved his sister, her tendency to plan and organize other people's affairs was vexing. He just hoped Ella didn't think he had anything to do with the scheme.

He noticed Ella's expensive-looking leather boots as he followed her out the door. "Um, will those be okay for walking around? The main sidewalks will be cleared, but I can't vouch for the side streets."

"I think they'll be okay. If not, you might have to carry me."

Right there in the glint in her eyes, Ben saw the teenage Ella. He smiled. "I'm sure I could handle that."

She quickly glanced away as if she didn't want to be caught smiling, too.

"Anywhere in particular first?"

"You're my tour guide. You decide."

"Maybe up to Town Square, then backtrack

down to Main Street and my favorite bakery and coffee shop."

"Sounds good. Lead on, then."

A thin layer of old, packed snow remained on the sidewalks, enough to worry about slipping if you weren't careful. That prompted Ben to place his hand against the small of her back, but as soon as he did so, Ella gave a slight twist, shaking off his touch. The subtle move reminded him that as much as he wanted to believe they could revert to their teenage selves, they were eons away from that time. The most he could hope for, he now realized with a pang, would be a tenuous reacquaintance. The kind you experience with old friends at high school reunions.

They walked up Porter Street toward the square in the center of town. There hadn't been a fresh snowfall in days. People in town were complaining, but as Ben's mother kept saying, "Be careful what you wish for." It was a sentiment Ben totally agreed with. The construction business ran more efficiently without a lot of snow on the ground, and Winters Building Ltd. couldn't afford to lose any more business.

Ella suddenly spoke. "I've never seen the Cove in winter."

Ben turned to look at her. "I hadn't thought of that. You always got to see it at the best time of year."

"True. I'm not a big fan of winter, but there's a kind of rugged beauty to it."

"Me neither," he admitted. "But you're right, it can be beautiful."

"I take it you haven't been here much in winter yourself the last few years. Grace implied you only came back when your father had his surgery."

"Dad's surgery was in January last year, so this is my second winter. I've come back for a few Christmases over the years, but only for a couple of days."

"Sounds like you didn't get home much."

"No."

"Why was that?"

"Too many bad memories." The answer slipped out before he could stop it, and Ben silently cursed himself for raising the topic to be avoided at all costs. *That summer weekend.*

She fell silent and, keeping her eyes on the square ahead, suddenly marched forward as if in a hurry to catch a bus. Ben caught up to her when she halted at the south end of the square. A skating rink, framed by a series of long wooden benches, covered most of that area. Except for a couple putting on skates, the place was deserted.

"This'll be full of people on the weekend," Ben commented, noticing Ella looking at the rink. Then he pointed to the north end closest to the town hall. A crane hovered over the top of a giant Christmas tree while a man leaned from its bucket to install a large star. Other workers on ladders were weaving strings of lights through the tree branches. Yellow warning tape had been set up around the perimeter of the site, and beyond it, groups of people mingled, watching the decorating.

"That must be pretty when it's lit."

"It is. The official lighting ceremony is this Saturday night." He hesitated. "Will you be here for it by any chance?"

She glanced quickly at him before turning her gaze back to the tree. "I'm booked into the hotel for two nights, so no, afraid not."

His disappointment took him aback. Hadn't Grace already told him Ella was in town for two or three days at the most? He really had to stop kidding himself about her return. In fact it wasn't a return at all—just a short visit. Nothing more. "There's the new library." He pointed to the opposite side of the square. "We're hoping it'll be finished by early spring. Work on it has stalled at the moment, waiting for town council to approve some additional expenses we proposed."

"Is your father's company building it?"

"Yeah." Ben wished he could reply "You mean *my* company."

"What used to be there?"

"The old movie theater. Remember The Clarion? I'm sure it was still here in our...when you..." He stopped abruptly, overcome by a memory flash of sitting in a cool, dark cinema on a hot summer day, holding hands with the girl standing beside him. Not *this* Ella, though.

"Oh yeah" was all she said, clearly untouched by the same association. "It'll be nice for the town to have its own library," she went on to say. "No more begging parents to drive to Portland for library books."

Her smile nudged Ben's spirits. "True. Grace sometimes complained about that, in spite of being a regular customer of Henry's."

"I envied her that, but she was always generous lending me the books she bought with her allowance, which was substantially larger than mine. How is Henry, by the way? Grace wrote that he'd retired."

"Just the same, though right now he's recuperating from a hip replacement. He's in a rehab hospital in Portland."

"Oh?" She frowned. "Well, I'm glad to hear he's recovering." She pivoted around, scanning the rest of the square. "It sure looks different in the winter. Bleaker, less inviting."

"Yep. Definitely not as welcoming as in the summer."

"My brother and I used to love the July Fourth parade and the stalls—especially the food and candy ones. Does all that still happen?"

The past July Fourth festivities were still very much on Ben's mind. He and his parents had met for the first time the man engaged to Grace—Drew Spencer, the Coast Guard officer whose mission to demolish the lighthouse had resulted in the family upheaval. One that was still reverberating. He pushed the memory aside. "Yes, with the same or maybe even more hoopla. By the way, how is your family? Your brother and parents?"

She looked away again. "My brother and his family are in Boston, but we don't see much of each other. They have busy lives."

"And your parents?"

"They divorced. My mother's still in Boston, too, but Dad moved back to Syracuse, where his family was from. He passed away two years ago."

"I'm sorry, Ella."

She swung around. "Why should *you* be sorry?"

The intensity in her face stunned him. "Just an expression. I feel bad for you, that's all."

"Dad's death was tough, but the divorce happened a long time ago."

After an uncomfortable moment, Ben ventured to ask, "So where to now? Want to see a bit of the new development the company's building? Then there's the harbor. Or the coffee shop?"

"Maybe the new subdivision. I could use more of a walk. Then the harbor. It's on the way back to the hotel."

Ben's vision of a chat over pastry and coffee at Mabel's vanished. *Time to stop kidding yourself, Winters.* "Let's head back to Main Street, then."

As they walked up the hill leading to the highway and the subdivision, Ben pointed out some of the newer businesses that had cropped up since Ella's last summer in the Cove. Other than an occasional "uh-huh," she seemed uninterested. Ben felt as if he were trudging through snowdrifts rather than shoveled sidewalks, his whole body weighed down further and further by the silence.

"No Tina's Ice Cream anymore?" she suddenly asked.

"They've retired. Moved to Florida."

"Hmm." She paused at the crest of the hill to the town below. "Can't say I blame them."

Ben knew then that the Ella his mind had preserved all these years was no more than an adolescent dream. He forced himself to disregard her obvious disdain for the town. Knowing what he did, could he blame her for that?

"My dad began that development four years ago." He pointed to the housing across the highway. "There were only about twenty houses then, and we've expanded to about a hundred, with plans to extend farther. Maybe to Portland city limits."

"Do you like working for your father?"

The unexpected question startled him. He recalled a few talks with sixteen-year-old Ella about his father's controlling ways. "It's only been a bit less than a year. I came back just before his heart surgery last January. It's been an adjustment for both of us." Ben kept his eyes on the housing project. Poor health and aging were taking their toll on Charles Winters. His low-key response to Grace's confession months ago was testament to that.

"And your mother? How is she?"

Ben appreciated the sudden warmth in her voice. There was still some trace of the old Ella in it. "She's good. The same. But she needed help with my dad, which is why Grace and I came home."

"And how was that for you? The homecoming?" Her eyes seemed to bore right into his.

"It's been fine," he lied. "I was looking for a change anyway. Shall we head back? You must be getting cold." He began heading down the hill, knowing any further explanation would be futile. He doubted she was really interested in how he felt about returning home. They were not the same two people who'd once shared confidences. That reality was sinking in very quickly.

When she caught up to him partway down the hill, she said, "Maybe I'll go back to the hotel now. I have some things to do before meeting Grace for dinner."

Ben stifled a sigh. Definitely no coffee. When they reached the hotel, he impulsively said, "Speaking of dinner, I'd love to take you out somewhere tomorrow evening."

There was the slightest hesitation before she said, "Sure. I'd like to see you again before I leave."

He felt a whoosh of relief at the chance to see her one last time. "Great. I'll get the details to you tomorrow. Have a nice evening with Grace."

"I fully intend to."

Her cool tone puzzled him, and he suddenly wanted to make up for not asking about her life after that summer. He grasped her hand. "I'm hoping we can catch up more tomorrow night. And thanks for coming back, Ella. It meant a lot to Gracie."

She casually withdrew her hand. "And me, too," she said, turning abruptly away to head up the steps to the hotel entrance.

Ben was confused by all her mixed messages, but perhaps dinner together would resolve this awkwardness between them. Then he remembered what he'd told Grace days ago. There was nothing to be gained by seeing Ella Jacobs again. Only everything to lose.

CHAPTER THREE

ELLA SAT ON the edge of the bed and painfully pulled off first one boot, then the other to gently massage her feet back to life. Contrary to what she'd told Ben, her footwear was totally inappropriate for more winter walking than from taxi to building in Boston. At least she'd had the sense to wear a thin pair of nylon socks rather than going barefoot inside the ankle-high, narrow-heeled leather boots.

If only she could as easily rub away her adolescent yearnings for Ben Winters. The walk around town was proof that their long-ago relationship—if it could even be called that—was basically dead. Stone-cold dead. Except for that frisson of heat when he'd grabbed hold of her hand just before she'd entered the hotel. Its jolt had unnerved her, and once out of his sight, she'd leaned against a lobby wall to catch her breath. Then she'd realized that this unexpected reaction was a reminder that coming back to Lighthouse Cove to do what she intended wasn't going to be easy.

Today had been the first challenge. Getting an apology tonight from Grace for what happened that summer would be another. And as for Ben…she wanted to know why he'd failed to support her that horrible Labor Day weekend. Face-to-face. Up-front and personal.

In spite of the heat blasting from the radiator in her room, Ella couldn't stop shivering. She slipped out of her clothes and stood under the shower until the stream of hot water ebbed to a trickle. Her skin was bright pink when she finally emerged from the bathroom, knotting the threadbare towel around her bosom. The hotel definitely had seen better days, she thought. She remembered the swift looks Ben and Grace had exchanged when she'd uttered that comment back at the bookstore, and Grace had mentioned something about the hotel's owner, Suzanna Winters, having difficulties. Ella hoped Suzanna would be far too busy with guests to be lurking in the lobby or reception area. Brandon's older sister was one person she didn't want to encounter during her stay. Ella knew that she—along with everyone else in town—probably still blamed her for what had happened to Brandon.

Every detail of the end-of-summer bonfire that Labor Day weekend was etched in her memory, as if it had happened months ago. She remembered the thrill of finding the note from Ben in the bag of books she'd borrowed from Grace and thinking how clever he'd been to hide it there. Obviously, he'd changed his mind about going to the bonfire, and once she found the note, she'd decided to go, too.

Grace and her friend Cassie hadn't been overly surprised to see her appear at the bonfire, a fact that Ella later realized should have been the first tip-off that something was up. But that night her thoughts were only about meeting Ben and maybe finding a dark, romantic corner of the beach to have some private time with him before he left for college.

She'd loved the old-fashioned touch of the note, something she'd never received from Ben before, and that, too, ought to have signaled something was off. Even when she bumped into Brandon on the path to the lighthouse, it had taken a few seconds for the realization to sink in that Ben had not sent her the note. Brandon had an identical one, signed *Ella*. A sudden burst of laughter from nearby bushes confirmed her suspicion that she and Brandon had been the victims of a prank. Years later, she connected the rush of humiliation at that moment to her response, tormenting herself with the awful thought that if she hadn't been so mean to Brandon, he might not have run off into the night toward the lighthouse. The place where he died.

Ella forced her thoughts back to the present. She'd worried before returning to the Cove that her mind would slip back into the past, and it was already happening. If she'd known Suzanna was now the hotel's owner, she'd have booked into a motel on the highway to Portland. *Too late now.*

After digging fresh lingerie out of her suitcase, she impulsively decided to get under the duvet on the queen-size bed. At least the comforter looked new and was invitingly soft and puffy. She'd been keeping a daily journal since the start of her book tour and temporary leave from the *Globe*, using her notes when she wrote her weekly op-ed piece. It was also a way to record her experiences during her travels, the dos and don'ts, should she ever have the luck to have another one.

As much as she'd enjoyed writing *Always Be Mine*, the work had essentially been a catharsis for everything she'd pent up inside over the past seventeen years. But during the tour, she'd received enough encouragement to foster the hope that perhaps she could write another novel, one that had nothing to do with that summer. It was something to think about when the pressures of her job at the *Globe* got to her.

She picked up her pen, cracked open a new page in the journal and wrote *Lighthouse Cove*. Tapping the end of the pen against her teeth, she thought back to the moment she saw Ben emerge from the basement at Novel Thinking. Until he'd smiled, he could have been a complete stranger, he'd changed so much. But that tentative smile along with the wisps of curls falling over his brow took her instantly back to the moment when she'd seen him for the first time at the start of the summer and known right then that Gracie's older brother would never again be just a shadow moving around the Winters home. He'd suddenly become her number one reason for hanging out at Grace's.

Ella jotted down a few words describing the adult version of that unexpectedly breathtaking presence: *rugged, taller, worry lines, larger nose, shorter hair, stubbled cheeks, broader shoulders*. Personality wise? She couldn't say yet. There'd been a couple glimpses of the younger Ben when he'd remarked, *You know Gracie*, and again when he'd flushed at her gibe that he might have to carry her. And the teenage Ben of her memory had reappeared briefly when they'd surveyed the subdivision his family company was building. She'd seen pride in his face and the same enthusiasm in his voice he'd had years ago, talking about his dream of being an architect.

Ella couldn't explain why, but for some reason the question about working for his father had popped out at that very moment, as she'd remembered the problems with his father that he'd once confided in her. His demeanor had shifted instantly, prompting her to ask about his mother. Ella had good memories of a kind and gentle Evelyn.

But she also had her own unhappy recollection of Charles Winters. He'd accompanied Brandon's father, Fred Winters, to see her parents the day Brandon's body had been found. Ella had hidden behind her mother as Brandon's father demanded to speak to Ella. Someone had told him she'd sent a note to Brandon arranging a meeting near the lighthouse. Ella would never forget his pained shouts, his voice cracking with emotion. She'd run to the back of the cottage, as far away from his anger as she could get. Later that afternoon while her parents were packing to leave the Cove, a day early at Ella's insistence, the police came. They showed the note to her and her parents. Could they ask Ella a few questions for their inquiry into Brandon Winters's drowning? It was a day permanently engraved on her mind and throughout all of it, she'd waited in vain for Ben to come to comfort her, to tell her he believed her.

Ella sighed. There was no point going over that time again. She'd returned here in order to move forward, knowing at the same time that occasionally glancing back would be part of the process. The key word here was *occasionally*. She couldn't go through with her plan if she was bogged down by memories.

She wrote a new heading: *Changes in the*

Cove. The library headed her list. It was a good change in town, though its construction was ongoing and Ben's comments implied it might not meet its opening deadline. Tina's Ice Cream Parlor was sadly gone, but Ella figured she had Mabel's to look forward to, given there was no breakfast in the hotel. Novel Thinking seemed to be exactly as it was when Henry Jenkins had owned it, and perhaps she'd have an opportunity to see him before she left. Ella drew an asterisk beside his name.

As for the subdivision that Ben was so clearly proud of, she was undecided if that was a good change to the Cove or not. Its layout seemed no different from Boston's suburban areas, and the housing designs were just as generic, which made his enthusiasm for it difficult to understand. What had happened to Ben's lofty dreams of becoming another I. M. Pei? Had he lost his vision? She sighed. It was unlikely she'd ever find the answers to those questions. The book talk was set for tomorrow at eleven, and Ella was thinking that despite Ben's invite to dinner, she might cancel and go back to Boston right away.

She'd handed in her op-ed piece for this

Saturday but hadn't yet come up with an idea for next week. Admittedly, she'd been seriously preoccupied with her return to Lighthouse Cove and meeting Grace—not to mention the possibility of seeing Ben—and had let her usual organized self go astray. Traipsing down memory lane, she'd lost her focus. Or had she unconsciously switched it from work responsibilities to her longtime desire for revenge? Ella thought about that. No, not revenge so much as vindication.

Ella guessed part of her agenda for coming back would be dealt with over dinner tonight. She had no idea how the scene might play out, but she did know she'd have to be fully alert and clear-minded. She wriggled down under the duvet and laid her head on the pillow. A good nap would help.

HER CELL PHONE alarm woke her half an hour before she was due to meet Grace. The fact that she'd actually slept shocked her. She hadn't napped since the last time she'd had the flu. Pondering her limited clothing options, Ella wished she'd asked Grace where they were going for dinner. She was saving the tailored slacks and cowl-necked sweater for the book talk, which she figured would be an informal affair with probably no more than a couple dozen attendees. If that. So the skirt and filmy blouse tonight. Dressy but casual at the same time.

At six on the dot, Ella was stepping out of the elevator and buttoning her red cashmere coat—an impulsive purchase after her divorce was finalized—when she spotted Grace walking across the lobby.

"Beautiful coat," Grace said when she drew close.

"Thanks. A present for myself."

"The best kind!"

"Nice scarf, Grace. I like that color on you."

Grace flushed. Ella remembered then how Grace was often embarrassed by compliments, as if she didn't think she deserved them.

"It was a present from Drew."

"Drew?"

"Drew Spencer. My fiancé. I guess there's a lot to talk about over dinner. I've got reservations for us at The Daily Catch."

"Is that a new place?"

"No. Remember the fish 'n' chips shop on the waterfront?"

"Right! I'd forgotten its name. A family restaurant I think?"

"Yeah. The Nakamuras. Their oldest son, Tom, is running it. He was in Ben's class at school. Anyway, it's now more of a high-end seafood bistro. I think you'll like it. Assuming you like seafood? Guess I should have checked first."

"I do, for sure."

"All set, then?"

Ella had planned to cancel her second night at the reception desk on the way out but decided to wait until later. "Yes."

Partway across the lobby, Grace said, "The bistro is close, but it's on the boardwalk, which might be slippery. Will you be able to manage?" She eyed Ella's boots.

"I'll be fine. I wore these on the walk with Ben." Had he made some comment later to his sister? She held back a sigh and followed her out the door.

But she kept Grace's remark in mind while descending to the boardwalk and held firmly on to the stair railing. There was a breeze sweeping in from Casco Bay, causing the strings of multicolored Christmas lights along the upper rail to gently bob up and down.

Most of the places along the walk had closed for the day. None of the business names were familiar to Ella.

"Are these all new?"

"Relatively." Grace paused to scan the row of dark stores. "I think the harbor-boat-cruise place was still here when you came to the Cove." She gestured to a shuttered storefront. "It's obviously closed for the season now."

"I vaguely recall it, though we never went on any of the cruises."

"Same here." Grace laughed. "As teens we wouldn't have been caught dead going on one with our families."

"True." The sentiment was exactly right, but it caught Ella off guard. She had a sharp memory of the number of times her mother had suggested the cruise as a family outing. One that never happened and now never would. Her mother had been astounded when she'd heard of Ella's planned visit and book talk. *Why would you want to?* she'd asked. Ella had muttered something about promoting her book without giving the real answer—*because I have to.*

Ella strode on, hearing Grace's boots clattering behind. "Is that the bistro?" She pointed to a small, brightly lit storefront. Two potted poinsettia plants flanked the entryway, which was partially enclosed by canvas panels to block the wind. The glass panes of the door behind the panels were rimmed with frost.

"This is it." Grace pulled open the door, letting wafts of warm air mixed with the heady aromas of garlic, seafood and wood smoke escape.

Once inside, Ella paused to take in the cozy refuge. She had a distant memory of standing at a counter with her father, waiting for an order of fish and chips that came wrapped in fake newsprint and greasy paper bags. "I think I sometimes came here with my dad," she told Grace as they were shown to a corner table.

Ella liked the interior—predictably reflecting the ubiquitous lobster-fishing themes she recalled from her summers at the Cove—because it wasn't the least bit pretentious. The artifacts even looked genuine, not that she knew much about antiques. *Old things*, as her mother would say disdainfully. The times she'd spent at the Winters home had exposed her to the heirlooms and valued assets of past generations, and although she'd never been drawn to their aesthetic, she'd envied Grace's link to history. Ella could trace her family tree back only two generations and knew little about her older ancestors.

She was still staring at the small piece of paper that was the menu when a waiter brought a bottle of wine to the table and began to uncork it.

"You seemed lost in thought," Grace was saying, "so I went ahead and ordered my favorite sauvignon blanc. Hope that's okay?"

So much for being clear-minded, Ella. "That's fine, thanks. Um, what's good here? I see few choices."

"The catch of the day is what I usually get. But as you can see, they have scallops, shrimp and lobster. Some of that will be frozen of course, given the season."

"The catch of the day sounds okay for me, too. I noticed the lack of fishing boats in the harbor. Are they up for the winter or something?"

"No. Most of the fishermen have either retired and moved south or gone into other work. The fish comes from Portland every day, so most of it's fresh, even now in winter."

"Guess I've never thought much about winter here."

"Well, why would you? Your family were summer people."

Summer people. That was a phrase Ella had heard many times during her family vacations. When she'd been young, she hadn't given the label much thought, but as a preteen and teenager, she'd begun to understand the implied meaning—summer people weren't regular people. They were seasonal, coming and going like the tides, with no lasting connection to the place.

"True, but we did come every year from when I was six until I was..." She didn't need to finish.

Grace dipped her head to her menu. After a long, uncomfortable moment, the waiter returned to take their orders. But Ella knew the interruption was a mere postponement of what would inevitably come. They ordered the fish special with a Caesar salad to share. Ella sipped her wine, looking coolly at her old friend. She wondered when Grace would get around to the topic they were both consciously avoiding—that Labor Day weekend. After dinner, perhaps, because otherwise one of them might stomp out and waste what promised to be a delicious meal. That was okay with Ella. She'd waited seventeen years for Grace's apology. Another hour or so would be nothing.

The food came and they were exclaiming over the whole grilled fish sided by a variety of grilled vegetables when a man in a chef's jacket appeared.

"Gracie! I was hoping you'd come by one of these days so I could congratulate you. Great news! I imagine your family is thrilled."

Ella watched the surge of red creep up Grace's neck and into her cheeks. The engagement, she surmised.

"Um, yes, they're pleased."

But not *thrilled*? Ella wondered.

"Tom, this is Ella Jacobs. She and her family used to come to the Cove in the summers."

When he looked her way, Ella thought his smile wobbled a bit, but he covered nicely. "The name's familiar. Welcome." He didn't offer a handshake. Then his attention shifted to their waiter gesturing toward the kitchen. "Oops, got to go. Congrats again, Grace. Let me know when you've set a date." He dashed away.

"Tom went to school with Ben." Grace ran a fingertip around the rim of her wineglass.

"So you said." Ella waited a beat, adding, "We should eat while this is hot." She noted the flicker of relief in Grace's face. She clearly didn't want a dinner ruined by a serious conversation either.

The food was delicious, and as they ate, the talk was all about taste and aromas. When the waiter took away their empty plates, Ella said, "Thanks, Grace. That was a wonderful dinner. Their fish and chips were good back then, but this was superb."

Grace smiled. "We must be sure to tell Tom if he pops by again. He'll appreciate the compliment." She scanned the room. "It's pretty quiet in here tonight, for a Wednesday. Sometimes it's difficult to get reservations, especially on weekends."

"It's not very big. I guess that adds to the demand." Ella sipped her wine, then said, "Tell me about your engagement."

"Well, it happened just recently. We haven't made any definite plans yet. Still waiting for the news to sink in with both our families."

"Is he from here?"

"No. Drew's originally from Iowa, but he's with the Coast Guard in Portland."

"Is he an officer, or does he work there as a civilian?"

"He's an officer. Used to be search and rescue, but now he's in charge of lighthouse maintenance. He just got a promotion."

Ella bit her lip at Grace's proud grin. "How nice for you both," she murmured, reaching for her wineglass again. "How did you meet?"

There was a long enough pause that Ella wondered if Grace had heard her.

"He came to the Cove to inspect our lighthouse." She made a funny throat-clearing sound. "It's a long story. I'd inquired about restoring the lighthouse in order to erect a memorial there. For Brandon. The lighthouse has been decommissioned, and we've been fundraising since the summer to buy it. The last payment was just made, and now it officially belongs to the town."

Ella kept her gaze firmly on Grace's face throughout her story. Judging from the woman's flushed cheeks and rapid breathing, she guessed she wouldn't have to wait long for the apology.

Grace suddenly blurted, "I'm so sorry, Ella. There's no way I can justify what Cassie and

I did. I've tried to rationalize my actions over the past few years, putting them down to jealousy and poor judgment, but all of those excuses really mean nothing. In the end I simply had to admit that I did something wrong that resulted in a death, and even though no one could have foreseen what happened, the fact is that our thoughtless prank upset Brandon enough to make him run off to hide his humiliation. He clearly wasn't thinking straight, or he'd never have gone to the lighthouse, but my theory is that he wanted to avoid the beach-party gang and he also didn't want to go home. If only I'd thought how he might react! I've spent the last seventeen years asking myself why I didn't consider that he'd be crushed. That he wouldn't just laugh it off. But he was fourteen, with all the frailty of a teenager. I ought to have been empathetic, but I was too wrapped up in my jealousy."

Ella couldn't speak. She felt as if she'd been breathlessly running alongside Grace through the whole outburst, and her head was spinning. Where to start? She chose the last point. "What were you jealous about?"

Grace stopped the nervous toying with her cutlery. "I was jealous of you and Ben. He got all your attention, and I felt like I was just someone you hung out with when Ben was unavailable."

"Cassie was there."

"But you and I were best friends for all the years you'd been coming to the cove. It was always just the two of us."

"Until that summer, when I came here to find that you were friends with Cassie."

"She was kind to me that school year. I had a hard time in ninth grade, getting bussed to high school in Portland. All those kids I didn't know. I was an outsider and Cassie paid attention to me. She was a year older—like you—and she didn't care at all about being on the outs with kids."

"Well, that's how I felt when I realized you and Cassie were tight. *I* was the outsider."

"But you were always so bubbly—laughing at Cassie's antics and going along with her schemes. It didn't seem like you felt left out."

"Because I was trying to make the best of the situation. I wanted to keep your friendship, but two's company and three's a crowd, right? There's no more apt cliché than that when referring to teenage girls."

"You're not saying that *we* drove you into Ben's arms?"

The mix of irony and disbelief in Grace's voice rankled. "I'm not taking the blame for what you and Cassie did. I was a teenager, too. Teens have crushes. You know that—you used Brandon's crush on me to set us up."

Grace flinched. "You're right, Ella. And I'm not blaming you. I'm just explaining how my fifteen-year-old mind was working. I didn't even realize at the time that Cassie also had a huge crush on Ben, which I think was what led to the whole stupid idea. So I'm apologizing on her behalf, too."

How typical of Grace, Ella thought, to include her coconspirator, not that she cared about getting an apology from Cassie anyway. "Whatever happened to Cassie?"

"She left the Cove for college and as far as I know, has never returned." Grace looked down at the table for a second and when she raised her head, her eyes were glistening. "I can't possibly make amends. I can't go back in time and make it all good. But I know I'll carry the burden of that night with me for the rest of my life. Even knowing my family still loves me, despite what I did, cannot free me of that."

Ella had to look away from the vulnerability in her old friend's face. The talk paused when the waiter brought the dessert menu. As soon as he left, she leaned across the table and said in a low voice, "I understand what you're trying to tell me, Grace. You were fifteen with the faulty judgment of a teenager. As for carrying the burden all these years, you're not the only one. I was vilified because everyone thought I was responsible for Brandon being out at the lighthouse. The police came to our cottage and showed me the note you gave Brandon. When I told them I'd also received a note but had destroyed it, I knew they didn't believe me."

"What exactly did you tell them?"

"I told them the truth, Grace. I told them someone else was responsible and that Brandon and I had been tricked. That I heard laughter coming from the bushes but I didn't see who was hiding there."

"No one came to ask *me* any questions."

"Of course not."

"What do you mean by that?"

"You and Cassie were townies and I was a

summer kid. Brandon was your cousin. You were a Winters. Do the math."

"My family knew nothing about *any* of this."

Ella fought to stay calm against the heat in Grace's face. "Maybe not, but they could have tried to find out the truth. *You* could have told them, Grace. Why didn't you?"

Grace turned her head aside. "I was afraid to."

"Well, there you have it. Your fear not only brought years of guilt on to yourself, but it also left a gaping wound in my own past." She saw that Grace was struggling to compose herself. In an instant, the years vanished and her summer friend reappeared: the bright smile when Ella knocked on the Winterses' door every first day back in the Cove; Grace's keen interest in Ella's school year and the circle of friends Grace had never met; the breathless excitement when Ella unpacked the books she'd hoarded over the winter, all destined for Grace's bookshelves.

A flood of emotion rose up, and Ella knew she couldn't sit a second longer or she'd be wrapping her arms around her old friend and forgiving her everything. But she wasn't ready to do that yet. She stood up. "I should go. I have some preparation work for tomorrow. Assuming you still want me?" The misery in Grace's face almost made Ella relent and stay longer.

"Of course, I still want you to come. But please…just think about what I've said tonight. Try to forgive me."

"I will, but…" Ella changed her mind about what she wanted to say. "Thanks for dinner." She plucked her coat and purse from the back of her chair and passed their startled waiter on her way out. Well into the night, the thought that surfaced didn't concern the apology but the fact that, in spite of what Grace had done, she had managed to find love. Could Ella say the same?

CHAPTER FOUR

THE BELL JINGLED as the door closed behind him, and Ben stifled a curse as a couple heads turned his way. He tiptoed to the center of the store, where Ella's book talk had already begun. He realized at once that there was no seating available and stood at the rear next to Grace, whose stern face rebuked his late arrival. He scanned the group in front of him. Most seemed to be female teens—and some a bit older—which made sense because Ella's novel was for young adults. He preferred nonfiction, but he'd read Ella's book and had liked it.

He'd known since that long-ago summer that she was a good writer, not that he was qualified to judge. There had been times when she'd been brave enough to read him some of her scribblings, as she'd called them, and he'd been in awe of her ability to produce images and ideas from mere words. He hadn't been surprised to learn that she'd become a journalist and not only because she'd often talked about it.

Yet as much as he'd been drawn into her novel, he'd felt uneasy reading it. It centered on a teenage boy being bullied at school. The character eventually finds someone who believes in him enough to give him the courage to proclaim his love for her as well as defy his tormentors. The main character was an eccentric—a nerd—and Ben instantly thought about Brandon. It surely was no coincidence that Ella chose that theme, as generic as it was, and fashioned that character. But what had prompted her to write such an obvious homage? And why now? He had the uneasy feeling she might have some kind of agenda in accepting the book-talk invitation.

Ben pushed that unpleasant thought aside. Right now he was trying to connect the poised, eloquent woman speaking at the front of the room with the girl of his teenage dreams. All the what-ifs he'd tormented himself with over the years rushed back. If that night had never happened, he might have grown into adulthood with Ella. He might have traveled with her, lived and worked with her in exotic places. They might have married and raised a family. A stab of pain caught his breath and he closed his eyes until he felt a tap on his shoulder.

Grace was frowning at him, her eyes big with questions. Ben shrugged and looked away. All those possibilities could have been realities if it hadn't been for his sister and Cassie Fielding. His feelings about Grace since he'd learned the truth had ricocheted from disappointment to anger to pity. He'd tried to calm that inner storm of emotion and hide it from Grace because he figured the cost to her of carrying that awful secret and then confessing to it had been great. But the last few months had sometimes felt more tumultuous than the days after Brandon had died, as Ben grappled with the realization that his life—and Ella's—might have been so very different. The scenario he avoided thinking about was what he himself should have done at the time.

A small round of applause brought him back to the moment. Ella was ending her presentation and opening the floor to questions. There was a general buzz of excitement and hands flew up across the room. Ben guessed from her smile and flushed face that she was pleased with her talk. He felt a twinge of guilt that his focus had been on the lilt of her voice and the sparkle in her eyes rather than her actual words. He decided to stay a bit longer, although he had a meeting in Portland with some potential investors.

The first few questioners were teenagers gushing about the book and how they could relate to its message. That got Ben's attention. He suspected the message was as universal and timeless as bullying itself. As he buttoned up his coat, Grace whispered, "Thanks for coming. I'm sure Ella appreciated it."

He nodded but doubted Ella needed affirmation from him. "I have to go," he whispered back. "But can you tell her I'll text about dinner tonight? I'm not sure if she's remembered that I invited her. Or have the two of you made plans?"

"No, we met last night. It's too complicated to give a recap now. Another time."

She must have told Ella what she'd done all those years ago. He wondered how that had gone. Perhaps he'd find out tonight from Ella. He was starting to leave when an abrupt silence fell over the room, followed by Ella's strained voice saying, "I'm sorry. Could you please repeat your question?"

"Of course," replied a woman whose back was to Ben. "Your book is fiction but bears a striking resemblance to an actual incident that occurred here several years ago. My research indicates that you might have been involved in that incident—one that ended in tragedy for a young teenage boy. Is your book, in fact, based on that event?"

Ben heard Grace's sharp inhale, but his whole being focused on Ella's ashen face.

"My *novel*—and I stress that word—is fiction. The characters are fictional and so is the story," she said with a steady voice.

"Yet a true-life experience can be fictionalized."

Ben peered over the heads in front and saw that the woman was holding a pen and notebook. Someone from *The Beacon*? He was about to inch forward to identify her when his sister's voice rang out.

"Sorry to interrupt, but we're short of time. If any of you would like Ella to sign your book, could you please line up on the far side of the room? And the cash register is now open." She gave a small laugh and headed for the counter opposite.

A group of teens leaped out of their chairs to swarm Ella. Ben noticed the woman who'd asked the question tucking her notepad into a handbag, and as she stood up, he caught her glancing his way. She looked vaguely familiar, and when she gave him a slight nod, Ben suddenly recalled meeting her several weeks ago when Paul Collins, managing editor of *The Beacon*, had introduced Ben—the paper's new partner—to the staff. Although Ben had promised Paul a free hand running *The Beacon*, he was tempted to swoop over and confiscate the woman's notebook.

Maybe this is why you ought to have listened to Dad, who warned you about conflict of business interests in a small town when you decided to buy into it. Ben sighed, knowing there was nothing much he could do about the situation. Besides, Ella was a seasoned journalist who'd certainly fielded many tough interviews. As he navigated his way to the front door, he saw her sitting at the table of books, chatting with a young teen. She noticed him look her way, and her smile stayed with him all the rest of the day.

ELLA PACKED UP while Grace locked the door behind the last of the morning's customers. Once she'd gotten into the rhythm of chatting and autographing, she'd managed to shove aside that woman's question. But now that she no longer needed to maintain her neutral-but-friendly smile, Ella wanted to flee to her hotel room, lie on the bed and close her eyes against all of it: the sorrow in Grace's face last night, the uncertainty in Ben's eyes when he'd grasped her hand yesterday and, most of all, the intent expression on that woman's face when she'd referred to Brandon's drowning and ruined Ella's presentation.

Ella knew returning to the Cove was a gamble and she ought to have been prepared for questions like the one today. A couple internet searches could easily uncover the tragedy of that summer, and although most of the people at the book talk consisted of young women who'd been born well after the incident, some in the audience could have known about it. It seemed she was never going to erase the memories. Even Grace's apology couldn't shift her mood. She was beginning to think she shouldn't have come back.

"Congratulations, Ella! I think that went

well," Grace said as she moved to the book table. "Lots of sales, and your talk was wonderful. I got raves about it from some of the customers."

"Who was that woman?"

The smile vanished from Grace's face. "Oh, don't worry about her."

"Do you know her?"

"Not really. I think she might be a reporter for *The Beacon*, but seriously, forget about her."

"The Beacon?"

"Remember the town's weekly newspaper? We weren't into it back in those days. As I said, don't worry about her."

"Okay," Ella muttered. "One of the teenagers was quite charming," she went on to say. "Her name was Becky. She told me her mother allowed her to skip classes this morning just for my talk and she persuaded her friends to do the same."

"Becky Oliphant. She's a lovely young girl. I met her last summer and she was actually the one who drew my attention to your book. She works for me some Saturdays."

"Nice."

"I loved working for Henry in the summers."

"I don't remember you working here."

"Um, well, it was the summer I turned sixteen, after—"

"I left."

Grace's smile vanished. "About last night…"

"I'm sorry about rushing off," Ella quickly put in. "There was a lot to process."

"I don't blame you for wanting to leave. It really wasn't the best place for that kind of talk, but the opening came up when I mentioned Brandon's memorial and…well…I just went with it."

There was the teenage Grace's impulsiveness Ella remembered. She softened her tone. "It's okay, Grace. The topic would have been difficult for both of us whenever it arose. I appreciate your honesty and your apology."

"Thank you, Ella. That means a lot to me."

The pause that followed was awkward. "I suppose that's it for me, then." Ella gestured to her packed tote bag.

"You have another night here, don't you?"

"I do, but—"

"Ben asked me to remind you that he'd invited you out for dinner tonight. He'd love to spend more time with you."

Ella wasn't so sure about that, given she'd

been so snarly with him yesterday, but she was pleased that he remembered his invitation. "Oh right. Well, I guess I could keep my hotel booking for tonight."

"That's great. And why don't I take you for lunch. I have an hour before reopening this afternoon. We can talk about what we've both been doing these past several years."

The thought of having a normal conversation free of more bad memories was appealing and knowing that tonight's meeting with Ben was still on unexpectedly boosted her spirits. "I'd like that, Grace, and I want to hear all about Henry. But it's my treat today."

BEN HAD SERIOUS misgivings about the meeting's success. Things had gone well until the slide revealing the latest numbers for Winters Building Ltd. He'd had qualms about including it but knew not to hide anything. Business was slow, but it would pick up come spring. Ben was certain about that. If only he could convince the Portland Credit Union. As much as everyone had smiled and shaken hands afterward, he'd caught a glance between two of the men that worried him—raised eyebrows that implied doubt about his numbers perhaps.

When Ben pulled out of the credit union parking lot, he debated whether to inform his father about the meeting right away or head for his office in the Cove to discuss it with his second-in-command, Andy Talbot. He was tempted to go for the latter, since he and Andy would be on the same page, unlike Ben and his father.

The other matter on his mind was that reporter's pointed question about the book. Ben had wanted to rush to Ella's rescue, but she hadn't needed his help at all. At least he had the evening with her to look forward to, if she was still willing to have dinner with him.

He used the short drive back to the Cove to mentally review the meeting for his discussion with his father and Andy. By the time he arrived at the exit to Lighthouse Cove, Ben had still not come up with a recap that would satisfy his father. His best shot would be a simple outline, the kind Charles preferred. *Cut to the chase* had been his father's advice as far as Ben's memory reached. He glanced at the subdivision that his father had begun and that Ben was currently expanding. Although he was proud of the well-built homes, he loathed their cookie-cutter design. When the company first began developing the land, Ben had tried to persuade his father to vary the plans. He'd even drawn up a few prototypes and blueprints but to no avail. *People don't care about owning a Frank Lloyd Wright knockoff, Ben. They want a house they can afford*, his father had protested.

Steeling himself for the inevitable battle of wills, he climbed out of his car and opened the front door of his childhood home—*the castle on the hill*, as his friends used to tease. Ben had been occupying his old third-floor bedroom since his return, but he had recently purchased a new, winterized bungalow near the beach, so he'd be moving soon. That had been another decision his father had protested. *You could have had one of our own rental places for nothing.*

Then I'd never be out from under your thumb, Dad, he'd thought.

"Hello!" he called out as he headed for the solarium, a favorite roosting place for his parents.

"This is a nice surprise." His mother was writing in a notebook and looked up when he walked into the room. His father was dozing in an armchair and roused at their voices.

Ben leaned down to kiss his mother's cheek. "What're you working on?"

"I'm planning an engagement party for Grace and Drew."

"Oh? Does she know about that?" He couldn't resist the tease, knowing his sister disliked being the center of attention.

"Of course she does. I wouldn't dare otherwise."

"Have they set a date?"

"For the wedding? Not as far as I know, but then—"

"We would be the *last* to know," Ben finished.

Evelyn laughed. "I made her promise not to elope. Any kind of wedding is fine by me as long as I can be there."

"Finished for the day already?" Charles broke in.

Ben felt his face heat up. "I've just come from a meeting with the Portland Credit Union and thought you'd want to be filled in." He glanced at his mother.

"I'm going to make a pot of tea," she said, getting up from her chair. "Anyone else interested?"

"I'll have one."

"Charles?"

He shrugged. "Fine." Then he redirected his attention to Ben. "I thought we already had a discussion about asking for more credit."

Ben sat on the chair Evelyn had vacated. "It wasn't a discussion, actually, Dad. I told you I planned to find investors for my new project, and you told me the project wasn't a good idea. End of conversation." He pushed on despite his father's frown. "I know you'd rather keep expanding the subdivision, but we still have a dozen unsold houses there. As I've told you before, there's a new generation of potential buyers interested in the green components of my new designs—the solar panels, the gray water system—"

"All that green-and-gray talk! I'm getting tired of it."

"Well, you can't compete if you're not in the game." Ben got up. "I'll see if Mom needs any help." He thought he heard Charles sputtering as he left the solarium. It hadn't been fair to use another of his father's favorite sayings against him, but he couldn't resist. He decided not to tell him more about the meeting until he had answers for the inevitable questions. And a tea break was exactly the diversion he needed.

Evelyn looked up from pouring boiling water into a teapot. “Couldn’t wait? Or needed a break?”

“I could use something stronger than tea, but it’s a bit early.”

She set the kettle back onto the stove. “He’s struggling, Ben. Eventually he’ll accept what we’re all trying to tell him.”

He perched on a bar stool and ran his index finger along his forehead. There was so much he wanted to say to his mother, but she had enough on her mind. His parents were still processing Grace’s revelation from a few months ago and didn’t need his personal worries added in.

“What is it, dear?” Evelyn was smiling sweetly at him across the island counter.

“Nothing, Mom. Just a bit tired. Can I take that for you?” He stood up and reached for the tea tray. No reason to spoil her day by telling her Ella Jacobs was back in town.

CHAPTER FIVE

ELLA SIGHED. IT WASN'T The Daily Catch, and the pub Ben had suggested—The Lobster Claw—fell short of the candlelit, linen-tablecloth venue her adolescent self had sometimes dreamed about enjoying with Ben. Not that she'd been expecting a romantic evening, nor did she want one. As far as she was concerned, this night was solely for business—the business of extracting an apology. She hung her down jacket over the back of her chair and sat down, facing the interior of the pub, which seemed very busy for a Thursday night.

Grace had been surprised when Ella had told her she was meeting Ben there. "I'd have thought he'd want someplace quieter," she'd said.

But Ella guessed he wanted a place where there would be less likelihood of a serious conversation. Her lunch with Grace had been pleasantly free of that very kind of talk.

They'd spoken about Ella's presentation, the enthusiasm of the young audience and, again, the annoying reporter. The incident had upset Ella because it had been a blunt reminder that she wasn't going to escape the past in Lighthouse Cove. The reporter had been correct in assuming the book was loosely based on the real tragedy, but for Ella *loosely* was the key word.

Her intention for writing it hadn't been only personal therapy but the chance to give Brandon an alternate life through fiction. When she'd agreed to do the presentation, she'd known there would be a possibility someone in the Cove would make the connection to Brandon. Not that it mattered. The book talk hadn't been her main reason for coming back anyway.

The server came with water then, forcing Ella's thoughts back to the pub.

"Would you like to order a drink?" she asked.

Ella declined. She needed every one of her senses to be functioning clearly. After the server left, she checked the time on her cell phone. Ben was late. No surprise there, she thought, recalling his teenage lack of punctuality. She scrolled through her email and noticed a new one from the head library in Worcester, Massachusetts. Her presentation there next week was canceled due to a municipal work stoppage. The visit had been the last stop on her book tour. Ella sighed again. She didn't have to report back to work until after the new year, although she still had two more Saturday op-ed pieces to write.

The problem was Christmas. That family-oriented holiday had been the bane of Ella's life since her parents' divorce, which had required travel between two residences. Her brother was now tied up with his own family, and her mother's current love interest had grandchildren. Although Ella knew she'd be welcomed to spend Christmas with either of them, she also knew she'd feel like an outsider. The holiday was two weeks away, and she wondered if she ought to contact her single friends to organize something. The idea wasn't appealing.

She scanned the busy pub and the knots of people of all ages celebrating either nearing the end of a working week or the coming holidays, and she envied them. Except for the publication of her novel, her life and career had followed a steady but unexciting trajectory. Even her divorce had been without drama. She and Jake, her ex, had simply grown tired of one another. *You're feeling sorry for yourself, Jacobs, just because you saw how happy Grace is.* She was checking around for her server so she could order a glass of wine after all, when she spotted Ben pushing through the crowd. Several people stopped him to chat or say hello, including at least two women, but Ella saw that his dark eyes remained fixed on her the whole time.

"Sorry I'm late," he said as he reached the table. Droplets of melting snow sparkled on his dark hair and the broad shoulders of his overcoat. He unbuttoned the coat and shook it, causing a light spray to flick across the table and onto Ella, who flinched.

"Sorry about that." He laughed. "Have you been here long?"

"Umm, not really." She couldn't take her eyes off him and his charcoal-gray suit and immediately wished she'd worn her skirt and blouse rather than the same outfit she'd worn to the book talk.

"Here." He picked up his napkin and stretched

across the table to dab her cheeks, where some of his coat's water droplets had landed.

The intimate gesture startled her, but not as much as the expression in his eyes. Tenderness? No, she must be wrong. She instinctively pulled her head back and muttered, "Thanks, I'm okay."

He dropped the napkin and sat down, loosening the collar of his pale blue shirt and tugging at his tie. "I meant to change, but I figured I was late enough."

"Business meeting?"

"Yeah, but then I went to see my folks for a bit and after that had a last-minute meeting at the worksite."

"How are your parents?"

"Good. My dad is still recovering from his heart surgery last January, as Grace may have told you. His doctor thinks he has other issues, as well, hence the slow recovery. Mom is fine despite coping with his extended convalescence."

Ella smiled at that, thinking Charles Winters would be a challenging patient.

"Listen," he began, leaning forward. "I'm sorry about the interruption during your book talk this morning."

"You mean when you arrived late?" She smiled to let him know she was teasing, but he flushed anyway.

"No, um, that woman—"

"The reporter from *The Beacon*?"

"Um—"

"At least, Grace thinks she works there."

"Right. Well—"

"*You* don't have to be sorry, Ben. You had nothing to do with her. Anyway, she didn't bother me."

"It's just that—"

"Ben. Forget it. I already have." That wasn't quite true, but Ella suddenly wanted to enjoy this dinner with him—their first in seventeen years and probably their last—without spoiling the evening. His apology could come at the end. Maybe after dessert. She picked up her menu. "Shall we order?"

"Sure."

Ella watched him reading his menu and immediately regretted her abrupt tone. Why was she so touchy around him? The glow in his face when he'd arrived had fizzled out and been replaced by something Ella couldn't quite identify. Trepidation?

"What's good here?" she asked, aiming for a friendlier tone.

"Pretty much everything, if it includes seafood. I usually get the clam chowder and salad followed by the shrimp sandwich."

So he was a regular, as she'd suspected from the way several people had greeted him. "That sounds perfect."

"Wine?"

"Please. White."

He signaled the server who'd brought Ella water minutes ago. The young woman flashed a bright smile when she reached their table. "Hey, Ben! How's it going?"

"Great, Amy. Can we get a glass of the house white and a beer for me? And I think we're ready to order."

"Sure. The usual?"

"Yes, thanks."

"And?" Amy's quick glance at Ella showed new interest.

"The same," Ben put in.

"Coming up." Amy collected the large leather-bound menus and strode off.

"Come here often?"

"It's a small town. Not too many places to choose from. Took me a while to get used to things like that, after living so long in Augusta." After a beat, he added, "But now I've got my favorites, so I guess that makes me a true resident of the Cove again." There was a trace of dismay in his grin, as if he couldn't quite believe it himself.

Ella remembered that grin, and a burst of warmth shot through her along with a quick pang of sadness. *So many years.* Pausing a minute to compose herself, she asked, "I take it you weren't expecting to stay on so long?"

"I thought a couple of weeks would be enough, but then it became obvious that Dad wasn't recuperating as quickly as we expected. That's when I persuaded Grace she should come home, too." His grin reappeared. "To be honest, I was hoping she and I could switch places and I'd go back to Augusta. But it didn't work out that way."

"What happened to make you stay?"

"When I realized Dad wouldn't be going back to work right away, I took over the business. In fact it was my mother who asked me to step in, not Dad. I think he was sore at her for days after. Admitting any kind of weakness is anathema to him. The move was supposed to be temporary, but now it feels permanent."

Amy arrived with their drinks, and Ella waited until she'd left to ask, "How did you feel about that? Coming back and running the company?"

"At first I was in shock. Not just from realizing that Dad wasn't the same strong father I knew but also guessing my life in Augusta would change."

"How so?" Ella was particularly interested in what he'd left behind in Augusta.

"I reevaluated my career with the architectural firm where I'd been working since graduation. It was family run, with plenty of 'heir apparents.' The chances of being made a partner were nil. At the same time, my marriage was breaking up." He paused to drink some beer. "The divorce was pretty much a cliché, which I won't bore you with, except to say it wasn't a surprise for either of us." He set his beer glass down. "And what about you? I know you're a reporter for the *Globe* and that you're also divorced."

She hadn't told Grace she was divorced, so he'd been searching the internet. Ella sipped her wine. Where to start and how much to say? Realistically, this game of catchup was a pointless exercise. Tomorrow she'd be gone and none of what they were sharing tonight would matter. On the other hand, the talk could be a warm-up to her main goal of the evening—getting an apology or even an explanation from him for abandoning her that Labor Day weekend.

"Same old story." She looked at him over the rim of her wineglass. "And a boring one. I graduated in Journalism from NYU, interned at the *Globe* during summer vacations—we always lived in Boston—then started there as a rookie after graduation. Worked my way up to reporter and got married along the way. The reporting part was a success, but the marriage not so much." She gave a quick shrug. "All water under the bridge now, as they say. Currently, I'm writing weekly op-ed pieces while I'm on tour with my book, and I hope to continue doing a column when I go back."

"Will you also continue writing novels?"

He knew her too well. Or perhaps he was simply remembering the teen version of Ella Jacobs, the one who'd shown him her creative writing, or "scribbling" as she'd called it. "Maybe."

Amy brought their chowder, and Ella was grateful for the chance to shift away from her future plans. Besides, even if she knew what those plans were, there was no reason to share them with Ben. "Delicious," she murmured after her first mouthful.

His smile was faint. Ella guessed he was struggling to keep up with her mood changes, from being chatty to clamming up. That was okay. She wanted to keep this uncertainty about her as a distraction, so that when she did get around to asking why he'd abandoned her that summer, she might get an honest answer from him.

Their main courses arrived, and Ben thanked Amy and complimented the food almost profusely, something Ella doubted he usually did, considering he probably ate the same thing every time. Amy's dimpled smile seemed to confirm Ella's impression that the woman was interested in Ben Winters. *Good luck there*, she thought, noting the warmth in Ben's eyes was friendly but nothing more. She'd always been good at reading him.

"I'm not sure I'll be able to finish this." She eyed the sandwich and mound of french fries.

"Lunch tomorrow?"

"To eat in my car on the way to Boston?"

"Right." His dark eyes searched hers. "This visit seems so short."

Visit? We're not exactly old friends having a reunion, she was tempted to say. But she shrugged. "Part of the plan." She bit into a large morsel of shrimp and chewed slowly. The sandwich was delicious. Maybe she could finish it after all.

Ben tucked into his meal as if enjoying it for the first time and not the umpteenth. They ate without further talk until she surrendered to reality. "I'm done. I can't take a single bite more."

"Same here."

She looked at his half-eaten sandwich. "Seriously?"

His smile was sheepish now. "Cutting back. My life in the Cove isn't as active as it was back in Augusta." He pushed his plate aside and leaned forward. "I meant it about staying on, Ella. It would be fun to show you around town a bit more, and there will be some festivities at the tree ceremony Saturday night. Christmas is a side of the Cove you've never seen. I know Gracie would be thrilled."

And what about you, Ben? Would you be

thrilled? was her immediate thought, and the earnest appeal in his dark eyes and his hands folded on the table in front of him, so close she could touch them if she dared, momentarily upturned her intended outcome for that night. She waited for her heart rate to return to normal. "Speaking of plans, Grace told me about Brandon's memorial."

She might as well have tossed a bucket of cold water into his face. He straightened up and reached for his drink. "Then she also told you what she did," he said after swallowing the last of his beer.

"Yes." This was the opening of a conversation she'd been anticipating since accepting Grace's invite, but he was taking his time. She stifled her impatience.

"How did you feel about her confession?" he finally asked.

Did he want the truth or a nice, evasive answer? His face wasn't giving anything away. "How do *you* think I felt, Ben?"

He shifted his gaze to a place beyond her and rubbed a finger across his forehead. Then his eyes met hers. Ella saw misery in them and sadness. *But not remorse.*

"Anger at first," he said in a low voice.

"Disappointment in her later. You two were close back then, right?" He paused. "I guess you must have felt a whole range of emotions, too—some of them conflicting." Another beat. "But now I'm hoping you'll eventually be able to forgive her, even if you can't forget. She's suffered in ways neither you nor I can imagine."

Grace was my best friend and not the only one who suffered. She stifled her irritation and stared down at the worn surface of the wood table. Suddenly she felt the warmth of his hand on her forearm.

"Maybe an extra day or two will give us the time we need to talk. To lay to rest all of our sad memories…or try to anyway."

Ella wanted desperately to believe that was possible. She hesitated, knowing a frank talk would inevitably end any chance of a reconciliation with Ben. But his hopeful face touched her. "I don't really have the right clothes for a longer stay," she murmured for want of anything better to say.

"We could drive to Portland tomorrow to pick up whatever you need."

He sounded optimistic, but her mind filled with all the reasons in the world why this was not such a good idea. Still, her heart refused to listen. She managed a tentative smile. “I’ll think about it.”

CHAPTER SIX

BEN MUDDLED HIS way through the first part of the morning. He'd gotten out of bed well before sunrise. Despite tiptoeing down to the kitchen from his bedroom, he wasn't surprised to find his mother sitting at the bistro table, drinking coffee and thumbing through the daily *Portland Press Herald*, which had probably just landed on their doorstep. Raising children had instilled this early-morning habit.

"Ben!" she exclaimed, looking up from the paper. "I know it's a weekday, but—"

"Couldn't get back to sleep after waking up around four." He went to the coffee machine on the counter by the stove, where two empty mugs sat waiting for him and his father. There were some benefits to moving back home as an adult, he conceded.

"Something on your mind?"

He sighed as he poured milk into his mug.

And then there were drawbacks, too. “Oh, this and that.”

She wasn’t deterred. “If it has to do with your funding problems or the disagreement with your father over the subdivision—”

“It’s okay, Mom. Don’t worry about all that. I’ve got some ideas.” He saw her wince slightly at his sharp tone and regretted being so touchy. Yesterday’s meeting hadn’t encroached on his sleep at all. What had really kept him tossing and turning had been Ella’s lovely and very enigmatic face. But he couldn’t open up to his mother. She didn’t know Ella Jacobs was back in town, and there was no way he was going to be the person to pass on that explosive bit of news. No. Grace created the situation and she could deal with it. But keeping that from his mother added to his grumpiness. He stood at the counter and swallowed as much of the hot coffee as possible before setting the mug into the sink. “Okay, well, I’m off.”

“But you haven’t had any breakfast!”

Another point for the drawback side. Still, he smiled because his mother was wonderful and just being…well, motherly. “I’ll pick up something on the way, Mom. I’m not going to go hungry." He patted his abdomen and grinned.

"Something with protein," she added as he made for the hall outside the kitchen.

"Yep," he called back. Maybe only half a point for the drawback team with that, because she was right. The house was silent as he walked through the ground floor to the front door. His father had begun sleeping late after his surgery. Although it had been successful, Ben knew—as did everyone else in the family—that Charles's physical stamina wasn't the same. As for the man's mental stamina, Ben could only smile. Keeping a sense of humor about his predicament was vital, though he wouldn't want to place a bet on how much longer he could maintain that attitude.

There had been a light snowfall overnight, and he turned over the engine to warm up the car before clearing the windshield and windows. He gazed up at the dark sky. Clouds had also drifted in, hiding any stars and even the moon. The shortest day of the year was coming up, and considering the amount of work ahead of him, Ben doubted he'd be leaving for the office in daylight for a very long time. He didn't like winter very much and never had, even as a kid. Grace had been the one who'd wanted to play outside and build forts or go skating at Town Square.

He climbed into the car, clicked on the seat warmer and headed for the road leading to the highway. A new outlet of a national fast-food chain had recently opened up just southwest of the Cove, on the highway to Portland. Judging by the lineup of vehicles at the drive-through, the place was already a booming success. Ben was happy about that—he assumed many of these customers came from the subdivision. Perhaps they'd tell their friends and colleagues about the conveniences of living a short drive from Portland, where rent and house prices had skyrocketed.

When his car rolled up to the drive-through window, Ben scrolled through the menu choices and clicked on the egg sandwich. In less than five minutes, he was heading back toward the Cove and the modular unit off the highway that was his office. It sat where it had been constructed two years ago, at the entrance to the subdivision. The company had intended the site to be temporary but kept it there with the hope that the slowdown in sales would change.

Though Ben figured if the dozen unsold houses eventually did go, and if he secured the investments he needed and his application to build the condo unit down the road was approved, he'd have the office relocated to the new construction site. *More ifs*, he thought. *The most important one being* if *Dad lets me take over.*

He swallowed the last bite of his sandwich and had another slurp of coffee, but his thoughts weren't on breakfast. The whole dinner scene with Ella resurfaced. Trying to make sense of the night was what had kept him awake for most of it. The way her moods kept switching from friendliness to silence had his emotions yo-yoing along at the same time.

When he'd walked her back to the hotel, after she'd declined his invite for a nightcap at a nearby bar, he'd been doubtful about her staying for the tree lighting. Still, when he'd made his last-ditch plea—*Text me in the morning if you decide to stay*—her nod had given him an iota of hope. He wasn't ready to give up on her yet.

The sun had risen by the time he reached the office. At least, what passed for a sun on what promised to be another gray and gloomy day. Much like his mood. Andy hadn't arrived yet, but Ben was surprised to find the company's new bookkeeper sitting at one of the four desks.

"Glen!" Ben closed the door behind him and stomped his feet on the mat just inside. He ought to have worn boots but couldn't be bothered lacing them up and bringing shoes to change into. A random thought of Ella's fancy but inappropriate footwear reminded him of his promise to drive her to the Portland Mall if she chose to stay.

If. That word again. He sighed as he hung his jacket on one of the hooks behind the door. "Glen, I know I said I needed some numbers for the presentation, but I didn't mean you had to get here at the crack of dawn to go through the books."

Glen Kowalski looked up with an unconvincing smile. "Yeah, well, I was up anyway. At five again this morning."

Ben felt for him. Glen and his wife had a one-month-old baby as well as a toddler. "I've been told things get better after a few months, but what do I know?" Ben quipped.

"We thought it would be easier the second time around, but..."

Andy had confided that Glen's infant daughter had some potential medical problems, which were presently being investigated. Ben didn't know if the matter was a secret or not but decided to be discreet and leave it up to Glen to divulge any personal issues. "Well, let me know if you want to take some time off. I can get Andy to look at the books instead."

Glen shook his head. "Appreciate it, Ben, but frankly, I can't afford to take the time. I've already used up my sick days for this quarter."

He managed a smile, but Ben saw through it. The benefit program that employees paid into and was matched by the company wasn't extensive. Ben knew many of his workers would need to supplement with private insurance. Perhaps he ought to review the benefits. Then he realized he didn't actually have the authority to do so, because his role in the company was temporary and unofficial. Frustration rose up. *Face it, Winters. If you want the situation to change, you have to make that happen yourself.*

"I'll see what I can do. But seriously, take the time. We can work out some kind of flexible schedule if necessary," he added at the man's drawn face.

The door flew open then, ending further talk about Glen's problems. "Meant to get here earlier, Ben," Andy said as he unzipped his jacket. "Oh hi, Glen. Early morning again for you?" He bent down to remove his boots and slipped on a pair of loafers from the shoe rack, just below the coat hooks.

Ben eyed the cramped winter gear arrangement, thinking if they did move the unit to the condo site, perhaps a closet should be installed. As it was, they had to pile hard hats and safety vests on the counter beside the microwave and sink. The place was too small, he realized, and he envisioned yet another expense in the near future. More issues and no real power to deal with them. He stifled a sigh and said, "Andy, let's sit down and go over the presentation from yesterday. I want your thoughts on how to improve it for my meeting with the bank next week."

ELLA WOKE LATE. That's what came from ruminating over every spoken word last night and chastising herself for not getting Ben to explain why he hadn't come to see her that Labor Day weekend before she and her family left. Her reference to the memorial project, intended to elicit what she'd been waiting for, had led to Grace's apology but not a hint of one from Ben last night. As if he'd forgotten all about his abandoning her. And she'd taken the coward's way out, avoiding a confrontation, because deep inside, she feared the truth. The more she considered the possibility he could have forgotten what happened back then, the more she disliked the logical response—to go back to Boston. What was she waiting for here? A lame "I'm sorry if I hurt you"? Would that make her feel better or compensate for all those years she nurtured her resentment against both Grace and Ben? No. She wanted something more. She wanted Ben to *feel* what she'd felt.

But so far she hadn't come up with a way to make that happen. As she pushed open the hotel's front door to go for breakfast, another woman was entering. Ella caught a glimpse of long reddish hair beneath a winter hat as the woman suddenly pivoted as if to speak. Ella hesitated on the other side of the door. There was something familiar about the woman staring at her, and if Ella had been anywhere else but the Cove, she might have opened the door and asked, "Do I know you?" But except for Ben and Grace, there wasn't another person in town she wanted to meet. The woman continued on and so did Ella, heading for Mabel's.

Finishing up her breakfast of fruit and yogurt with a side of freshly baked croissants, Ella thought about the past two days. They'd been emotional but not traumatic. Although she felt some skepticism about the sincerity of Grace's apology—*no one had forced her to do what she did*—she could accept it at face value, given how the tragedy had affected Grace.

Grace had moved on and found someone to love her while Ella was left with no one. Her brief marriage had confirmed for her there could be no replacement for Ben Winters. Despite the therapeutic act of writing a book, all the feelings from that summer still hovered, pouncing on her at random times. The morning's encounter at the hotel with that familiar woman was a good example of how paranoid she was becoming about confrontations. After she paid her bill, she headed for Grace's bookstore to say goodbye.

"I'm so glad you came by," Grace said. "I was about to text to see if you wanted to have lunch before you left."

"I've just come from a late breakfast at Mabel's, and I doubt lunch will appear on my agenda today. But thanks anyway."

"Yeah, Mabel's can do that to you." Grace flipped down the lid of her laptop and came around from behind the counter. "Thanks again so much for yesterday. I have a gift for you, so I'm doubly glad you dropped by. Saves me the trouble of mailing it."

Ella felt an unexpected pang at Grace's nervous laugh and that their past friendship—something she'd once treasured—had grown into this awkwardness. "I came to say goodbye and also to tell you to keep the rest of the books I brought. I'm sure my publisher won't care, and you could sell them or even give some away to your teen customers."

For a frightening moment, Ella thought Grace was about to hug her, but she headed for the table where the novels were still on display. A gift bag sat among them. Grace shyly presented it to Ella. “It’s not much. I know you didn’t want any remuneration for your talk, but I wanted to give you something.”

After a slight hesitation, Ella opened it and pulled out a book titled *Recipes from The Daily Catch* and featuring a mouth-watering photograph of a seafood platter on its cover.

“Tom Nakamura published that a few months ago. So many people in town as well as tourists had been asking him for his recipe for the house tartar sauce or the cheddar-corn biscuits—to mention a couple—that he decided to produce his own book.”

Ella had begun to flip through some of the pages while Grace was speaking. The gift surprised her because she liked to cook, a fact that she doubted Grace knew. Her interest in cuisine had been slow to take hold, accelerating during the lonely days following her divorce when Ella had impulsively signed up for a cooking class. “This is lovely, Grace. Thank you so much.”

“It was Ben’s idea. I passed a few suggestions by him, but he came up with this. Honestly, I never would have thought you’d be interested in a cookbook, but I'm glad you like it."

Ben's idea. The comment resonated so strongly that Ella was at a loss for words. She had a sudden memory of sharing a plate of fries with him at the diner all the kids went to back then. She couldn't recall its name, but it was near Tina's Ice Cream Parlor. Ben had made a joke about their standard order and how he hoped one day they'd move on to some more sophisticated food. She'd felt a flush of excitement at the implication that she might be in his life whenever that day came and had added that maybe she'd learn how to cook and make something special for him. Had he remembered? Or was this just a coincidence?

"Please thank him for me."

"I'm sure you'll get a chance to do that yourself."

Ella frowned at Grace's slight smile. "Oh?"

"I assumed you might be seeing him today before you left. After your dinner together last night."

Grace must not have spoken to her brother yet; otherwise she'd have known that their dinner had been anything but a success. That was a relief because she was regretting her abrupt good-night, capping off a whole evening of barbed comments. He must have felt immense relief when he'd left her at the hotel, yet he'd still made that last pitch to get her to stay longer. Even her disappointment at not getting his apology was no excuse for such poor behavior. *When did you become that kind of person, Jacobs?*

"We didn't make any plans to see each other again."

"I'm sorry. I'd hoped—"

"What?"

Ella knew the sharpness in her voice came from irritation with herself, not Grace, and was about to tone it down when Grace continued, "That my apology might have implicitly included Ben's. I mean, I know you never got to see him again and that you had plans to visit him at college. He'd told me that. But it never happened because...well...I suppose because of what I did."

Grace was taking on a lot more blame than she needed to. "Maybe Ben should account for his actions himself."

After a moment, Grace nodded. "You're

right, Ella, and I hope you'll give him that chance."

I wanted to last night, Ella would have said, but there was no way she was going to confide about Ben to his sister. Not now and not ever. "Okay, well, thanks again, Grace. If you make it to Boston someday, give me a ding." But they both knew that wasn't going to happen.

She picked up the book and gift bag to head for the door and reached it just as Grace called out, "Ben said he'd asked you to stay for the tree lighting tomorrow. I promised him I wouldn't tell you how much he was hoping you would say yes, but..."

Ella swung around. Her immediate thought was how the Winters siblings had both made last-minute pitches. The similarity was kind of cute, she thought. Clearly, their desire to have her stay was genuine. "I...uh... I'll think about it, Grace. Bye."

She did think about it all the way back to the hotel and at some point while she was packing up, she impulsively sent a text to Ben.

Is it too late to change my mind about staying through the weekend?

Setting her phone down, Ella realized she'd just made the decision she'd been avoiding all morning. Leaving now would mean all the unanswered questions about Ben—the whys and what-ifs—would plague her for the rest of her life. If she wanted him to know how he'd hurt her, she'd have to stay to make that happen.

CHAPTER SEVEN

BEN GOT ELLA'S text just before noon as he and Andy were finishing up reviewing the next funding presentation. He spent such a long time staring at his cell phone that Andy asked, "Problem?"

Ben raised his head. "Uh, no, but I'm thinking I might take a drive into Portland this afternoon, see how things are going at head office." He started typing his reply to Ella but was interrupted again.

"Okay," Andy said. "Want me to stay here, then, in case anything comes up?"

Except for a few small jobs left to do in the unsold houses, construction had basically ground to a halt in Lighthouse Cove. There was an ongoing office-building project in Portland, but it was being handled by the company's crew there. Ben thought for a minute. Andy would normally be overseeing the subdivision jobs on-site today, but now he'd be troubleshooting for him here and maybe helping Glen with the books. This trip to Portland with Ella wouldn't complicate anything at the office.

"Sure. When Mike shows up, get him to take care of the light installations you'd planned to do. Also, I'm expecting a call on the office line, confirming my meeting with Portland National Bank. If anything urgent comes up about that, call me on my cell. And maybe you could give Glen a hand, if you have the time."

Glen looked up from his computer at this. "I think I'll be fine, boss."

Ben puzzled for a minute at the man's guarded expression but was already texting Ella to tell her he'd pick her up in front of the hotel in half an hour. She wrote back immediately, and when he put his phone down, he realized the men were staring at him.

"Listen, if things are slow, just close up. It's Friday and I'm sure you both would appreciate a short day."

Now they looked a bit worried. Booking off early could mean there wasn't enough work. Ben wanted to reassure them but figured they'd see through any attempt at painting a rosy picture. They knew as well as he did business was slow. "I'm also expecting to hear from town council about our request to go over budget for the library. I got an email late yesterday telling me the outcome looks promising. So..." Ben had planned to inform his crew when he got the final word but guessed they needed some bolstering now rather than in a day or two.

"All good." Andy smiled at this new information.

"Okay, then, I'll head out. Call if you need to. Otherwise I'll see you both on Monday. Unless we bump into one another at the tree lighting tomorrow night." He tucked his cell phone into his jeans pocket.

"Think I'll pass on that," Glen muttered.

"Maybe. If Trish wants to go." A frown crossed Andy's face.

Andy had confided a few months ago that he and his wife were in couples therapy. Ben would have asked how things were going if they'd been alone or suggested a buddy lunch to talk things over, but today he had plans. Exciting ones.

He decided to go home to change from his worksite attire of jeans and hoodie into a suit.

Although the visit to head office had been his impulsive excuse for leaving work early, Ben figured he ought to make an appearance anyway. After the unsatisfactory meeting with Portland Credit Union yesterday, he'd emailed Winters Building Ltd. VP, Harold Ferguson, to give him a recap and had promised to follow up with him later.

Ferguson had been with the company since Charles Winters had taken over as president, but while Charles had landed the top job through inheritance, Harold had slowly worked his way up through the ranks. The two men had become friends and there was no person in the company that Charles—and Ben—trusted more. Harold was the reason that Ben could indulge his preference for hands-on work by spending more time on-site than at headquarters. The older man had also become a kind of sounding board for Ben's frustrations.

Not that Ben had ever pointed to Charles as the source of those feelings. He loved his father in spite of their differences of opinion over the company and would never be disloyal. But then, he didn't need to be frank with Harold. The man had worked with Charles a long time and knew him well enough to figure things out for himself. He'd hinted recently that he was thinking of retirement, but Ben hoped that wouldn't happen until his own position in the company was finally secured and settled. Whenever that day dawned.

Ben dismissed all those negative thoughts as he drove home, because the weekend was suddenly looking brighter.

ELLA PICKED UP her cell phone twice after Ben's text, intending to cancel, but both times she turned it off, stopped by an image of the disappointment on Ben's face. Despite wanting Ben to know what she'd gone through she also knew leaving now would be leaving forever. On her way to meet him, she stopped at the reception desk to extend her booking. "I can give you the room until Sunday," said the hotel clerk, Rohan, as he peered at the computer.

"That's fine." She'd be leaving Sunday anyway. Her stay in the Cove would be two days longer than she'd anticipated, and by the time she left, no doubt she'd have accomplished her two goals in coming—getting apologies from Grace and Ben. She ought to feel satisfied about that, but when Ben's car pulled up a few seconds after she exited the hotel, all she was feeling was a giddy headiness.

"I'm happy you changed your mind," he said as she climbed into his car.

"You and Grace can be very persuasive."

"Oh?" He glanced quickly at her while making a U-turn on Main Street to head up the hill to the highway. "You saw her this morning?"

"Yes, initially to say goodbye. She gave me a thank-you gift. A lovely book of recipes from The Daily Catch."

"Nice." He looked at her. "Do you like it?"

"I do. And she told me I had you to thank."

He focused on his driving again, but not before she caught his quick smile of satisfaction. "Well, it was a suggestion, that's all. I'm glad it was a good one." He cleared his throat. "Um, so I have to stop by company headquarters briefly, but there's a mall nearby. How about if I drop you off there, and we can text to organize a time to pick you up?"

"I hope you haven't had to change any plans, just for this shopping trip."

"No, I needed to see someone there and remembered the mall was close by."

Ella was a bit disappointed that he wouldn't

be shopping with her but then realized that would make the outing too much like a couple thing. And they definitely weren't a couple. "That's fine," she said.

Stopping at the top of the hill before turning onto the highway, Ben pointed to the subdivision down the road. "That's where I usually hang out, in the modular unit we use as an office. But the company's official headquarters are in Portland. We used to own a two-story building there, but my grandfather sold it. Now we rent space in an office tower." He looked over at Ella and smiled. "Cash-flow problems. Even back then."

She saw the flicker of worry in his eyes. He clearly had a lot on his mind. On their walk he'd implied working for his father was challenging, so financial problems on top of that would be stressful. "If you're usually here, who's in charge in Portland?"

"A man who started in the company almost at the same time as Dad, except he worked his way up. His name's Harold Ferguson and he's the VP."

Ella wondered where Ben fit into that scenario, considering he had no official title. She was curious but hesitated to ask in case the subject was a sensitive one.

"We work together, more or less," he went on, as if sensing her curiosity. "He knows I like to be with my own team on the construction site more than in an office building, and he also knows my dad well enough to figure out my situation. At least, that's my take on it. Harold's always been very discreet where my father is concerned. They've been friends a long time."

Ella realized that fact alone could be part of the dilemma Ben referred to. Harold and Charles Winters were friends as well as business partners. Threesomes were complicated, especially where power and money were involved.

She had a sudden flashback to that summer when she'd arrived at the Cove to find that Grace had another best friend—Cassie Fielding. Ella had always assumed that Grace had friends she hung out with during the school year—just as she had herself—but once summer came, those friends seemed to blend into the background. But Cassie had been there the first day Ella ran to Grace's house to tell her all about her school year in Boston and, to her dismay, Cassie had stayed. Then Ella had started spending more time with Ben, which had turned out to be a bonus for her.

They didn't speak again until the outskirts of Portland. "There's the new mall." Ben pointed to a large complex of stores ahead, on the west side of the road. "How about if I drop you off at the main entrance? Text me when you're ready."

"I wouldn't want to take you away from something important. I can be quick when it comes to shopping and besides boots, I don't have much else to get. How flexible can you be?"

"My meeting with Harold was last-minute, so I can pick you up whenever."

She studied his profile as he steered off the highway onto the mall's main road. The clenched jaw and fingers gripping the wheel were further signs of stress. He was taking time away from work to ferry her to a mall so she could buy appropriate footwear for a Maine winter. All because she was going to stay for some Christmas-lighting thing that she actually wasn't very interested in. It was a considerate gesture, and she felt a moment's regret that her motivation for the extended stay wasn't so innocent. He clearly wanted her to be there, and she… Well, she wanted satisfaction.

BEN TAPPED LIGHTLY on Harold's office door. It was ajar, but he knew the older man was a stickler for formality. Hence his change into a suit.

"Yes?"

Ben hesitated. Harold sounded a bit testy. Well, too late now, he told himself. He pushed open the door and stuck his head in. "Got a minute, Harold?"

"Ah, Ben! Come in and close the door behind you." Harold looked up from a file he was reading, his eyeglasses perched on the end of his nose. Light from the ceiling reflected off the top of his balding head. He'd taken off his suit jacket, loosened his tie and rolled up his shirt sleeves.

Getting down to work, Ben thought. Any evidence of a bad mood had disappeared, which reassured Ben, and he sat on the chair on the other side of the desk. "Twice in two days?" Harold quipped, referring to Ben's email yesterday.

"Yeah, but if you're busy, I can come by next week as we'd planned."

Harold set his pen down next to the file he'd been reviewing. "No, now is good. What's on your mind?"

Ben liked that about the older man. He got to the point right away.

"I've gone over my presentation to Portland National Bank next week and wondered if you have anything more to add. I just emailed it to you, and you might not have had a chance to look it over. It's more or less the same as the one I made to the Credit Union, which we reviewed a bit yesterday."

"Well, I skimmed through it, but I was going to email you my thoughts. However, now that you're here, there is something else I'd like to discuss."

Unease stirred deep in Ben's gut. He'd hoped to bring up the possibility of extending employee benefits in the new budget simply to get Harold thinking about the idea ahead of time. Then he'd broach the subject with his father. But the serious expression on Harold's face told him his plan might have to be deferred.

"Go ahead," he said, though a big part of

him wanted to cut the conversation short as he recalled Ella's remark that her shopping would be quick.

Perhaps Harold read something in Ben's face. "I'll make this short for now. I had a phone call from one of our suppliers today. A problem with their shipment orders not correlating to invoice payments. He wants to investigate further and then get back to me. Can you ask the new guy who's reviewing invoices at your end..." His face creased in thought. "What's his name? The one who replaced Matt Valetta."

"Glen Kowalski."

"Okay. Check it out with him. Maybe we're missing some paperwork or whatever. I've already asked our guy in accounting, and he hasn't noticed any problems. I can see you're anxious to get going, so I'll email you the details."

Ben gave an embarrassed laugh. "I do have another stop to make on my way home. I'll let you know my thoughts as soon as I get your info. Maybe by Monday?"

"Sure." As Ben got up to leave, Harold added, "Say hi to your folks for me. Especially Charles. How's the old man holding up? Chomping at the bit to get back here?"

Ben's face twisted into a smile that didn't fool Harold.

"Hang in there, Ben. Sooner or later he'll get the message."

"Yeah."

"Don't get discouraged." Harold's eyes fixed on Ben's. "Want me to mention something? I can be diplomatic as all heck when I need to be."

"I appreciate the offer, Harold, but I should be the one to talk to him. You have enough on your plate, and besides, no point in ruining a good friendship."

Harold's bark of a laugh filled the room. "Oh, your dad and I have jousted in many verbal tournaments over the years, Ben. We're still speaking to each other, even if we're not always on the same page."

If only Ben had a similar relationship with his father. But then, sons and fathers were a different combo altogether. "I'll set up a meeting with you after I've had a chance to go over the information you're sending."

Harold's expression sobered. "Do that, Ben. We have enough money troubles as it is. Lost or missing invoices and payments that don't match shipments are the last thing we need right now."

Ben thought of Glen hunched at his desk first thing this morning. Something was clearly on the man's mind besides a newborn. He said goodbye and, while he waited for the elevator, texted Ella to say he was on his way.

As soon as he saw her tall, slender form standing outside the mall's main entrance with two shopping bags clutched in her hands, all thoughts of the company and this new problem vanished.

She stowed her bags in the back of the car and climbed into the passenger seat. "That was fast!"

Ben's heart was full at the pleasure in her face. "Successful expedition?"

"Very."

Her blue eyes stayed on his, and she beamed a smile Ben remembered from years ago. *This is the grown-up Ella Jacobs I've been waiting to see.* He wanted nothing more in the whole world than to draw her close and kiss those cherry-red lips. They stared at one another, their breathing the only sounds in the car. Ben sensed that if he reached for her, she wouldn't resist. Then another driver honked from behind.

"Guess we should get going," Ben muttered as he shifted into Drive. He'd just turned onto the highway when she spoke.

"How was your visit?"

Small talk? Ben guessed it was better than acknowledging what they'd both been feeling seconds ago, and he felt a pang of sadness at the gulf between them. One that he wondered if even a kiss could span. But the day wasn't over yet, and better still, Ella was staying.

CHAPTER EIGHT

ELLA STARED AT the purchases scattered across her bed. The boots weren't pretty, but they were appropriate for a Maine winter, and while she might never wear the pale blue hoodie again, she figured it was a good fit for the Cove. The shopping plus the room fee for her extra nights in town were adding up, and Ella questioned her impulse to stay longer.

Who am I kidding? Money has nothing to do with what I'm feeling right now. She'd seen the kiss in Ben's eyes—the intent and, most of all, the desire. Every cell in her body had frozen, waiting for him to lean across the car console and carry through with it. What had really shaken her as they drove away was the letdown when he hadn't. She'd wanted that kiss as much as he had, to find out if the magic of her sixteenth summer was possible again. Was that really the reason, she asked herself, for all the back-and-forth debate about returning to Boston or staying longer in the Cove? Maybe she was kidding herself, too, in thinking she was waiting for an explanation about his behavior back then, when in reality, she simply wanted to be with him. To soak up his big, strong presence and dark eyes that conveyed such a blend of tenderness and passion. She only had to close her eyes to transport herself back to that summer and the shivery warmth of his arms around her. She bit down on her lip, letting the quick stab of pain distract her from troubling thoughts that she knew could lead nowhere.

By the time they reached the Welcome to Lighthouse Cove sign, reason had intervened. She couldn't risk giving in to long-forgotten feelings when in less than forty-eight hours she'd be gone for good. As he dropped her off at the hotel, his expression was wistful, and Ella was tempted to kiss him on the cheek as a thank-you—a gesture a friend might make. But she didn't. Kisses would definitely sabotage her plans.

"Meet you in the lobby about six?" he asked as she opened the car door.

"Sure. And, Ben, thanks for taking the time today."

He nodded thoughtfully. "I'd make time for you—"

"Anytime?" she quipped.

"Anytime, anywhere," he murmured.

Flustered by his intense gaze, Ella stammered, "Um, okay, then. See you in an hour." She closed the door and watched as his car turned onto Main Street. Then she headed into the hotel.

An hour later she'd showered and changed into jeans and her new hoodie. He'd suggested having dinner at a new place near Town Square. Nothing fancy, he'd added, which Ella interpreted as a hint not to dress up. That suited her because a quick peek out her hotel room window revealed it was snowing again.

Her new boots clomped across the lobby's marble floor. She was adjusting the hood of her sweatshirt over her jacket collar when she spotted Ben talking to a woman in the center of the lobby. He noticed Ella, and the expression on his face made her pause. At the same time, the woman craned her neck around and Ella realized she was the same woman who'd been entering the hotel that morning. Ella's jaw clenched when she read her ID badge. Suzanna Winters. Brandon's sister.

Suzanna had just completed her freshman year at college and had been away from the Cove the summer Brandon drowned. Ella had met her only a few times during her vacations and remembered her as an aloof, older teen who hung with a different crowd.

Ben cleared his throat as Ella drew up. "Do you remember my cousin Suzanna? I was just telling her you were back in town for a few days."

Ella made a show of trying to remember though she knew she wasn't fooling the other woman. "I think so. You were usually with the older kids."

Suzanna gave a curt nod. Her gaze never wavered from Ella's face, and for a horrible moment, Ella wondered if she knew the whole story. Grace had told Ben and likely her parents, but surely Suzanna and the rest of the family also knew the truth about the prank.

"Are you enjoying your stay at the hotel?" she asked.

Not much of a greeting, Ella was thinking, but she said, "Yes, and it's wonderful to be back in the Cove."

After a long minute's appraisal, Suzanna

said, “Good. Well, I’ll leave you two to your dinner.”

Ella watched her stride away. “Does she know what really happened that summer?”

Ben’s face was sober. “Yes, but I think she’s still trying to understand. Zanna’s always been hard to figure out.”

“How long has your family known?”

“Since July.”

“I guess she’s still processing all of it, which I can understand, but still… Now she knows the truth.” She took a deep breath, about to go on when she noticed the flicker of unhappiness in Ben’s face. She didn’t want to ruin one of her two remaining evenings in the Cove. “Shall we go?” she asked, managing a faint smile as she pushed open the hotel door.

Outside, the night sparkled. Strings of lights swayed gently along Main Street, splashing color onto the black water of the harbor. Rows of shops, houses and cottages glowing with Christmas displays arced east toward the lighthouse, though the tip of the rocky peninsula was dark and unwelcoming. Ella shivered and flipped her sweatshirt hood up. The chill caught her breath.

"Cold?"

"Yes, but it's also very beautiful." Ella shoved her hands into her gloves and tucked them under her arms to speed up their warming.

"A different kind of beauty from summer." He stared up at the starlit sky.

"I remember sitting on the porch of our cottage with my dad, trying to pick out the constellations we could see on clear nights." The memory pulled at Ella and she suddenly teared up, remembering all she'd lost. She felt his eyes on her but couldn't risk looking his way.

"You must miss him."

"I do." When the moment passed, she announced, "I'm famished. Where are we eating tonight? And by the way, it's my treat." She descended the few steps to the sidewalk and looked back at him. "Come on!"

BEN TRIED TO focus his attention on the menu, but his eyes kept flicking to Ella. As soon as they'd walked into the new Italian place on a side street off Town Square, he'd felt his tension ease. The roaring fire at the end of the room and the intimate arrangement of tables welcomed them, and Ben smiled. The best part was that the proximity to other diners precluded private or intimate conversation. Here, the talk had to be superficial. He was relieved at that.

Ella raised her head from reading the menu. “I love places like this. A bit retro and charming.”

“As long as the food is good.”

“It doesn’t even have to be. Just being here on a cold winter’s night with a fire blazing and the aroma of sauces bubbling is enough.”

“It does smell amazing in here. I don’t see the kitchen, though.”

“Maybe they’re bringing the food in. You know, from the owner’s mother’s house down the street.”

“I like that image. Here’s to the food surviving the trek from Mama’s place tonight.” He lifted his water glass in a mock toast. Her giggle prompted a memory. “Remember when we met at that new pizza place near the harbor and some kids were passing by, so we sank down in the banquette seats because we didn’t want them to see us?”

Her face clouded suddenly and she peered at the menu again. He wanted to kick himself for spoiling the laugh they'd just shared, but then she looked up.

"You have a good memory, Ben."

Maybe too good, he thought. The woman across from him bore little resemblance to the giggling teenager lying on the seat of that pizza place. They'd thought they were pulling something off on the other kids by hiding their rapidly growing mutual attraction—the heady rush of adolescent hormones that had governed their lives that summer. He remembered the thrill of their fantasies about a possible life together beyond the Cove. But the joke had been on them. Fate had decreed otherwise, writing another future for them.

The server came to get their drinks order and, after he'd uncorked the bottle of wine Ben had chosen, left to fetch their shared appetizer.

Ella raised her wineglass. "Here's to old times anyway. They weren't all bad."

Ben clinked his glass against hers. "Cheers, and let's think about the good ones tonight."

She bit down on her lower lip. Ben wondered if unhappy memories were always at the forefront of her mind. Her face was flushed, either from the fire's glow or his remark, and he noticed her hand tremble as she set her wineglass down. If she were staying in town longer and if he thought they had a real chance at exploring some of those memories—good and bad—and laying them to rest where memories belonged, Ben would take her back to his new bungalow near the beach after dinner and talk. Bare his soul. *If only I had the courage to do just that.*

Their orders began to arrive—the *burrata* with crostini, her sweet potato gnocchi and his seafood linguini—and the tense moment gave way to small talk and the pleasures of eating good food.

"My mother and I took a trip to Venice the spring after my divorce. I needed to get away from Boston, and she'd always wanted to go to Italy. This food is as delicious as any we had there."

What she said was loaded with potential conversation starters—or enders. Ben opted for the one least likely to affect the mood. "How did you like Venice?"

"Beautiful city, way too many tourists. So many crowds that we jostled against one another crossing narrow canal bridges. But of course, we were two more, so I guess I can't be too judgmental." She paused. "Have you done any traveling outside the States?"

"Not yet. Maybe someday." Their eyes met, and Ben wondered if she was having the same thought as he was now about their many plans to explore the world together. He was beginning to wonder if time spent with Ella Jacobs was ever going to be without these memory bursts. They were in a kind of limbo—no going back and no way ahead. *But there's still tonight and tomorrow*, he told himself. That would have to do.

Ella broke the spell, pushing her empty plate aside and groaning. "So many carbs—"

"And so much pleasure."

"Especially on a freezing wintry night."

"Maybe a walk around the square? Burn off some of that?"

"I'd like that."

"Dessert?"

"No way," she groaned.

He scanned the room and managed to catch the server's eye.

"My treat," she reminded him as the server approached.

They were on their way out the door when another couple entered. Ben was holding the door for Ella and wasn't paying attention to them.

"Ben!"

He turned sharply. "Hi, Julie."

His sister's friend gave him a clumsy hug as the four of them stood in the tiny entryway. The icy blast from outside was a good excuse to keep moving, but for some reason, Julie stalled. She introduced her date while staring the whole time at Ella.

"Ella, this is Julie Parker, an old school friend of Grace's, and this is Ella Jacobs." Ben noticed Julie's frown. "Ella used to spend her summers here."

"So I heard." Her eyes skimmed across Ella before aiming a smile back at him. "Is the food here as good as people say?"

"It is."

"Great," she enthused. "See ya, Ben."

He placed his hand on Ella's back to usher her onto the sidewalk, where she suddenly rounded on him. "Wow! If looks could kill."

Ben suspected Grace hadn't revealed her story to Julie and tried to dismiss her rudeness. "She's a bit of an airhead."

"I thought people in small towns were supposed to be welcoming and friendly."

"People are the same everywhere, Ella. You know that."

"Yeah, you're right. But twice in one night?" She gave him a long, appraising look and began to walk.

Ben caught up to her and grasped her hand. "The night is still ours, Ella. Don't let anyone take it away."

"It's just that people here don't want me to forget." Her blue eyes glistened under the streetlight.

Ben tugged her closer. He wanted to kiss her trembling lips and tell her everything would be okay. But they had a long way to go before a kiss could make unhappiness disappear.

He squeezed her hand. "Come on. The night is still ours, right?"

She squeezed back. "To the square?"

"You bet." He looped his arm through hers and they strode along Main Street, up Porter, past Grace's bookstore, all in darkness. The music from the oompah band at the square reached them first, then the smoky fragrance of roasted chestnuts from a cart at the eastern corner of the plaza. People drifted around the perimeter of the skating rink, watching the skaters, munching on street snacks or just strolling while the cheesy tunes from the band filled the night. A large portable spotlight had been set up, its beacon aimed at the massive Christmas tree, which a handful of people on ladders were still decorating.

"What time is the official ceremony tomorrow?"

The interest in her voice gave Ben new hope for the next day. "I'm not sure. After dark, obviously. I'll call you when I find out."

Suddenly she was pulling him toward the rink. "Let's skate." She was pointing to the small skate-rental booth.

Ben closed his eyes. Not a good idea. But how could he dampen the first signs of pure pleasure he'd seen in her? All too quickly they were sitting on a side bench and lacing up skates—something Ben hadn't put on his feet since he was a kid, and even then, he'd only done so reluctantly. He'd never been into winter sports. Baseball and track had been his preferences in high school and college.

Ella grinned as he struggled with the laces. "See you out there." She glided a few feet away, drew a tight circle and disappeared into the crowd. Ben sighed and resumed lacing up.

By the time he got onto the ice, Ella was still nowhere in sight. He slid one foot ahead and then the other, keeping within arm's reach of the waist-high snow fence surrounding the rink. It wouldn't support him if he slipped, but at least he wouldn't topple onto the other skaters. He was jostled as a young boy about eleven or twelve whizzed past him. He must have heard wrong but thought the kid had said, "Sorry, Gramps."

Gramps? He'd almost completed half a lap around when someone breezed up to him and tucked an arm around his—the arm windmilling at his side while the other extended to the fence, just in case.

"You made it!"

Ben risked a quick glance. "Made a fool of myself is more like it."

"I take it skating isn't on your list of favorite winter sports."

"Nothing about sports is on my list of winter favorites." They'd reached the benches where people were putting on or taking off skates.

"Funny, I never knew that about you."

"And I never knew you were some kind of Olympic figure skater."

That brought another laugh. "Not much ice-skating in the summer here."

"True enough." His eyes met hers for a long, thoughtful moment. He was wishing he had time to discover all the other unknown sides to Ella Jacobs. "So, what now?" he asked as they sat down to take off their skates.

Ella looked up from knotting the laces on her boots. "Hot chocolate?"

The childlike lilt in the question warmed his heart. "It's a deal. I think Mabel's might be open late for the festivities." Hand in hand, they wound their way through the crowds, pausing briefly to watch great blocks of ice being lifted from a truck onto wooden platforms along the perimeter of the square.

"Those are for the ice sculpture contest next weekend." Ben wanted to ask if she might stay or at least come back to town for it, but he didn't want to be disappointed if she said no.

They strolled toward Mabel's and the harbor area. There were no empty tables at the diner, so they ordered their drinks to go and carried paper cups of the thick, rich chocolate down to the harbor. The stiff breeze had died down and they found a bench overlooking the marina boardwalk. He smiled at the soft humming sounds Ella was making as she held her cup between both hands and sipped.

"Delicious." He chugged the last mouthful and crumpled the cup in his hand.

"Finished already? That was fast."

"When I enjoy something, I want to dive right in. No dainty sips or nibbles for me."

Her laugh bounced from bench to bay and back. Ben pulled her closer. "Warm enough?"

"I am now." Her face tilted up to his, golden in the soft pools of light from the street behind them. A tiny streak of chocolate lurked in the corner of her mouth and as Ben dabbed it with his finger, her lips parted in a hesitant smile. He dipped his head and kissed her. Every nerve in his body came alive. His mouth filled with the smoky richness of chocolate and the tastes of Ella he'd dreamed about for years. He was spinning back in time to other kisses, furtive and exciting. Later he couldn't remember taking the cup from her hands and setting it on the bench beside him. But he must have, because her arms reached up around him and her hands gently held his face against hers, as if to keep him right there, locked on to her.

Eventually he reluctantly pulled his mouth away from hers. “That was better than any hot chocolate I’ve ever had anywhere.”

There was that smile again, the one that gave mixed messages. But her eyes told the whole truth. They were incandescent. Ben tucked her into the crook of his arm, holding on as tight as he dared. Giant snowflakes circled lazily from a black sky speckled with stars, and Ben wanted the night to last forever.

CHAPTER NINE

ELLA COULDN'T RECALL when she'd had a better sleep. She stretched under the duvet, raising her arms to touch the headboard and extending her legs till her toes poked out at the end. Except for bumping into Suzanna Winters and that friend of Grace's who'd given her such a dirty look, there had been no bad moments last night. Uncomfortable ones for sure, especially when Ben had walked her back to the hotel from Mabel's, but not bad.

Something indefinable had happened between them. Ella couldn't point to exactly what had led to this newfound comfort and ease with Ben. Maybe the skating, when she'd seen a vulnerability in him that she'd never noticed when he was young. He was no longer the boy she'd once known whose physical bearing always exuded confidence and strength. The new Ben had taken her teasing with humor and grace. All the pieces of last night had fit together perfectly, with the kiss completing the picture.

She'd been looking for that last piece for years and finally she had an answer. Yes, she could—and did—feel the same as the teenager she'd once been. Except last night's kiss had been so much more than the breathless excitement of their stolen kisses back then. There had been promise in it…and hope.

But these are my *feelings*, she thought. Did the kiss mean the same to him? Ella pondered that question as she got dressed. Perhaps she was reading too much into the kiss. It could have been only a spontaneous expression of pleasure at a fun night together. But no, she thought. A kiss like that would have been on her forehead or cheek. She stared briefly at her reflection in the bathroom mirror as she brushed her teeth. *However you want to analyze last night, Jacobs, not much in your current life will change because of a single kiss. Remember that.*

Because it was her last full day, and Ben had told her he had work, Ella decided to go for a walk after breakfast. A peek out the window revealed a bright, sunny day, but plumes of frosty air swirling up from the open patches of water in the harbor indicated cold temperatures. Ella reconsidered her wardrobe and reached for the hoodie she'd worn last night, knowing she'd need something on her head.

Mabel's Diner was just opening when Ella arrived. "Making up for a late night," explained the young woman who held the door for Ella.

"Well, I appreciated the hot chocolate last night, so thanks for staying open." She sat at a nearby table and scanned the chalkboard for breakfast options. Something hearty to prep for her walk. She was sipping the coffee the waiter had poured when she felt a presence at her side.

"I recommend the eggs Benedict." Grace was beaming down at her. "And I'm so happy you decided to stay, Ella."

Ella remembered her decision to remain in town for the weekend was mainly due to her unfinished business with Ben, something she'd forgotten in the headiness of last night. "Join me?"

"Thanks, but I've just come for some takeout coffee and cocoa. Becky's helping me this morning, and I always provide treats. I assume you'll be coming to the tree lighting tonight, then?"

Ella nodded.

"Wonderful, 'cause Drew's coming, too, and you'll get a chance to meet him."

The evening ahead was developing by the second. Ella had been planning a confrontation with Ben before leaving town and felt an unreasonable twinge of resentment at having little control over how her last few hours in the Cove would play out. "Great" was all she said.

"Okay, well, see you tonight."

Ella watched her friend go to the take-out counter and felt unexpectedly happy for her. She knew Grace was a decent person who'd made a mistake that ended badly, something that could happen to anyone. *Even me.* Brandon's wounded face after her angry taunt that night burst into her thoughts. Ella's breath caught and for a split second she was standing on the lighthouse path, his pained, accusing voice ringing in her ears. She closed her eyes.

"Are you ready to order?"

Ella opened her eyes. The server was standing beside her. "Yes, thanks. I'll have the eggs Benedict."

THE TOWN LOOKED so much smaller from the lighthouse path. Or perhaps viewing it from up there as an adult had something to do with the perspective. Ella's heart rate slowed after the challenging slog through midcalf-deep snow. Fifteen minutes ago she'd been gazing up at the snow-covered dunes towering over the beach and thinking a route to the lighthouse would be easier from the Cove's upper road, near the highway. But to take it, she'd have to walk back through town. Of course, she could have driven to the junction where the dunes met the highway and trekked to the lighthouse from there, which also would have been easier, but challenges appealed to Ella.

Turning away from the scene below, she stared at the lighthouse several yards ahead. It wasn't as pretty as she remembered. The red band that circled it had faded to a dull salmon color and its cap of snow gave it a slightly comical appearance, like a cartoon character. She almost expected the lighthouse to start singing and dancing. It definitely wasn't the image she'd been stressing over. Perhaps returning to the Cove in winter, when everything looked so different, had its positive side. But when she eyed the ice-covered black rocks circling the cement base, Ella shivered.

Was that where Brandon had been found? Or had he been discovered at the foot of the dunes, closer to the beach? *This may not have been such a good idea.* She shivered in spite of the exertion of the climb. Deciding to head back, she spotted something red in a drift of snow and moved toward it, noticing what she hadn't before. Footprints. They weren't fresh, and their imprints had been lightly filled in by last night's snowfall. They stopped right at the flash of red—a bouquet of frozen roses.

Ella looked around as if she might discover someone hiding nearby, then tittered nervously at the foolish notion. There was no one else here, as far as she could see, and few places to hide anyway. *Get a grip, Jacobs.* Whoever had been up here was long gone. Perhaps the flowers were meant as some kind of memorial. For Brandon? If so, then the person could have been Grace, because she was the organizer behind the memorial. Ella would ask her about the flowers when she saw her later. For now, the chill was filtering through her extra layers. Ella retraced her steps, noticing that more footprints were coming from the direction of the road. It was an easier route for sure, but did Grace own a car? Or maybe someone drove her. Hadn't she said her fiancé was in town?

Ella was focused on these questions and missed the precise place where she'd climbed up. She realized her mistake as soon as she stepped onto the snow-covered slope and her foot hit an invisible patch of ice. She slipped, fell backward and slid down the dune. If she hadn't been startled by the tumble, she might have laughed at her comical descent. When she hit the bottom, she waited a moment to assess any damage. All to her pride, she decided with relief. On her way toward the center of town, she paused in front of Cassie Fielding's place.

Staring at the shuttered bungalow, Ella realized she hadn't once considered what had become of her. She knew there'd been just Cassie and her mother, with no word of a father. Ella had never been inside their home. Cassie maintained her mother wasn't a tidy housekeeper and didn't like guests. Besides, the Winters home had always been so welcoming. Grace's mother had been warm and friendly, frequently baking cookies and other treats for them.

Plus, Ben had sometimes been around. He was the draw for Ella that last summer and, as it turned out, for Cassie, too. If she'd known back then about Cassie's own crush on Ben, she might have reacted differently the night of the bonfire—been more conciliatory to Brandon and empathetic to Cassie. Ella sighed. That was her adult self revising history. Teenagers didn't think like that. She suddenly wondered if Cassie had married and had children. Somehow that image didn't fit the teen Ella remembered. *But then, here you are, Ella Jacobs—unmarried, childless and unloved.* The sting of tears forced her on. Self-pity was unproductive.

Most of the sidewalk beyond the Fielding house had been cleared, so she made better progress. As she walked, she scanned the rows of permanent bungalows and summer cottages, looking for the one her family had always rented. It had been small for their family of four. Ella and her younger brother had shared one of the two bedrooms, which had been an annual source of annoyance. On warm summer nights, she'd often camped out on the tiny screened-in porch, but later, when she was a teen, she'd sometimes slept over at Grace's. Ella's crush on Ben and his obvious interest in her had charged the sleepovers with an exciting tension that she identified later as adolescent hormonal stirrings. If only she'd had an older sibling or friend who could have taken her aside to advise, *Look, these feelings you have are perfectly natural, but don't let them cloud your judgment. They're not going to last forever.*

When she reached the roadside staircase leading up to the Winters home, Ella stopped. Her old cottage must be here somewhere. She remembered it was near the bottom of the hill where the Winters home perched, making access to Grace so convenient. She walked back and forth, studying each of the bungalows. One that was bigger and newer seemed to be in the approximate location where hers had been, but she couldn't be certain. Finally, she gave up and continued on her way. Another hot chocolate at Mabel's was beckoning.

BEN PARKED BEHIND the black SUV that belonged to Drew Spencer, Grace's fiancé. The Coast Guard officer was in town from Portland for the tree lighting and was staying at Grace's apartment, while she was bunking in her old room across from Ben's. He knew their mother liked the arrangement. Not because the couple wasn't married and she was old-fashioned but because, for a few rare hours, she got to relive the past when both of her children were home. The house was too big for just his parents, and Ben sometimes wondered how long they'd want to stay in it, given his father's ongoing health problems. Maybe he'd be able to persuade them to move into one of the new condos he hoped to be building in the very near future.

His meeting with Andy that morning had gone well. They'd tweaked the bank presentation for Monday, deciding to highlight the condo design rather than the company's current financial downturn. *If the numbers scare them, they won't be objective about your ideas*, Andy had told Ben. *They won't see the potential.* That was the key word they'd agreed on as a focus. Ben knew the company had a good reputation here and in the greater Portland area, and its equity was solid. He wasn't worried about paying bills or making payroll. *For now.*

He and Ella had arranged to meet at Mabel's prior to the tree lighting, which was scheduled for seven. They'd pick up a coffee and walk to the square, then have dinner later. Seeing Drew's vehicle, Ben decided to invite the two of them, as well. It might be Grace's last chance for a visit with Ella. *And yours.* The thought jolted him back to reality.

Last night's kiss had been replaying in his head all day at the most inconvenient times. There'd been a moment when Andy had caught him staring off into space and he'd been forced to come up with a vague reply to his question, *Something up, boss?* Ben was determined not to let anything dampen these last few hours with Ella, especially the sobering fact that a kiss was no guarantee of a future with her.

He climbed out of his car and went inside. As usual, the house was quiet. Ben thought he heard the TV in the den and as he walked along the hall, he could hear the radio in the solarium. These were the rooms his parents dwelled in more and more, along with the kitchen and master bedroom, of course. He went to the kitchen first for a glass of water and then on to the solarium, where his mother was reading the newspaper in her favorite armchair.

"Hello, dear. You were up and out early this morning."

"I had a meeting with Andy to discuss our next presentation."

"When is it?"

"Monday morning." Ben sat on the chair across from her.

"Do you feel prepared for it?"

He had to smile at his mother's concern. Her expression took him right back to final exams in twelfth grade. "I feel optimistic."

"Will you pass it by your father beforehand?"

That was a loaded question. She was well aware of the ongoing battle of wills with Charles. Was she suggesting he *ought* to see his father first, or was she merely curious? Ben leaned forward and ran a finger across his forehead. This part of his life badly needed fixing. He was about to make some noncommittal reply when his mother surprised him.

"You don't have to, you know. That's all I'm saying. He made you temporary head, and I know how challenging it's been for you.

I've lived with your father for forty-two years and no one knows him better. Do what's best for you and the company. Trust yourself."

While he stared at her, his mouth embarrassingly agape, she went on to say, "Suzanna phoned me with some startling news."

Ben was still focusing on his mother's advice about Charles and was slow to pick up on the abrupt change in her expression. "What?"

"She told me that girl is back. Well, obviously she's a woman now, but—"

"Are you referring to *Ella*?"

"I am, Ben. She's staying at the hotel, and—"

"And I was with her when we bumped into Suzanna." Ben felt a rise of hot annoyance. No. *Anger.* This was what happened to people living in small towns—*with their parents.*

"So Suzanna told me. Why didn't you mention anything to us?"

Now his irritation was directed at his sister. "Grace invited her and I figured it was her job to tell you and Dad."

"We all know how diligent Grace is about keeping people informed." Evelyn sniffed.

He took a deep breath. "Mom, we also know the truth about what happened. Ella

Jacobs had nothing to do with any of it. And no," he quickly put in, seeing she was about to interrupt, "don't bring up that old chestnut about 'where there's smoke, there must be fire.' You know very well Ella wasn't to blame at all. For anything."

"That's not how people in town see it, Ben. After I got off the phone with Suzanna, Janet Jeffery happened to call about book club and asked me if I knew Ella Jacobs was in town. She'd heard from a friend who'd noticed a poster in the bookstore window about her coming for some presentation. Janet was shocked that she'd have the nerve to show her face here. I haven't had a chance to speak to Grace yet, but I will. I can't for the life of me comprehend why she invited her here. Bringing up old hurts."

"I hope you put your friend straight about Ella, Mom. That she played no part in what happened to Brandon."

When Evelyn looked away Ben knew she hadn't and felt a rise of frustration.

Finally, she said, "There are many sides to this story, Ben, and though we think we know them now, because of what Grace has told us, we may not. Ella Jacobs may regret accepting

Grace's invitation after she reads this." She held up a copy of *The Beacon.*

Ben's stomach tightened. He wished he could have done something about the review, but interfering wouldn't have been right. In his anxiety over the funding presentations, he'd completely forgotten. He reached for the paper, turning to the page his mother had folded over.

Fact or Fiction? the headline read. Ben skimmed the article.

> *The debut young adult novel by E. M. Jacobs is, on one level, a standard coming-of-age story of a young teenager's fight against peer bullying. But Jacobs's eloquent version deals with other societal issues, like individuality battling conformist norms and the courage to speak up in an era when silence is rewarded. Jacobs handles teen angst deftly and empathetically, and that should be no surprise, given that the author—Ella Mae Jacobs, a former summer resident of the Cove—possibly sees herself as a victim of bullying and society's condemnation.*
>
> *And this is where fact and fiction*

merge. Ms. Jacobs spoke recently at Novel Thinking bookstore here in Lighthouse Cove. The presentation was attended mainly by awestruck teenagers far too young to know about the real-life connection of Always Be Mine *to a tragedy some seventeen years ago. A tragedy—the drowning of a teenage boy—that Ms. Jacobs was allegedly at the center of.*

When asked by this reporter, Ms. Jacobs denied any such link. "My characters are fictional and so is the story." Perhaps. But the facts speak for themselves and those of us who remember the events of that sad summer will decide for ourselves.

Ben stopped reading. He didn't trust himself to speak. He got to his feet and strode out of the room. *This is* not *going to ruin the next twenty-four hours with Ella*, he vowed, his hand clenched tightly around the paper. But doubt was already creeping up on him.

CHAPTER TEN

ELLA STOOD IN line at the counter, along with a handful of others who'd had the same idea to take a hot beverage to the tree lighting. Ben was late but not by much. She was debating whether to get him a coffee, too, if he didn't show up by the time it was her turn, when she saw him entering with Grace, who was holding hands with a tall, attractive man. She remembered Grace saying something that morning about meeting up at the tree lighting and felt a stab of disappointment that she and Ben wouldn't be alone.

"Hello," she said, managing a smile, as the three joined her in line.

Grace made the introductions as Ben stood close to Ella, his hand resting lightly on her shoulder. The gesture made her feel a part of the foursome, even though Ella knew she really wasn't, and she flashed Ben a quick smile while shaking hands with Drew Spencer.

The Coast Guard officer's grip was warm and friendly. "A pleasure to finally meet the friend Grace has told me so much about."

Ella's instant thought was, *Has she told you everything?* but his voice held no hint of sarcasm or innuendo. If he knew the whole story—and Ella assumed he did—he'd clearly accepted it and her without any judgment. She liked him at once.

She turned around to the people waiting behind her. "Mind if I get their orders, too?" she asked.

Someone farther back in line quipped, "If you get ours, as well," and everyone laughed. The joking continued as Ella handed coffee to Ben and Drew and hot chocolate to Grace. As they made for the door, there were a couple goodbyes plus a shouted "See you at the square, but hopefully not in a line," which set off another round of laughter.

The four were grinning as they paused on the sidewalk for the first sips of their hot drinks, their breath puffing vapor into the frosty night. A sense of belonging struck Ella, and the warmth that flowed through her had nothing to do with her hot chocolate. But she caught herself with a reminder—*all of this is temporary, so enjoy it while you can.*

Ben fell in step beside Ella as they headed for the square. "I hope you don't mind. I thought Grace would appreciate the chance to see a bit more of you before you have to leave tomorrow."

From the way Grace and Drew leaned into each other as they walked, Ella figured Grace's happiness lay solely with the man at her side and not at the chance of seeing Ella again. Envy was as pointless as self-pity, but for a long minute she gave in to it, feeling its sharp edge. She eyed Ben's profile, his gaze fixed on the street rather than on her. Despite the brief pressure on her shoulder in Mabel's, he'd made no effort to touch her or hold her hand. Last night's kiss and that second of closeness in the line had sparked a hope that she and Ben might be no different than any of the other couples making their way to the tree lighting—for the next few hours anyway.

Then he suddenly glanced at her. His smile was guarded, and his eyes, lit by the street's decorations, seemed troubled. Something was on his mind. Was it her leaving tomorrow? Or perhaps his thoughts were similar to hers at that moment, dwelling on all the what-ifs. He reached for her hand, squeezing it gently, and Ella reciprocated.

The sounds of Town Square reached them, quickening their footsteps. Turning around to grin, Grace began to run. Drew shouted some exclamation Ella couldn't catch and dashed after her. With his long legs, he caught up to Grace in seconds.

Ella looked at Ben and smiled.

"Her first Christmas back in the Cove in a couple of years," he said, shrugging.

She thought Grace's glee had more to do with sharing her first Christmas with Drew Spencer and felt that envy again. *Try harder to put the past behind you. For this one night.*

"It's my first Christmas here ever, but I'm not running."

"Me neither." He released her hand.

Grace and Drew were nowhere in sight when they reached the square. Knots of people mingled around the edges, but the greatest number were clustered in front of the massive tree. Some dignitaries were standing on the steps of the town hall, and a silver-haired man holding a microphone was addressing the crowd. There was so much chatter around her that Ella could barely make out what he was saying.

"George Andrews, our mayor." A shiver at Ben's warm breath in her ear shot through her from head to toe. Ella moved closer to him. The brush of his down ski jacket against her cheek took her instantly back to other days when physical contact with Ben came as naturally as their frank and honest talks. For a single, blinding moment she craved that feeling again, but when she glanced at his profile, fixed on the mayor, as if the person leaning into him was merely any woman, Ella felt such a stab of pain—or was it regret?—that she inched away from him, pretending to take an interest in the people around them.

They were all ages, and no doubt many had witnessed numerous tree-lighting ceremonies, yet the excitement in their eyes and voices seemed fresh and new, like the tree itself. She wondered if growing up in a big city had inured her to civic celebrations like this—not that she could recall the last one she'd attended.

The mayor's mic squealed feedback as a school band behind him struck its first note and the entire crowd began to sing "Deck the Halls." When the music ended, someone holding the mic began a countdown that was instantly taken up by the crowd. At the roar of "One!" hundreds of lights on the tree flickered momentarily before beaming steadily, filling the square as well as the dark sky above it with rainbows of color. A millisecond of silence fell over the crowd, followed by a rumble of exultation. Ella turned to look up at Ben, locking eyes with him as they broke into laughter. The crowds began to break up into small groups. Ben reached for her hand.

"Shall we go look for Grace and Drew? If we don't find them, I'll text her to say we're heading to the restaurant."

His warm hand enveloping hers lifted her out of the past. She smiled back, squeezing his hand. "Where are we eating tonight?"

"There are one or two places here in the Cove that we haven't hit yet, though if you stayed longer, we could check out places in Portland."

"Perhaps I should stay just for that opportunity." She was teasing, but his face clouded over.

"I'd like that," he said, his voice low. He stared at her as if waiting for her to declare

"Okay, I'll stay longer, then!" and at that very moment, Ella would have, but a nearby shout broke the spell. Grace was marching their way, with Drew in tow.

"ABSOLUTELY NOT!" BEN shook his head once more because Grace wasn't taking no for an answer. She looked at Ella as if to plead for her intervention.

Fortunately, Ella shrugged and said, "We went skating last night."

"I've had too much to eat and drink to skate around a rink with dozens of other people," Drew put in.

Ben was happy that Grace didn't have the man completely wrapped around her baby finger. He scanned the remains of their barbecue dinner at Joe's Smokehouse, the new place he'd read about a while ago in *The Beacon.* His sense of well-being was suddenly marred by this first thought all night of the book review in the paper. He ought to tell Ella about it but figured why spoil her last night here? She might leave in the morning without seeing it. No point in creating unnecessary problems. He ran a finger along the rim of his beer glass, thinking he didn't need another complication in this brief reunion with Ella Jacobs, until suddenly he was aware of the silence that had fallen after someone—*Grace?*—had spoken.

He blinked, rising out of his thoughts, as Ella replied, “Um, well, that’s very nice of your mother but I’d planned to leave early. Besides, I only have the room for tonight and I think the hotel is filling up.”

Ben watched the slightly embarrassed lift of her shoulders. He wished he’d been paying more attention. Had his mother invited Ella for Sunday dinner? After her complaints to him that very morning about old hurts?

“Persuade her, Ben. Drew could stay with us if he decides not to go back to Portland, and Ella can use my place.”

Ella was the only one not looking at him. Instead she was playing with the fork angled on her plate and Ben couldn’t see enough of her face to determine if she wanted persuading or not. It was one of those socially awkward moments that he hated, and he was annoyed at Grace—and especially his mother—for not mentioning the idea to him before. Then there was the review. Had Grace read it, too? He ought to have known something would come up to throw the night off-kilter. Whatever he might say would either focus more unwanted attention on Ella or dampen Grace's earnest appeal.

It was Drew who saved him. "No pressure, Ella. But let me point out that changing plans after a big meal and a few glasses of wine may not be a good idea. Best wait for the morning to decide."

Grace gave him a playful punch on the shoulder. "You're always so sensible."

Ben let out his breath.

The awkward moment passed until Ella suddenly said, "I went for a walk earlier today, up to the lighthouse."

Silence fell over the table, and Ben noticed Drew's quick frown as he draped an arm across Grace's shoulders. "Not a hospitable place this time of year," Drew commented.

"No kidding. But the view of the town was great. I did notice something odd, though."

"What?" Ben asked, wondering how the conversation got turned in this direction.

"There was a bunch of flowers up there. Red roses. Frozen stiff. Guess they'd been there for a couple of days."

Grace cleared her throat. "That's weird.

Last summer I found flowers a couple of times. Strange that someone is still leaving them."

Ben noticed his sister's attention drift, going back to what had been an emotional summer for her. Then the server came to remove dishes and present the bill, which prompted a spontaneous verbal tussle over who was going to pay. The interruption had been timely, Ben thought as they put on their coats. He didn't understand the significance of the flowers at the lighthouse, but he did know the place and its memories were still a sensitive topic for Grace.

Seconds later the flowers were forgotten as they stood on the sidewalk, stomping their feet against the cold. Grace suggested a post-dinner espresso somewhere. Ben couldn't tell from Ella's impassive face what she wanted to do. He was about to decline when Drew once again came to the rescue.

"I don't know about the rest of you, but I've had a long day and coffee at this hour wouldn't be a wise idea for me." He must have noted Ben's frown, because he added, "After I left work, I picked up Henry at the rehab place in Portland and got him settled back into his place here."

"How's he doing?" Ella asked.

"Fine. He can manage on his own, with the help of a walker and a cane. But we plan to check up on him. He doesn't have anyone else in town," Grace answered.

"He's one of the people here I'd have liked to have seen, but—"

"Another reason to stay longer!"

Ben decided to intervene. "Tonight was great. I'm glad you two could join us." He didn't look at his sister but felt her eyes on him as she and Drew said goodbye.

After they left, Ben asked, "Want to go for a bit of a walk? That was a lot of food."

Her face brightened. "I'd like that."

"The harbor? It's always pretty at night."

"Yes!"

Her enthusiasm was encouraging. Was she thinking of last night's harbor visit like he was? He placed his hand on the small of her back, guiding her down to Main Street. The area was still busy. Ben wondered if there were more people at the tree lighting than in other years. If so, was that due to the new subdivision? The Cove was growing and he was happy to be part of its expansion. When they reached the marina, they stopped to look out across the inner bay and Casco beyond.

"It's pretty but kind of scary at the same time," Ella murmured.

"Because it's so big. The great unknown."

"Like the future." She stared silently across the water.

Ben shifted from one foot to the other. He didn't want the evening to end on a melancholy note. "Hey, would you like to see my new house?"

"You have a house? I thought you were living with your folks."

"I am through the Christmas season, but come the new year, I'll be independent again." He laughed. "Thanks goodness. Not that I can complain but—"

"You can't go home again."

"Not as an adult, that's for sure. At least, not permanently."

"Is it close by?"

"Remember where your old cottage was, at the foot of the hill leading up to our house?"

"I looked for it on my walk this morning but couldn't find it."

"Yeah, because my dad sold off most of his

rental units and the people who bought your place tore it down to build a winter home. But then they sold it in the fall to me." He smiled as her eyes widened in surprise.

"That place is yours? I'd love to see inside, even if it's not the same cottage."

He folded her hand in his, and they weaved in and out of the knots of people until they were standing in front of the house he had yet to move into.

"I wondered if this was where our place had been, but I thought my memory was playing tricks on me."

"Nope." He led her up the steps onto the porch. "I'm thinking of enclosing part of this with screens for the summer. Like yours had. Remember?"

"I do. I loved to sleep out there on hot summer nights."

Ben had a sudden image of the two of them sitting on the two-person swing that had been at one end, holding hands and pondering the future. "There's no furniture or anything yet, but other than some minor details, it's good to go." He dug into his jeans pocket for the key and stood aside for her in the compact entryway. When he flicked the light switch, her soft gasp more than made up for the hours of work he'd personally put into the place. "The couple who built it did a great job, so I didn't have to change a lot. I decided to keep the hardwood floors because they're solid oak and durable. I also kept the gas fireplace for now."

"I'm assuming it's winterized."

"Better be, because I'm moving in in a few weeks. Come and see the kitchen. It's my favorite room."

She hesitated, looking down at her boots.

"Don't worry about them. The floors have been treated, and I have a cleaning team booked for the week before my move."

He led the way along a short hall, past a closed door—"downstairs powder room"—and another room—"office or den"—to the rear of the house and the kitchen. "This is where I made most of the changes. New appliances, and I had the island lighting replaced. But I liked the granite counters so I kept them. There's a deck beyond those sliding doors." He turned to see her making a slow pivot, getting the full 360-degree perspective.

"I like the island counter."

That amused him. "What about the rest?"

She turned back to him, her face glowing. "It's beautiful, Ben. I can't believe this is our old cottage."

"Well, it really isn't, Ella. That was torn down, remember? But I like to think it is, in spirit anyway."

"That's a lovely thought." She moved closer and placed her hand on his forearm.

His heart swelled. "Ella, I—"

"Shh." She tapped her finger on his lips, her upturned face shining with pleasure.

He lowered his mouth onto hers, but after a minute, she pulled back and he could barely hear what she was murmuring over the pounding in his chest.

"This isn't a good idea, Ben."

He closed his eyes, pressing her against him, reluctant to let go. Then he dropped his arms. "Yeah. You're right. Guess we better head back." He swallowed hard against the lump in his throat. She was leaving the next day, and he had a sinking feeling that kiss might have been his last chance to prove they could go back in time.

CHAPTER ELEVEN

ELLA STOWED HER things in her car and decided to leave it in the lot on the side street next to the hotel while she had a last breakfast at Mabel's. She'd have to look for a similar café in her Boston neighborhood, though she suspected nothing else would compare—in her mind, at least.

She hadn't slept well. Ben's kiss had almost led her to believe they really could put the past behind them. The passion that had soared through her had felt, for a frightening moment, uncontrollable. Until her brain kicked into action, saving her from interpreting a couple of kisses as a sign that everything could be so easily fixed.

Her failure to follow through with her more important reason for returning to the Cove—getting an explanation from Ben—was what had compelled her to stop kissing him last night. She'd been sidetracked, thinking all the social events—the dinners, the skating, even the shopping—were the outings of an ordinary couple. But she and Ben weren't an ordinary couple, and unless she got what she'd come for, they never could be. She'd wrestled with that dilemma all night, knowing that a confrontation with Ben might bring her some satisfaction but could also—and this frightened her most of all—destroy any possibility of a second chance with him. A second chance she was beginning to realize she wanted.

After packing up, Ella had remembered she hadn't properly thanked Grace for her gift, so she'd texted to invite her to join her at Mabel's. Perhaps the decision about whether or not to leave town was best made on a full stomach.

Greeted by the same young woman from yesterday, Ella impulsively asked, "Is there a Mabel? Just that this place is so great, I wanted to thank her for such wonderful food."

"There used to be a Mabel, but she's retired. The new owner is Sam, but he decided to keep the diner's name."

"Well, please pass on my compliments. I'm waiting for a friend, so I'll order when she arrives."

"Will do. Sit anywhere you like. I'll be over with coffee in a sec."

Turning away, Ella noticed a few copies of *The Beacon* on the counter and picked one up to read while waiting for Grace. She started to flip through it when a photo caught her eye. A picture of her sitting at the book table in Grace's store. Then she noticed the headline—*Fact or Fiction?*

When she finished reading, she lowered her head onto her hands. The reporter with all those questions at the book talk. The one Grace had insisted was nothing to worry about. Yet here she was, speaking through the town's only newspaper and drawing conclusions about *Always Be Mine* that Ella had preferred not to be drawn—certainly not while she was still in the Cove. Plus, there was her photograph, and not a very flattering one either. She peered around at the handful of other diners, wondering if any would recognize her.

You're being silly, Jacobs.

Her mother had once said when Ella was a teen, *Life isn't always about you, Ella.*

But life in the Cove—past and present—felt very much like it *was* all about her. The guarded expressions when her name was uttered, the cool greetings and the brush-offs were testament to that. By the time her coffee arrived, she'd read the review again and was debating skipping her planned visit to Henry and returning to Boston right away.

She folded the paper and set it aside. If Grace didn't come soon, she'd leave a note with the server and go. But she'd no sooner had the thought than Grace breezed through the door, full of apologies.

"Sorry, Ella. A bit of drama at home. My dad fell in the shower this morning."

"Oh no! Is he okay?"

"Some bruises. Luckily he didn't hit his head. He refused to be driven to emergency in Portland, so Mom called their family doctor and he came to check him out. Dad has to go for an X-ray tomorrow, and we're supposed to keep a close eye on him." She sat down opposite Ella and unzipped her jacket. Then her gaze fell on the folded newspaper. "Oh."

"Did you—"

"Uh-huh." Grace gave a half-hearted shrug. "She liked the novel."

"Yeah, that part of the article was okay. It's just all the rest that bothers me. Raising baseless issues and implying I had something to do with what happened to Brandon."

"I'm sorry about that, and just to let you know, Ben had nothing to do with it."

"Why would *Ben* be involved?"

"Well...um...because he owns the newspaper. Kind of."

"Ben owns *The Beacon*?" Ella saw Grace wince and lowered her voice. "Since when?" She noticed the server heading their way. "Let's order first."

After the young woman left, Grace explained. "Ben owns it, but he doesn't run it. He bought controlling interest a couple of months ago when the owner—a former school friend of his—needed financial help to keep the paper from going under. *The Beacon* has been in the Collins family for a couple of generations, and Ben hated to see it disappear or sold to some conglomerate."

"Has Ben read it?"

She nodded. "Yesterday, but as I said, he didn't know about it before."

"Yet he didn't say a word to me last night."

"Maybe he didn't want to...you know...put a damper on the evening."

Or see his chances of getting another kiss evaporate. *Get a grip, Jacobs. You're not a teenager anymore.*

"He was angry about it," Grace added.

"How do you know?"

"Something my mother said. He jumped at her about…" Her voice trailed off.

"About what?"

"Just things. Family and business issues," Grace said.

Ella had no doubt she'd been part of that conversation—otherwise Grace wouldn't look so uncomfortable. She decided to let the matter drop. Grace wasn't the problem and, she had to admit, neither was Ben. The article simply highlighted what she'd been experiencing since her return. She was still being blamed and she had no idea how to set that right. At least, not with the town. Ben was another matter. For now, she'd end this last visit with Grace on a friendly note. She decided to change the subject. "I just found out that the real Mabel is retired and her counterpart is really a Sam."

Grace smiled. "Yeah. He's new to town. Well, new a little more than a year ago."

Ella wondered how long a person would have to live in the Cove to be considered a genuine "townie." Would she ever know? Not likely now.

"You mentioned at dinner that you'd like to see Henry before you leave," Grace said. "Are you still up for that or do you have to go right away?"

Ella didn't want her goodbye to Grace to end on a sour note, and she genuinely wanted to see Henry. "I can stay long enough for a short visit with him. Listen, don't worry about the review. I've gotten negative comments about my writing over the years. My skin is pretty thick by now."

"Okay," Grace said, her voice sounding relieved. "I'll give you directions, but I can't come with you. I promised Mom I'd help out with Dad this afternoon. Also, she asked me to let you know that she'll have to take a rain check on dinner."

Ella had forgotten all about the dinner invitation and didn't recall accepting anyway. "A rain check? Your mom was always so wonderfully… What's the word I'm looking for here?"

"Old-fashioned?"

"Yeah, but in a nice way, not a stodgy one. I have warm memories of her."

"She is a good mother, especially when I was a teen. Not too intrusive. Just enough to reassure me she was thinking about me. That she knew I had stuff on my mind."

Ella thought of the weeks after her parents split up. The undercurrent of anger from her mother and Ella's belief that she was being blamed for it. *Not true*, her mother had told her years later. But it had been hard for Ella to believe her, the words coming so long after she'd needed to hear them.

"How did your parents react when you told them what really happened that summer?"

The unexpected question clearly threw Grace off. She flushed and peered down at the table for a minute before answering. "They were stunned. Couldn't believe it at first. I think they still struggle with that. Their darling girl doing something so mean."

Ella thought back to what Ben had said about Grace suffering, too. Cassie had taken full advantage of Grace's teenage insecurities.

"No one knew Brandon would do what he did," Ella said. She reached across the table to clasp Grace's hand. "We were just kids, and not bad ones either. Maybe it's time to stop beating ourselves up about it." She kept her eyes on Grace's. "You asked for my forgiveness and...well...I'm sorry I haven't come out and said it, but…" Grace's eyes welled up and Ella felt the sting of her own tears. "I want you to know that I do forgive you." There was a moment of silence before she added, "So how do I get to Henry's place?"

"I'LL GET ONE of my men to install grab bars in the shower and by the toilet. And we need to get mats for the shower and bathtub, too."

Evelyn was shaking her head and Ben felt a rise of irritation. "It's not a big deal." He and Evelyn were sitting in the solarium after they'd persuaded Charles to rest.

"Your father won't like all this fuss."

"He doesn't have a say in this, Mom." He took in the worry lines in her pale face. His father's fall that morning had frightened her badly, as it had Ben and his sister. The fact that Charles hadn't seriously hurt himself was meaningless next to the possibility that a fall could happen again and with more serious consequences.

Evelyn pursed her lips, obviously unhappy about riling her husband. *Too bad*, Ben was thinking. It was time to let Charles Winters know he was no longer running things at work and even here, at home.

"We can't take away his independence, Ben. That's what gets him up in the morning. He needs to know he has a say in things."

"A say is merely that. It's not him telling *us* what he will or will not do."

"The doctor says the fall might have been due to low blood pressure. I know Charles had problems last year with that."

"Grab bars are simply safety measures, Mom."

"You're right, Ben. I'm just glad you and Grace were here. I couldn't have gotten him on his feet by myself."

Any thoughts that he could resume a life beyond the Cove had slowly faded over the past several months as Ben gradually came to terms with the reality of being available for aging parents. He was thirty-five years old, divorced and essentially still working for his father. And living at home, though that would change soon.

He hadn't really considered what living in Lighthouse Cove permanently would be like for him. Was there a woman out there for him? Someone who could make all thought and memory of Ella Jacobs disappear? He doubted that now. The hard facts of his situation hadn't hit him until Ella had arrived and he'd seen how his life might have been.

Earlier that morning Ben had decided to see Ella before she left. Their parting last night had been awkward. First, she'd wanted to say good-night outside the hotel on the sidewalk—in the middle of winter. He hadn't been expecting an invitation up to her room or even somewhere for a nightcap after that impulsive kiss, but really? The sidewalk?

Then when he'd tried to hug her, she'd stepped back and offered a handshake instead. *Awkward* didn't do justice to the moment. Now he was doubting if going to see her one last time was a wise move. If his father hadn't fallen, he might have already been enjoying a last coffee with her at Mabel's. Though perhaps it wasn't too late. Perhaps his sister could take over here at home. "Where's Grace, by the way?"

"She went to meet up with Ella for breakfast. At Mabel's, I think." Evelyn pursed her lips disapprovingly. "I asked Grace to mention our dinner plans for tonight were off, since she was the one who'd suggested inviting her. All for the best anyway."

Ben had forgotten about the unexpected

dinner invite Grace had passed on to Ella last night. His mother never ceased to surprise him, but right now her tone did. When Grace had confessed about giving Brandon—*and Ella*—the notes from Cassie, his mother had forgiven her daughter in the space of a heartbeat. Whereas Ella couldn't seem to shake the role of villain in the whole sad affair. However, there was no point talking to her about it now that Ella was leaving. What really pained him was the fact that Ella had invited Grace to join her for breakfast and not him. But maybe he could fix that.

When he turned to leave, his mother asked, "Where are you going?"

"Uh, I have some work to do. You'll be okay, right? Dad's resting, and you can text me or Grace if you're worried about him."

"Go ahead. I'll be fine, Ben. I've decided to cook after all. Take-out pizza isn't my idea of Sunday dinner."

Ben smiled, knowing puttering in the kitchen had always been therapy for his mother. As he left the solarium he texted Grace, asking if she was still with Ella at Mabel's. His phone dinged at once.

I'm at my place with Drew. He's helping me unpack a shipment of books before going back to Portland. Ella went to see Henry.

Okay. He hadn't seen the old man since his return to town, so that would work. Minutes later he was pulling up in front of Henry's bungalow. Another car was already parked there that he guessed was Ella's.

"Ben?" She stood in the doorway, surprise and something else he couldn't identify in her face. Her lovely face, he amended.

"Um, thought I better pop around to see Henry before my work week starts." He cringed at the lame excuse.

She held the door for him to step inside, where he bent down to remove his boots and place them on the mat next to hers. She was wearing jeans and the blue sweater from the other day—the one that highlighted the dramatic color of her eyes. Her hair gleamed in the shaft of sunlight pouring in from the open door, and Ben wanted so much to bring her into his arms that he had to clench his jaw.

"Henry will be happy to see you. We were just talking about you and your father. How is he?"

"He's okay, thanks. It was more of a scare than anything." He was far more interested in hearing what they'd been saying about him than recapping his dad's fall.

"Henry's in the living room, and I was about to make tea. Would you like some?"

"Please." He searched her face for any sign of softening since last night's goodbye but found nothing more in it than simple courtesy. As if he were a neighbor popping in for a visit. She went down the hall leading from the entryway to the kitchen while Ben turned right into the cozy living room.

"Ben! What a wonderful surprise." Henry was sitting in a recliner, his legs propped up on the ottoman extension and his cat, Felix, sleeping on his lap. A cane leaned against one of the chair's arms and a walker stood nearby.

Ben had a pang of guilt at the pleasure in the old man's face. He'd seen him only a handful of times since Ben's return to town almost a year ago. The most recent was a visit to the rehab center where Henry had been recuperating after his surgery. Grace had always been closer to the former owner of Novel Thinking, because she'd been buying books from him since she was a kid.

"Ella has been telling me a bit about your father. How is he?"

Ben went through the morning's events, but most of his attention was tuned to the kitchen and the sounds of Ella making tea. He was relating his mother's concerns about Charles heeding the doctor's advice when Ella returned with a tray of cups and saucers, a teapot, milk, a bowl of sugar and a plate of cookies.

"I hope you don't mind that I rummaged through your cupboards and fridge, Henry."

"Good for you. I'm impressed that you could put all that together, and I'm sure those cookies didn't come from a cupboard."

Ben met Ella's eyes and they both smiled.

"I'm embarrassed to say Mabel's became something of a daily routine while I was here."

"Too bad you have to leave, just when I've come home." Henry shooed Felix from his lap as Ella handed him a cup of tea.

Ben thought he saw a streak of pink rising up her neck at the old man's reference to leaving. While they drank and nibbled cookies, Henry told them about his rehab experience and some of the other patients he'd met there.

"One lady was from the Sea View Retirement and Nursing Home in Portland. When I said I was from Lighthouse Cove, she mentioned that a woman at her nursing home was also from here. Violet Fielding." He paused. "But Violet had recently passed away."

The reference to Cassie's mother had Ben glancing quickly at Ella. Her face revealed nothing, but the hand holding the teacup was shaking. She set the cup onto a saucer. "I should really get on the road."

Ben hoped his own disappointment wasn't as obvious as Henry's.

"Will you come back for a longer visit next time?" the old man asked.

"Of course. I'll put all this away before I leave, Henry."

"Let me help with that." Ben got up, ignoring the look she shot him, and carried the tray into the kitchen. As soon as he set it down on the table, she hissed, "What're you doing here?"

"I came to see Henry."

"Did Grace tell you I was here?"

He nodded.

"We said goodbye last night, Ben."

"Ella—"

"And frankly there's nothing more to say."

But there was so much more to say that Ben didn't know where to begin. What she blurted next, however, solved that dilemma for him.

"I read the review in *The Beacon* this morning and wondered why you hadn't mentioned you were an owner. Not that it matters, of course, but then I also wondered if there were other things you haven't told me."

For a minute Ben thought she'd somehow found out about the rest of it—what he'd done himself that night seventeen years ago. But no, she couldn't have. Grace had promised not to tell anyone about the note handed over to the police. The note that had triggered community animosity for Ella.

Until she added, "Like why you disappeared the day after Brandon was found."

"Please." He kept his eyes on hers in spite of the anger he saw in them. "Let's talk. Come to my place."

"It's about time we did talk, Ben."

CHAPTER TWELVE

ELLA SAT IN her car outside Ben's house. She'd left first, but from the twinkle in Henry's eyes she doubted he was fooled by their abrupt departure within minutes of each other. From the half hour she'd spent with Henry before Ben's unexpected arrival, it was obvious the old man was pretty intuitive. She'd figured Grace had already told Henry about the prank she and Cassie had played on her and Brandon.

Ella had envied Grace and Henry's friendship as a teen, an age when connections with adults were normally fraught with tension or rebellion. Plus, Henry had never been the type to hand out unsolicited advice. He'd probably been a sounding board for Grace, whose relationship with her father had often been challenging though not as tumultuous as Ben's had been.

Henry had been too discreet to mention what happened all those years ago. When he answered the door, clutching on to his walker, he'd simply given her a pat on her shoulder and told her how happy he was to see her. His only reference to that time had been a quiet statement. *You were brave then, Ella, and you are now in coming back.* He was one of the few people in the Cove who hadn't leaped to conclusions about her—unlike the one person in town she'd relied on most of all for support.

Ben. Fancy him showing up at Henry's like that. She guessed she had Grace to thank. The whole brother-sister act was wearing her down. The relationship between Grace and Ben had been different when they were teenagers. Whenever Ella was around the Winterses, the communication between them had ranged from sniping banter to moody silences. Of course, they were grown up now and behaving as adult siblings should, but Ella wished she and her brother had as good an understanding of one another.

She checked the time on her car dashboard. Despite her excuses to Henry, she had no set schedule. The days up to and through Christmas were free because she wasn't due back at work until after New Year's.

Ella heard the rumble of an engine and

craned round to see Ben pull up behind her. *This is it*, she thought, as she got out of her car. The talk that would lead to his apology. Then she could get on with her life. But when he walked toward her, his face creased in a hesitant smile, Ella knew getting on with life now without Ben Winters in it might be a bigger challenge than the one she'd faced years ago.

"I appreciate your staying on a bit longer, Ella," he said when he drew near. "I…uh…I didn't want our goodbye to be unhappy. You know, the way it was last night. And then today, with that thing about *The Beacon*, I couldn't let you leave without clearing it up." When she failed to respond, he was silent for a minute before asking, "Want to go for a walk? We could talk inside, but as you saw, there's no furniture."

"A walk is fine, Ben. Anywhere in particular?"

"Along the beach? You're wearing your new boots, so you should manage okay."

Ella locked her car and zipped up her jacket. "I'm ready." She knew her curt tone had reinforced his obvious nervousness but didn't care. Now that the moment was finally here, she was determined to go through with it.

The waterfront was quiet for a Sunday morning. No more than a handful of people were out, some perhaps going to church and others to brunch somewhere. There were a few dog walkers on the beach boardwalk when they reached it. Ella shivered in the stiff breeze blowing off the water, wishing she'd worn her hoodie under her down jacket.

"Cold?" Ben put his arm around her shoulders and drew her closer.

She might have pulled away except she *was* cold, and his body heat wasn't only warm, it was comforting. They soon reached the end of the boardwalk and stepped onto the beach, crunching along on the mix of snow, ice and frozen sand. When they came to the place where the arc of beach curved into the peninsula, the lighthouse at its tip, Ben stopped.

"I thought I recognized that reporter at your book talk but wasn't sure," he began. "I want to clarify that I have a majority interest in the paper, but I don't manage it and I don't want to, and yes, I could have told you in passing, but was the connection between your book and what happened really that far-fetched? Don't you think that most people who knew the story would come to the same conclusion as that reporter did?"

Ella didn't want to hear that, because he was right. Had she been fooling herself, insisting the two stories were different when all along she knew she'd begun her novel as therapy? That she'd intended to breathe life into a character who had a happy ending, not one who drowned on a summer night? She looked across the bay, blinking back tears. There was kindness beneath Ben's blunt questions. That's what hurt most of all, because kindness wasn't part of her own agenda.

"Ella." He placed his hands on her shoulders, turning her to face him. He dabbed the corners of her eyes with his finger. "Don't make this bigger than it is."

Ella didn't want to hear that. "I'm sick and tired of being accused of something I didn't do! Everyone thinks that I wrote Brandon the note asking him to meet me on the lighthouse path and that it was my fault he ended up getting caught there at high tide. If Grace was so brave telling her family the truth, why couldn't she have told other people in town? Even just her friends." She couldn't stop the tears and strode ahead toward the snow-covered dunes. After a few seconds she heard him follow.

He was gazing up at the dune where she'd slid the day before. "Looks like someone had a tumble. People should know better than to go up there in winter."

"It was me."

"What?" He was looking at her now. "This was yesterday? When you told us about going up there last night, you didn't mention you'd fallen. And why did you go up anyway? Was it really for the view, as you implied?"

"I wanted to see the lighthouse. I thought if I looked at it close-up, I could exorcise the bad memories. Confront them and chase them away. Do you know what I mean?" She searched his face for some kind of affirmation. It was suddenly important to know that he could understand.

He glanced at the dune again, shaking his head. "You could have hurt yourself. Hit your head or broken something."

"But I didn't, Ben, and that's—"

"Yeah, not what we were talking about a second ago. I can't say I *know* what you went through back then, Ella. It was a scary and sad time for all of us but especially for you, because people were blaming you without having the facts. As for Grace, I don't know why she hasn't told anyone else. But that's her responsibility, not mine." He gazed out to sea. "I'm especially sorry that I didn't come to see you after. I don't know exactly why I didn't, but..." His voice trailed off. "You were waiting for me. At least, I guessed you were. I'm not going to blame anyone else, but there was a lot of pressure on me and Grace from the family. Questions. Crying. At the time, we both just wanted to hide from it all. And knowing what I do now—what Gracie did—I can understand why she stayed in her bedroom for days after. I wanted to see you, but people needed me at home. Then your family left." He turned away for a moment. "All of that doesn't justify what I did, though. Part of me refused to believe what everyone was saying—that you were secretly meeting Brandon—because I knew we cared for each other. I knew we had something special between us. But then the doubts came. I heard about the note you'd written and—"

"I *didn't* write it. You know that!"

"I do now, but back then I didn't. I'm sorry I doubted you. Sorry I let you leave the Cove without giving you a chance to tell me what really happened. Sorry I didn't contact you later, when the grief had gone. But by then, it felt too late."

Ella had been waiting to hear those words for years, but she didn't feel relief or vindicated. The turmoil in Ben's face and the quaver in his voice told her his apology was from the heart, but her own heart was still hurting. She couldn't help wonder if the apology she'd longed to get was going to change her life at all.

She managed a faint smile. "Thanks, Ben. I needed to hear that." She took a deep breath. "Now I guess I should get back to Boston." As she turned around to walk away from the dune, she caught a glimpse of his face. Was that what she'd *really* come for? To see his sadness?

"I'll help Grace. You go sit with Dad in the den."

"Thanks, Ben."

His mother cast a wary glance at him as she left the dining room. She'd been quiet since just before dinner when she'd casually asked him about Ella. Of course, she'd said *that Ella Jacobs*, which had riled him, and he'd snapped, *She's gone back to Boston.*

So now he was making amends. Apologies didn't come easily to him. The confrontation with Ella earlier was proof of that. Even though he'd meant every word, the whole apology had been wrenched from him, as if some invisible being was pulling it from his chest. He'd actually felt sick afterward but didn't know if that was due to the emotion involved or guilt. Apologies weren't confessions, and Ben knew that, unlike his sister, he wasn't ready to travel that path.

"This your way of saying sorry?" Grace looked up from loading the dishwasher.

"Huh?"

"I heard you just now snapping at Mom over Ella."

"Then you also heard what she said—'that Ella Jacobs.' It ticked me off."

"Yeah, I get that. It annoyed me, too. But you have to accept that Mom and Dad are still reeling over what I told them. And they're having a hard time believing I was to blame rather than Ella."

"It was months ago."

"Yes, but Ella's return here has brought it all back."

"You were the one who invited her!"

Grace put down the plate she'd been rinsing. "I had to, Ben. You know all this. I had to make amends to her, too. She was a victim, just like Brandon."

"Not the same thing."

She placed a damp hand on his arm. "I understand you probably have mixed feelings about Ella, but there's more going on here than her return to Boston, isn't there, Ben?"

"Well, she was upset over *The Beacon* article...but mainly because I hadn't told her I basically own the paper."

"And you couldn't have done anything about it. So you apologized, and then what?"

He hesitated. Talking about that summer night years ago was a topic very much avoided in the Winters household, even after Grace's confession. "I realized that the review wasn't the biggest thing bothering her."

"So, what was?"

"She wanted an apology from me. For my actions after Brandon died."

"What do you mean? Giving the police the

note? I've never told anyone outside of the family, Ben. I *swear*."

He wrapped his arms around her. "I know, and thank you for that. But I should have gone to see her the next day and I never did. You remember what it was like here. Dad calling the relatives, and everyone descending on the house. The police with their questions. The phone calls. Mom holed up in her room with Aunt Jane. Savanna home from Augusta, looking like she'd been hit by a truck. Uncle Fred..."

Grace teared up and Ben cursed himself for bringing those days back when he knew she was blaming herself again. But he persisted. She needed to know. "Ella deserved an explanation for why I didn't go see her the next day. For why I didn't call. I acted like everyone else here in town, assuming she'd sent that note."

"She felt abandoned."

Grace's voice was thick with emotion, and Ben felt for her. At the same time, she could have spoken up back then.

"Yes. And she was. Not only that, but you haven't set the record straight here in town, have you?" He saw her wince but didn't regret his words.

A moment later she asked, "How was she after?"

"What do you mean?"

"After you apologized. Do you think she was satisfied?"

Ben couldn't be sure. She'd accepted it, but was that the same thing? "I don't know. I thought so, but now..."

"She's gone back, and maybe you'll never know."

Ben nodded. That was the crux of the whole matter. He'd never know for sure how she felt, because she was gone.

She spun around. "Ask her to come back. Reach out to her."

Ben shook his head at the eagerness in her face. "I think it may be too late for that, Grace."

"Maybe I can think of a way to get her to come back."

Ben smiled at the faraway, thoughtful expression that he knew so well. This was the Gracie from last July—the schemer and plotter. But he doubted any idea she came up with would work. He pictured Ella's stony face and remembered her voice when she abruptly announced she had to leave. Those few words, delivered so coldly, made him realize his apology was all she'd wanted. There was no more unfinished business in the Cove. She'd gotten what she came for. And that made him unspeakably sad.

CHAPTER THIRTEEN

ELLA PUT A second load of laundry into the washer. Her monthlong absence from her rental condo had been broken only by the few days of preparation for her visit to the Cove. Except for the small pile of mail to sort through, there really wasn't a lot to do. That was a benefit of living by herself. She made her own rules and set her own schedules. She never had to compromise. The only person she needed to please was herself. She'd enjoyed those benefits since her divorce and had liked being on her own, until seeing Grace and Drew together.

The washer revved up, and Ella wandered from the compact laundry-storage room to the sliding doors leading onto her small balcony. She'd moved into the condo days after the one she and her ex had owned together was sold and was glad now she hadn't purchased it. For the first time since then, she felt the unit's size close in on her, smothering her like the memories of the past weekend in the Cove had. *Cut it out, Jacobs. Move on with your life.*

If only she could. Now she regretted booking time off over Christmas. She'd thought she'd need a rest after the tour, and there were always social events to look forward to in the season. Yet for some reason her calendar for the next two weeks was unusually blank. Then she thought back to the emails and voice messages she hadn't gotten around to answering.

Why? Her only explanation was that after receiving Grace's note weeks ago, she'd gone into autopilot mode. Life on tour hadn't been as glamorous or exciting as she'd anticipated: cycling through the book talks in a string of small cities and large towns; repeating the same story over and over; signing books and smiling. Then Grace's invite had overshadowed every thought and word. *I'm going back to the Cove* had been in her mind the whole time.

Ella stared at the sliver of gray water visible between the skyscrapers around her condo building—the "waterfront view" that had been the unit's lead in the rental ad—and thought of the units Ben hoped to build overlooking the peninsula and the lighthouse. There was no chance of skyscrapers blocking that view. She hoped he got investors and town approval for the project, because it was a good one and she knew how much it meant to him. She wished now she'd told him that rather than fixating on her obsession about his apology.

Funny how perspective alters emotions. What happened that Labor Day weekend had dominated her few days in the Cove. She couldn't seem to escape the past. Now that she was back in Boston, she realized she hadn't given Ben a fair chance. He wasn't the same person he'd been back then, and neither was she.

Too late for thoughts like these. She picked up her pile of mail to sort the junk into her recycling and scanned a handful of bills. Then she decided to make some phone calls. Christmas was less than two weeks away, and she knew people's social calendars filled up quickly. All except hers, apparently. No doubt her small circle of close friends and her even-larger group of colleagues assumed she was either promoting her book or working on another.

Less than an hour later, the realization that she'd probably be alone on Christmas Day had sunk in. The resultant phone call to her mother had been brief because her mother was on her way to the theater. "I thought I told you before you left for the Cove, dear, that Frank and I were having Christmas with his daughter and her family. And your brother is taking his family on a cruise. Didn't he tell you that months ago?"

Perhaps. Ella couldn't remember anything from months ago or even the days before her return to the Cove. Her mother had added, seemingly as an afterthought, "And how was your visit back? Did it all go well?"

"Sure." Ella had lied, knowing her mother didn't really want to know. The topic of that weekend had been taboo since they'd packed their car with the possessions they'd stored at the cottage for the previous ten years. Her family had loved their annual vacations and leaving forever—at Ella's insistence—had been bitter. She wondered if her brother had ever really forgiven her for the loss of carefree days and his own summer friends. Her parents' divorce months later had, for Ella, been tied to the whole mess. After her father's death, there'd been no obligation to trek to Syracuse for holidays, and she'd never gotten close enough to his second family to continue the tradition afterward.

The calls and emails to friends and workmates were equally disappointing. There'd been a flurry of apologies—*we thought you'd be with your family* had been the most common—and a few half-hearted invites. *You're welcome to join us anyway* had been the most humiliating, especially that tepid last word, *anyway.*

She spent the rest of Monday cleaning, buying Christmas gifts that she would now need to mail to her family and trying to come up with an idea for her next op-ed piece for the *Globe.* It was scheduled for the coming Saturday but needed to be filed by Thursday.

When Grace phoned her later that night, Ella was pleasantly surprised. "I know you must be busy getting settled after being away, but I wonder if you'd be interested in coming back here."

That got Ella's full attention. "Um—"

"It's just that my mother has been pestering me about an engagement party…and you know me. I hate the idea of a big party! I've managed to pare down her grand plans to a small dinner for family and close friends this Friday night. I'd love for you to come. You can stay at my place, and Drew will stay at the house with me and my folks." There was a quick pause while she seemed to catch her breath. "It's asking a lot, taking you away from your own social life at this time of year, but it would mean so much to me. And to Ben. There's an important town council planning meeting on Wednesday night that's open to the public, and his condo project is on the agenda. I don't know how much he's told you about it, but he's worked so hard! I hope the project will be a go for him, but that hinges on getting a permit from town council. I'm rounding up a lot of people here to attend the meeting and give their support to the plan. I know he'd be thrilled if you came, too."

Ella's head was spinning. Not from Grace's run-on explanation, but at the idea of a return to Lighthouse Cove. "Um, can I get back to you? That sounds great, but I have some things to tidy up here first."

"Of course! But let me know as soon as

possible so I can let my mother know. For numbers, she said." Grace laughed.

That gave Ella a second's pause. Family and friends—like Suzanna and Julie? "I'll call you first thing tomorrow."

She sat for a long while after the call ended, considering every potential consequence of returning to the Cove. Yet going back now would be different. Ben and Grace had apologized. People in town had seen her around and knew she'd reconnected with the Winters family. Well, with Ben and Grace at least. A second visit would be more comfortable. This time she knew what to expect and she felt ready for anything the town might throw at her. But most of all, this was her chance to be with Ben without the memories coming between them. Everything was resolved and for the first time in seventeen years, they could be like any other couple. They could get to know each other all over again. They'd at last be free to say what they felt for each other and maybe—Ella hoped for this more than anything—those words would lead to a future together.

TUESDAY HAD BEEN long and stressful, but Ben was optimistic. A phone call from Portland National Bank's team confirmed they'd liked his project and weren't concerned about the handful of unsold houses either. *House prices in Portland won't be going down anytime soon*, one VP had commented. Now all Ben had to do was get the project okayed by the town council.

On his way home, Ben stopped at the site office. Andy had already gone home, but Glen was there, looking unhappy enough that Ben decided to take a few extra minutes and find out what was bothering the man.

"It's not just the new baby, Ben," Glen said. "I've been finding some anomalies in the books."

That got Ben's immediate attention. "What kind of anomalies?"

"Invoices that don't correspond to orders received."

"Well, Andy does the ordering and checks the shipments. What did he say?"

"That he'd have a look."

Ben knew Andy had problems at home that he was trying to sort out. Ben's buoyant spirits sank as he locked up the office after Glen was persuaded to go home. This could be connected to what Harold had mentioned on Friday—the query from one of their biggest suppliers. The thought that he'd let the problem slide worried him. Harold had sent the information from Harbor Lights Supply and Ben had simply skimmed through it, intending to deal with the situation later. That was two days ago! He'd dropped the ball on what was potentially serious trouble for the company.

And why? Because every second of the last few days had been devoted solely to Ella. When he wasn't with her, he was constantly thinking about her. Now he was doubting his commitment to the family business. How could he expect his father to have enough faith in him to hand the company over if he allowed a teenage fantasy to dominate his every decision? Ben had no answers, but whatever was going on needed to be cleared up before the town meeting tomorrow night.

The aroma of beef stew greeted him as he opened the front door. His favorite winter meal—and if he was lucky, there'd be his mother's biscuits to go with it. Ben wondered if the stew was a kind of peace offering. He and Evelyn had always had a good relationship. Her support for him as a teen and later, when his marriage was falling apart, had been constant. She'd been the buffer between him and his father for as long as he could remember. Keeping the family on an even keel had been her life's goal. And that had been no easy feat, as Ben knew, in the days after Brandon's death. Evelyn had managed it all—Brandon's family and her own—when everyone else was falling apart.

Which was why he'd been feeling regret for the recent tiffs with her—the stilted talk and snapped replies to innocent questions, on both sides. He just didn't understand why she continued to focus on Ella now that she knew what really had happened that summer.

He called out a "Hello" as he hung up his coat and slipped out of his boots. Loosening his tie, he followed the voices he was hearing into the solarium. Grace was sitting next to Evelyn, who was writing in a notepad.

"Hey, Ben. We're making up the menu for Friday night."

He took in Grace's tight face and smiled. The dinner party had been an unsatisfactory compromise for both mother and daughter. Ben thought his sister and Drew would be better off eloping, if Grace could summon the courage to do so.

"How was your day, Ben?"

"It was good, Mom, and thanks for making stew! That's the icing on the cake as far as today is concerned." Her obvious pleasure made him realize he should compliment her more often. Like Grace, his mother had never liked the spotlight, but praise now and again was good for the soul. He suddenly thought of Ella and the missed opportunities when she was here to tell her how beautiful she was. Too late to change all that now, but he could mend things with his mother.

"Could you tell your father dinner will be in ten minutes, then, dear? He's in the den."

The *dear* convinced him his relationship with his mother could be salvaged. As for his father...

Charles was watching the news, something he'd been obsessed with since temporarily stepping down from running the company. As usual, the volume was full blast, and the first thing Ben did was pick up the remote to turn it down. His father jumped slightly, startled.

"For crying out loud, Ben! Don't sneak up on me like that."

"That's pretty funny, Dad. Mom says dinner's in ten minutes."

"Which means fifteen, because she's with Grace and they'll be talking."

He knows us all too well, Ben thought. He sat down next to his father, watching the TV news play without sound and wondering if he dared bring up his problem at work. Maybe not, he decided, looking at the old man's profile. The hard set of his jaw had softened over the past months since the heart surgery, and there were a few more lines in his face as well as silver strands in his hair. Otherwise Charles Winters looked pretty good for a seventy-year-old man who had heart and blood-pressure problems. His fall the other day had left him with some bruises, but that was all.

Ben was about to leave the room when his father asked, "Have you heard anything about your meeting with the bankers yesterday?"

He knew his father had misgivings about the condo development and would have preferred building more houses in the subdivision. But Ben felt otherwise, thinking the condos would draw a different clientele that would balance out the economic development in the Cove and even beyond. "They like my project and they're on board. Dependent on the permit, of course."

"Congratulations, Ben! And Gracie said you're on the agenda for the council meeting tomorrow night."

"Well, the company is, Dad. I'm simply representing it, as you know."

Charles was nodding thoughtfully, and Ben assumed the brief conversation was finished. "Yes, of course. Though speaking of the company..."

Ben closed his eyes, waiting for whatever came next. One never knew with his father.

"I called my lawyer this morning, Ben. He's drawing up the papers for a changeover."

Ben looked at his father, whose slightly flushed face was angled to the flickering TV screen. *Avoiding looking at me with bad news?* He knew Harold Ferguson could probably be persuaded to postpone his retirement if he was offered the chance to take over the company. But if that were to happen...

"I'm signing the company over, Ben," Charles said, facing him again. "To you. Full control. I promise." He cracked a wry grin.

From Evelyn's smile when he followed his father into the kitchen twenty minutes later,

Ben knew she'd known what was going to transpire. She was holding a bottle of sparkling wine, and Grace, spooning stew into bowls, gave him a thumbs-up. It had been a long time since his family had enjoyed a festive occasion, and Ben decided to relish every second.

Then the sobering thought about the problem Glen had mentioned plus the council meeting brought him back to earth. It wasn't until later, after Charles and Evelyn had gone to bed and Grace was wrapping up her daily phone call to Drew, that Ben had a few minutes alone in the den with his sister.

"Were you surprised about Dad's decision?" she asked, setting her cell phone on the sofa next to her.

Ben looked up from the *Portland Press Herald* he was reading. Or trying to, as his thoughts were everywhere but on the paper. Processing the big news of the night and wishing more than anything that he could share it with the one person who'd understand more than anyone—except maybe Gracie—what Charles's decision meant to him.

"*Floored* is a better word."

"You deserve it, Ben."

"I dearly hope so, Grace. But it's kind of scary, too."

"I bet. Don't be afraid to ask him for advice. Now that you're the boss, things will be different." She was grinning.

"You think so?"

"We can always hope."

They laughed—for their first time together in a while.

"I also hope you won't be upset by this, Ben."

That instantly dissolved the light mood. Maybe Drew found his sister's penchant for scheming a bit charming, but Ben had been wary of her so-called talent for a while—certainly since they'd both returned home.

"I invited Ella to come to the engagement dinner Friday night, and she's accepted."

He felt his jaw drop.

"And she's also going to attend the planning meeting tomorrow. I told her about it and how I was organizing a bunch of people to go to support you. I've offered her my place to stay, and I'll be here, helping Mom and so on. I really hope you don't mind, Ben."

Mind? He wanted to whoop and sweep up Grace and spin her around the room. Instead he smiled. "I don't mind at all, Grace."

CHAPTER FOURTEEN

Ella slowed as she approached the turnoff from the highway. There was a line of vehicles waiting to access it from the new subdivision. The dashboard clock read 8:30, and she realized this must be morning rush hour in the Cove area. Clearly, people who lived in the subdivision were commuters, and at some point, Ella figured the county would have to install traffic lights or stop signs on the highway.

She'd told Grace she'd be at the bookstore before it opened and would bring coffee from Mabel's. Finding a parking space outside Mabel's was tricky because many customers were running in for take-out breakfast, leaving their cars to idle at the curb. Not advisable in a big city, but it seemed okay for the Cove. These people must also be commuters, and it seemed they preferred to get coffee here rather than at the chain franchise closer to Portland. Weekday mornings in Lighthouse Cove were a revelation to Ella. When she'd been here last week, her days had begun a bit later. She finally found a parking space farther up the side street and decided to leave her car there for the time being.

Grace opened Novel Thinking's door right after Ella's second tap on its glass window.

"You made it!"

Her smile was big and warming, easing Ella's nerves. She'd been doubtful about returning ever since she'd called Grace to confirm, because her excitement at the chance to see Ben again was tempered by the possibility that he might not be feeling the same. Their parting had been coolly polite rather than friendly, and it had been Grace who'd called asking her to come back. Not Ben. Yet here she was, hauling her small suitcase into the bookstore.

"Good trip?" Grace asked, taking the cardboard tray of coffee and bag of treats from Ella.

"I left early enough to miss Boston rush hour but surprisingly found one here in the Cove. A lot of the traffic was coming from the subdivision."

"I know. People have been complaining about it. The commuters here in town are noticing it's harder to get onto the highway because of the stream of cars coming from there." Grace set the coffee and baked goods on the table in the seating area. "Come, let's eat and talk. I don't have to open till ten, but I want to show you around upstairs before then."

Ella took off her coat, slinging it over the back of a chair opposite Grace's. "Some county or municipal department needs to take care of that. What will happen when Ben's condo project is being built and even more commuters move into the area?"

Grace shrugged. "I don't know. Someone will figure all that out, I suppose. So, this is what I'm thinking about for the next few days."

Ella sipped her coffee and nibbled her muffin, half listening to Grace's plans, but her attention was caught when Grace mentioned Ben. "He's going to stay at work until tonight's meeting. Some problem, I think—he never actually said, but I could see something has been troubling him. He has some wonderful news that I can't tell you about because he ought to do that himself."

The rest of Grace's recap might as well have been hollered into the wind roaring outside for all that Ella absorbed. Her focus centered on the fact that he'd been *troubled.* Was that because of their talk? The tidbit about *wonderful news* was also interesting. Clearly, life in the Cove hadn't come to a standstill in her absence. Later she followed Grace around her upstairs apartment and settled in while Grace went down to open up. She decided to have a walk around town and arranged to meet Grace for an early supper before the meeting. After pocketing the keys Grace had given her, Ella laced up her boots, zipped up her down jacket and put on her hat and gloves. The wind was picking up, and she wanted to be dressed for a long, cold walk.

A woman with two small children was entering the bookstore as Ella was leaving. She turned sharply and stared as Ella squeezed past her in the doorway. "Excuse me, but are you Ella Jacobs?"

Ella froze. Not already. She murmured, "Yes," and braced herself.

"Just that I saw your photograph in *The*

Beacon. My daughter, Becky, is a big fan of yours. She came to your book talk and got an autographed copy, which she treasures. Thanks so much!" One of her children said something, and the woman continued on inside before Ella could respond.

She remembered the teenager who'd rushed up after Ella's talk—the same girl who worked in the bookstore. The brief encounter lightened her mood, and she walked toward Main Street feeling a bit less anxious about returning. Businesses were slowly opening up. Ella assumed weekday shoppers in the Cove were more likely to be the townspeople who actually lived there, rather than the newcomers in the subdivision. Most commuters probably did their basic shopping in Portland.

For many years Ella had thought her family owned their cottage; only as a preteen, she'd learned—to her dismay—that they rented it from Charles Winters. The fact had temporarily driven a small wedge between her and Grace. At least, in Ella's mind. That was the summer she also became aware of the unspoken but obvious division between the townies and the summer people. Somehow that latter group was different, a fact that was never truer than on Labor Day weekend.

Now, as an adult, Ella was beginning to see the Cove from a different perspective. It benefitted from its proximity to larger towns along the coast as well as nearby cities like Portland. Even Augusta was less than an hour away. People knew one another and their business here, reinforcing the small-town stereotype. Ella had become painfully aware of that her last summer in the Cove. *Enough, Jacobs. You've moved on from all that.*

She stopped in front of a gift shop to look at the window display and noticed some scented candles. Her mother loved them, and Ella decided to buy one to add to the Christmas gift she'd already purchased. There were a few customers inside, and Ella browsed a bit before finally selecting a couple of candles, which she took to the woman at the cash register. When she handed the woman her credit card, she saw her raise an eyebrow to someone nearby. Ella turned slightly to see two women about six feet away, whispering, their eyes fixed on her. Then the woman at the register handed back the card along with Ella's purchase.

She mumbled a thank-you and headed for the door, feeling their stares the whole way. Out on the sidewalk she took a deep breath, telling herself she was imagining things. They hadn't been talking about her. But despite the pleasure of meeting Becky's mother, it was the women's stares and whispers that stuck with her the rest of the day. When Ella met Grace back at the apartment for supper, she'd decided not to mention it. There were more important matters ahead.

They set out for the meeting an hour before starting time. "We want to get seats up front," Grace said. "And I promised to save some for my mother, Henry and Drew."

Those inevitable encounters heightened Ella's nervousness as they waited in line to go through security at Town Hall. Ella had never been inside the building and she paused at the top landing to take in the scene below. A crowd was already pouring in, and she wondered if Ben was among them or if he'd arrived earlier. A couple of security guards directed them to the public areas in the upper galleries on both sides of the chamber floor. The podium and council sections were still vacant.

Grace rushed ahead to the front row of their gallery. “Here, put your hat, scarf and jacket on some seats and I’ll do the same. We’ll save what we can.”

They sat side by side in the middle of the row, with their belongings saving the places next to them. She noticed Grace waving and saw Henry inching along with his cane followed by Grace’s mother, who peered past Henry and Grace to give a slight finger wave that Ella thought seemed friendly.

Then someone leaned over on her other side to ask, “Are these taken?” A silver-haired couple stood at the end of the row.

“Um, sorry, they’re being saved.”

The man shot her an irritated frown, and Ella saw the woman whisper something to him. They stared a few seconds longer before ascending higher up. Were they talking about her? She turned to mention the incident to Grace, who was waving frantically at Drew Spencer as he walked up the stairs. He leaned over to smile at Ella as he sat down beside Grace, and their two heads moved close as they whispered and giggled about something. Ella felt a rush of envy.

Sensing movement to her right, she saw

Grace's friend Julie. The woman hesitated when she noticed Ella. "Um, are these seats saved?"

Grace heard her. "Hey, Julie. Yeah, for you! Sit down."

Julie whispered to a man behind her, and he squeezed past her to sit next to Ella, who recognized him as Tom, the owner of the restaurant she'd gone to with Grace last week, The Daily Catch.

"Hello," he said before leaning across her to say, "Thanks for the seats, Gracie."

The abrupt greeting both irritated and embarrassed Ella. The rest of her side of the row filled up but she stared straight ahead to avoid any small talk. Just as the town councilors filed in, Ella spotted Ben in the front row of the gallery directly across from her. His head was down as he read some notes, and Ella was disappointed that she couldn't wave to him, to let him know she was there.

Everyone suddenly rose up when a white-haired man wearing an honorary sash entered the chambers and mounted the podium. Ella recognized him as the mayor from the tree lighting. He tapped on the mic to check the sound system and announced that, due to the unexpectedly high public interest in the Winters Building Ltd. application, the night's meeting would be dedicated to the company's presentation followed by questions. Regular council items would be deferred to a later date.

An enormous TV screen behind the podium suddenly came to life, showing a graphic of the waterfront near the lighthouse and a four-story cubic structure facing it, surrounded by a large, walled area of paths meandering around gardens, benches and small sitting nooks. There were low murmurings from the public because the design was attractive and looked idyllic.

Ben descended to the podium with a confident, professional air, dressed in his charcoal suit and crisp white shirt with a knotted gray tie. He kept his presentation brief, focusing on the eco-friendly aspects of the project. The entire unit was intended to be small, he said, to diminish its intrusion on the prevailing landscape. He flicked through various images on the screen, ending with an artist's rendering of the newly approved memorial to Brandon Winters.

There were a few louder murmurs at that.

Ella was afraid to turn around, after the whispers and looks she'd intercepted earlier. As if reading her mind, Grace reached for Ella's hand. The gesture warmed Ella, but she instantly thought, *Why am I feeling like* I've *done something wrong?*

Ben's talk ended with a scatter of applause, and some people began to line up at the mics. Someone in the gallery across from theirs unfurled a long banner proclaiming No More Expansion, which was received with mild booing and light laughter from the crowd.

Grace turned to Ella, raising an eyebrow. "Now the fun starts."

In spite of her rising anxiety for Ben, Ella thought many of the comments were balanced. Some concerns pointed to the increased traffic problems that had already made an impact on the daily commute. Ben's acknowledgment of the problem as well as his implication that the county planned a traffic study seemed to satisfy many. Then a middle-aged man, introducing himself as a longtime Cove resident, complained about the lack of parking spaces in town, especially on weekends. There was some jeering in response, someone calling out about that being the least of the town's problems. The room hushed while a young woman, introducing herself as a mother and new house owner in the subdivision, expressed worries about the spate of break-ins, and that issue dominated the next few minutes, until the mayor intervened to say that he had an upcoming meeting with the police chief about that very matter. He reminded the assembly that only ten minutes remained for questions.

Ben looked pale and tired. Ella guessed a lot was at stake here for his family's company. If she were alone with him right now, she'd draw him close to her and smooth his furrowed brow, chase his worries away. She saw Grace and Drew holding hands and realized she wanted to have that intimacy with Ben. To be a couple with him.

Henry's voice at the microphone brought her back to reality. "I guess my seventy-years-and-counting qualifies me as a longtime Cove resident," he began to some tittering in the crowd. "Those of you who know me can attest that I'm not a big fan of change. *Unnecessary* change! That's the key word here. I'm not going to go into a rant about the Cove back in my younger days, but change has been happening here since the day I was born. Some of us just haven't noticed it. If people from beyond our town limits want to find a better life here, raising families and doing business with us or the folks in Portland, I say welcome. Bring us your new ideas and plans. We need them. That's all I got to say."

The mayor waited for the round of applause and cheering to stop before reminding the audience of the next council meeting and adjourning. Ella saw Grace give a thumbs-up to Henry as he moved away from the mic. People prepared to leave, gathering up coats and chatting as they began to file down the gallery steps onto the ground floor.

"Meet you outside," Grace shouted over the din to Ella. Then she and Drew stood up to exit from their end of the row.

Ella watched Grace speaking excitedly to her mother before greeting and hugging other people around them. Julie and Tom had left, and Ella sat alone for a few minutes, waiting for most of the people to disperse. She couldn't see Ben anywhere. Finally, she got to her feet and put on her jacket. Grace and Drew were below in the middle of a group congregating around Henry. Ella watched them for a few minutes before descending to the main floor.

There was no group for her to be folded into. Although she wasn't a newcomer to the Cove, she felt like one. *An outsider.* She envied Grace's belonging and, at the same time, felt a pang at the unfairness of it. She didn't deserve to be an outsider. She'd done nothing wrong.

Realizing Ben's time would be taken up by the line of people waiting to speak to him, Ella decided to head back to the apartment. She still had her op-ed piece to write but also needed the cool night air to clear her head. The slights from Julie and Tom as well as that couple rankled. Yet how could she blame them for their thoughts about her? Clearly, Grace hadn't revealed her part in the prank to anyone outside the family. As she walked out of the building, Ella thought it was about time Grace did exactly that.

BEN STRETCHED HIS neck over the throng of people. He couldn't see Ella anywhere. The last fifteen minutes had been frustrating, trying to be polite, thanking people or reassuring them—depending on their stance on the issue—and all the while anxiously on the lookout for Ella. When Grace and Drew, followed by Evelyn, reached him, the first thing he asked was, "Have you seen Ella?"

Grace peered around. "She was sitting with us, but I haven't seen her since the meeting ended. So what do you think? Do you feel good about it? Your presentation was great. Do you know when you'll hear the council's decision?"

Drew laughed, drawing her against his side. "You're only allowed one question at a time, Grace."

Right. Good luck with that, Ben thought. "To be honest, I don't know. There was a mix of questions and concerns. I don't think any one side prevailed."

"Maybe not," his mother said as she drew nearer. "But Henry's comments at the very end were precisely what the crowd needed to hear."

"A typical Henry moment for sure."

"He said what needed to be said," Evelyn reiterated. "Your father is eager to hear all about it." She placed a hand on Ben's forearm, leaned into him and whispered, "He'd have been proud."

Ben was touched by that, but the one person whose opinion he really wanted didn't seem to be present. "Do you know where Ella might have gone?" he asked Grace.

"Maybe she went back to my place. She said she had some work to do. A deadline or something."

Ben stifled his irritation at Grace's nonchalance. He had an important meeting with Andy and Glen first thing in the morning but after that he'd go see Ella. Or he could interrupt her work and see her tonight. An even better idea.

His mother was tugging on his jacket sleeve. "Dear, can you give me a ride home? I came with Drew and Henry, but I'm tired and Charles is waiting up to hear all about it."

Ben pursed his lips and nodded. *Okay, so not tonight.*

ELLA LOGGED INTO her laptop shortly after daybreak. At some point during her wakeful moments overnight, she'd begun to spin ideas for her next op-ed column. *An unexpected benefit of insomnia*, she thought, sitting back to reread her title, "'Tis the Season." A second cup of coffee and piece of toast later, she'd typed the first few lines.

While others throughout the Christian world may be singing that familiar carol this Christmas holiday, the voices of residents here in Lighthouse Cove, a former fishing village and now small town northeast of Portland, Maine, are raised in ire these days over the town's expansion and current building projects.

All right. It was a start.

CHAPTER FIFTEEN

BEN ARRIVED AT the site office as dawn struggled above the horizon of another bitter winter day. He needed a couple hours by himself to go over some files. He was feeling relief after the presentation—which he personally thought had gone well. His father's quiet listening, followed by only a couple questions as Ben recapped the presentation, had only added to his spirits.

But by the time Glen's car rolled up to the office, followed seconds later by Andy's, his positive mood from last night's presentation had been destroyed. Ben had reviewed a dozen questionable invoices and payments in the material Harold had emailed him. He didn't doubt for a second that there would be more. He'd fired off an email with a few questions to Harold and was still waiting for a reply.

The scam Harbor Lights Supply had warned

the company about days ago revealed itself in more detail, with many orders that didn't match invoices. Ben hadn't figured out exactly how or when the fraud had begun but guessed it required two people, one in his company and one at Harbor Lights. He was sick at the thought that one of his employees—maybe someone he'd known and trusted for years—was involved. And there were a limited number of possible suspects.

Glen and Andy walked into the office and Ben's heart rate picked up. "Take a seat, guys. Sorry there's no coffee yet, but I wanted to finish going through this paperwork before you got here."

"How'd the meeting go last night?" Andy asked. "Sorry I couldn't make it."

"Yeah, me, too," Glen mumbled.

"There were some thoughtful questions and comments on both sides. No idea when they'll make a decision, though." Then Ben pointed to the papers on his desk. "I came in early to have a look at the books 'cause I didn't have a chance last night." Focusing his attention on Andy's puzzled frown, he clarified, "Glen told me that he'd already spoken to you about some anomalies in the invoices, Andy."

His old friend's face paled. "Well, he did, but, uh…I haven't actually had a chance to follow up yet, Ben. I will right away."

Was that guilt in his old friend's face? Ben knew one of Andy's jobs was to check shipments that arrived at the work site. Each one had an order attached and Andy matched items to the order before stamping the form Okay and sending it off to accounting at head office to await receipt of the invoice from Harbor Lights. But Ben had concluded that when many invoices arrived in accounting, they listed items that hadn't been on the original shipment order. The amounts paid to Harbor Lights were therefore higher. Someone at Winters Building Ltd. either missed the discrepancies or purposely ignored them. Ben stared at Andy and Glen. *No way*, he thought. But—

His cell phone suddenly dinged and he picked it up. After staring at the phone for a long moment, he set it down on his desk. "Yes, well, you won't need to do that now, Andy."

"What's going on, Ben? Help us out here."

Ben pointed to his phone. "Last week Harold Ferguson informed me he'd had a call from Harbor Lights Supply about some questionable invoice payments. He said he'd look into the matter and get back to me. I've spent most of this morning going over papers he emailed me, and you were right, Glen. There are some troubling anomalies. If I hadn't asked you to go through the books for my funding proposal, and if Harbor Lights hadn't stumbled on this at their end, the fraud could have gone on much longer."

Glen nodded thoughtfully while Andy looked pale. Feeling guilty about not catching the discrepancies himself? With this new information from Harold, Ben could put most of it together. "I just got a text from Harold saying that someone in Harbor Lights financial department has confessed. The man implicated an accomplice, because the scam couldn't have been done from just one end, of course." Ben let out a long sigh as his tension from the last couple days eased.

Andy jumped to his feet. "I swear I check every shipment that comes in very carefully before I send the paperwork to head office. I admit I may have skimmed through some of the orders, but…"

From his higher-pitched voice, Ben realized Andy thought he was being accused. "It's okay, Andy. The fellow at our end is in accounting at the Portland office. He okayed the payments and apparently the two men split the difference. The invoices were then buried in the files here and at Harbor Lights. None of this would have come to light but for two factors. Glen ran across some of them when he pulled files at random for his short audit for me. Then the guy at Harbor Lights was on sick leave for a week and his substitute noticed a problem on an order in their files. I don't know exactly how long this has been going on and I expect we'll have to bring in an outside audit team. Glen, I'm hoping you'll be able to work some extra hours to help with that."

"Anything I can do. How about I get the coffee going now?"

Relief swept through Ben. He couldn't help feeling a tad guilty that he'd been so quick to think either of them could be involved. Seeing how upset Andy had been at the idea he was being wrongfully accused, Ben thought about Ella. She'd been blamed by the town for the event that led to Brandon's death, and she'd lived with that blame for far too long.

ELLA READ HER column once more but still hesitated to hit Send. She'd pondered both sides of the controversy and, in the end, agreed with Henry's point about making newcomers feel welcomed. Many of those newcomers could have moved to the Cove for the same love of history and community touted by its longtime citizens, not only for economic reasons. The piece didn't have to be sent until midnight, so she had some time to edit further if necessary.

At some point in the morning, she heard Grace open up downstairs and, later, the tinkling of the doorbell as customers came and went. Ben's continued absence was disappointing. He hadn't even bothered to send a text or email. A long day loomed, so Ella decided to drive into Portland's new mall to look for a dress to wear to the engagement dinner tomorrow. Although she'd brought a dress with her, she was in the mood for some shopping therapy. Anything to get her mind off what could be an awkward evening, with Suzanna and her mother invited. On her way out, she dashed off a note to Grace in case she came looking for her.

Much later, she was strolling through the mall's lower level on her way to the indoor parking, pleased with her purchases of a stylish black cocktail dress and new shoes, when she saw two women heading her way from the garage. Ella tensed when she recognized Suzanna Winters. With no escape route in sight, she pasted a smile on her face.

There was no such greeting from either of the two women. Suzanna mumbled a surprised "Hello," but it was the other woman, a stranger to Ella, who stopped. "You have your nerve, going to a public meeting about the Cove when you don't belong there and never have."

Suzanna pulled her friend away, whispering to her and at the same time casting a parting glance that Ella was unable to read. Apologetic or smirking? Not that it mattered, because as soon as Ella was in her car, she cried anyway. Thoughts and words she'd wanted to say but hadn't—today, yesterday and last week—streamed through her mind all the way back to town.

When she arrived at the bookstore, Ella

rushed upstairs, thankful that Grace was busy with a customer and couldn't ask about her day. Half an hour later, a mug of tea in one hand, she booted up her laptop with the other. She clicked on her saved file and stared gloomily at the title—*'Tis the Season.*

Indeed, she thought gloomily. Overwhelmed by the temptation to rewrite it to cast the Cove as an unwelcoming town, she hit Send before she could change her mind and do exactly that.

It's not really the coward's way out, Ben rationalized as he called Ella. He could have emailed or texted, which would have been inconsiderate after not having contacted her since her return to the Cove yesterday morning. To make matters worse, he couldn't even tell her about the company fraud issue, a legitimate reason for not getting in touch the past several hours.

His guilt had been heightened by Grace's reply to his text asking if she knew where Ella was.

She's upstairs now. I just texted her to see if she wants company for supper, but she said she has a work deadline and will call me in the morning. Maybe she wants to be alone for a bit?

The message suggested going to see her might not be a good idea, so he opted to phone. Perhaps hearing her voice would reassure him that everything was still okay between them.

"Ben?"

He closed his eyes, savoring the lilt in that question. It was a promising start. "Hi. Listen, I'm so sorry I haven't gotten in touch with you sooner. Something came up at work that I had to deal with."

"That's okay. I know you were tied up with the presentation yesterday, as well. It was great, by the way. Have you had any feedback from the council yet?"

"I think they're voting on it when they get the results of a survey from residents in town and in the subdivision. Um, is there any chance of seeing you sometime tomorrow? I mean, before the dinner party."

"Sure. I'm a free agent."

"Grace said you had a deadline."

"Yes. My weekly op-ed piece for the *Globe*."

"How's it going?"

"Just wrapping it up now."

"I have to go to Portland in the morning but could meet you for lunch somewhere."

"That sounds nice, Ben. Where and what time?"

He thought about the meeting with Harold and officials from Harbor Lights. It could be a long morning. "How about if I text you when I'm finishing up? Maybe we could go to Mabel's or The Lobster Claw."

"Or someplace entirely different?"

He laughed. "Yeah, guess it's about time for a change. I'll think of a new place and if you spot any in your wanderings, let me know. We can decide tomorrow."

"Okay."

"And, uh...I'm really looking forward to seeing you again, Ella. Thanks for coming back, and for going to the meeting last night. I appreciate it."

There was a brief silence. "I'm glad I went, Ben. See you tomorrow."

He closed his eyes, cringing at his thank-you—the kind a person would extend to an acquaintance, not someone they'd known for most of their life. *Well, except for that huge gap of seventeen years.*

HALF AN HOUR into his meeting, Ben began to relax. He and Harold had met earlier to discuss options. They agreed that the company didn't need the publicity that a full investigation and police charges would bring. Ben and Harold had discussed the possible negative effects on their promised bank loan as well as permit approval from Lighthouse Cove's council. Then an executive from Harbor Lights broached the option of firing the men without laying charges. Both had confessed and were remorseful. Such a move would avert public attention and bad press.

His head was spinning with all the scenarios—none of them good—by the time he was getting into his car. It was just past noon and he texted Ella, suggesting The Lobster Claw, only because the pub wouldn't be busy at that time of day and reservations weren't needed. Her reply was a bit of a surprise.

I found a great deli in town and bought some food. We could eat here at Grace's.

He liked the idea of a casual lunch with just the two of them, though knowing Gracie, she might decide to pop upstairs. He wrote back.

Let's go to my place for a winter picnic. I'll turn the heat on! Meet you there about two?

A thumbs-up emoji was her reply. Ben felt better than he had all morning. There was time now to change and maybe talk to his father about what was happening at work. He turned his phone off and drove home.

His mother was on the phone in the solarium. She held up a finger, signaling him not to interrupt. Last-minute plans or glitches for the dinner party? Judging by her creased forehead, maybe so. He waved and went into the den. This time his father muted the volume first.

"If you're looking for your mother, she's in the solarium, I think. Some problem with one of the courses tonight."

"The caterers?"

"I guess. Maybe we'll have to order in from The Lobster Claw or The Daily Catch instead."

Ben saw the glint in his father's eyes and smiled. "I'd be okay with that."

"Me, too. Better than some fancy wee bit of a thing on a plate that leaves you hungry an hour later."

Ben smiled. *That's more like the dad I remember.* Although he and Harold were handling the situation, Ben was in a dilemma about his father. Should he confer with him as a courtesy? Or would the information lead to an argument? He decided to risk it. His gut told him Charles might appreciate being in on the problem.

"Something has come up at work," he began. His father clicked off the TV and looked expectantly at Ben. "One of our employees has conspired with an employee from Harbor Lights Supply to rig a false invoice and payment scheme. They've both confessed."

"Who was it from our company?"

"A guy in accounting. Someone we hired more than a year ago. The thing is, both men have financial problems and are remorseful. Our employee blamed his lack of health insurance. His wife is seriously ill."

"Maybe our benefits plan isn't enough these days, what with rising costs."

Ben hadn't expected his father to focus on the company benefit package, much less imply that it might need upgrading. Instead he'd anticipated a rant against employee theft. Encouraged by this, he outlined what he and Harold had discussed at the meeting with Harbor Lights executives—the plan to discuss with company lawyers the possibility of firing the employees rather than laying charges. They'd call police if necessary, once the scope of the fraud was known.

After listening quietly, Charles finally said, "Harold's got lots of experience, even in a situation like this. I'm glad you're discussing it with him."

Ben waited for more. "What do you think about our plan, though?"

"If you want advice, Ben, ask for it."

"Okay. I'm asking."

"Choose the option you can live with. This man's life will be affected by your decision. But you also have to consider the ramifications of handling this on your own, without laying charges."

That was it? Did he think the idea was good

or not? Ben worried about that for a minute until he realized perhaps he didn't need affirmation. Perhaps Charles trusted him to make the right decision all by himself.

The TV clicked back on, drawing Charles's attention once more.

Ben sat quietly next to him a moment longer before getting up. "Thanks, Dad," he said, lightly touching the top of his father's head as he left.

OPENING THE DOOR of his new house to greet Ella Jacobs was the highlight of Ben's difficult day. Her breathless "Hey!" and rosy cheeks from the brisk wind—or maybe at seeing him?—were exactly what he needed to put the morning out of mind.

"The furnace is on, and I thought to bring a couple of cushions and a blanket from home."

The color in her face deepened. She held out a large cloth bag. "Here, then. I'll let you do the honors."

He took the bag in one hand and reached for hers with his other, drawing her in out of the cold. They went into the kitchen, where he'd set a couple of plastic glasses and a bottle of chilled white wine on the island counter.

"Nice," she said, looking about. "If we had a sunny day—"

"It'd be even better," he cut in, smiling at her as he opened the wine and began to pour. "I'm designing a deck. Lots of room for a big one."

She peered out at the yard. "Uh-huh." She stared for a while longer before moving back to where he was now unpacking the food she'd brought and laying it on the counter.

"Glad you brought plates and cutlery. I didn't think of that."

"Grace found them for me."

"You told Grace we were having a picnic here?"

"I had to when I asked her if she had any plastic stuff."

"I'm surprised she didn't ask to join us."

"I think she wanted to but thought better of it."

"I'm sure she has enough to do for tonight. She asked Henry to take over the store so she could leave early. I've just come from home. Apparently, there might be a problem about the catering order."

"Nothing serious, I hope."

"Nothing that will affect our picnic here,

that's for sure." Ben handed her a glass of wine. "Let's get some food. I'm starving."

"Me, too."

Her eyes locked onto his. Ben was a happy man. They took plates of cheese, pickles, cold cuts and baguettes into the living area, where he'd laid out the blanket and cushions. They ate and made small talk, which was fine by Ben. It allowed the storm in his mind to calm. When she got around to asking him about his important meeting, he was able to dismiss it without breaking his mellow mood. "An employee situation that will be worked out eventually. And how about you? Did you send off the piece you were writing?"

"Yes, I did," she said while gazing down at her lap to brush away some cookie crumbs. "What time is the dinner tonight, by the way?"

"Mom says cocktails at six." Ben was about to ask more about her article when she abruptly stood up.

"I guess we should go. I'm sure your mother would like some help, and I'm planning to pamper myself beforehand. Maybe a long bubble bath. My room has one of those old-fashioned, claw-foot tubs as well as a shower." Her grin was mischievous.

Ben got to his feet and pulled her into his arms. "I'm happy you came back, Ella. After you left, I… Everything seemed so hopeless. I wanted so much to have another chance to show you…no, to *tell* you that I love you and—"

"I'm here now, Ben," she whispered, looking up at him.

His heart felt like it might burst. "I do love you, Ella. I hope you know that."

She nodded, but the expression in her eyes shifted and Ben's confidence faltered. Instead of kissing her, he rested his chin on the top of her head. He could have stayed like that with her for hours, feeling her heart beating against his, but he knew the moment had passed.

"Guess we should pack up," he murmured. He heard her sigh as she moved out of his arms, and he was about to reach for her hand to draw her back, when she began picking up the remains of their picnic.

Ben watched her, wishing he could replay the last few minutes, cursing himself for perhaps reading too much into every change in her face or tone of voice. He needed to relax and not make so many assumptions about what she was—or wasn't—feeling.

"Ella."

She was putting the used dishes and cutlery into the bag and turned to look at him.

"Thanks for this. It was exactly what I needed. And not just the food." He managed a small laugh over the lump in his throat. "The last forty-eight hours have been tough. Being with you, even for a short time, has made everything so much better."

"It's what I needed, too, Ben. The chance to be with you, just the two of us. Like an ordinary couple."

"We can be." He kept his eyes fixed on hers, the emotions he saw in them, the desire and doubt.

"I...I hope so, Ben. I'd like that."

His heart swelled. Inhaling a deep, steadying breath, he said, "Guess we should finish up here, then. You have a bubble bath to enjoy, and I'm sure my mother will have a list of tasks ready for me." He paused. "We still have tonight to...you know...talk some more."

"Yes" was all she said, but it was enough for Ben.

CHAPTER SIXTEEN

THE DRESS WAS a good choice. Elegant but not fussy; formfitting without being seductive. Appropriately sexy enough to turn heads—Ben's in particular, she hoped. She tucked a strand of hair into the loose knot at the nape of her neck and smiled at her reflection one last time before collecting her purse, coat and gloves. She'd decided not to wear boots. The sidewalk outside the store was clear enough, and Grace had told her the entrance to her parents' home had also been shoveled. Ben was picking her up in ten minutes, so she descended to wait near the front door.

The day had been almost perfect. There'd been no talk of the past, and she wanted to keep that harmony as long as she could. When he'd mentioned her column, she'd avoided talking about it. Although she'd opted in favor of the condo development, citing the benefits and advantages of community growth, she knew there would be people in town who might feel otherwise. They'd made their opinions clear at the public meeting, and the op-ed could lead to some pushback against Winters Building Ltd. Thankfully it was going to be published in Boston, a long way from Lighthouse Cove.

Car headlights flashed across the door as she tucked the phone back into her purse. Ben was here. Ella locked up behind her and, bracing against the wind, climbed into the passenger side. "Getting breezy out there," she laughed, buckling up and tidying her hair.

"Supposed to be a storm headed our way in the next couple of days. Maybe you'll have to extend your stay." The look he gave her wasn't at all subtle, and Ella felt a small thrill.

As soon as they walked into the Winters home, Ella realized they were among the first to arrive. Grace, who looked striking in a dark cherry-red dress, rushed to greet them. "I'm glad you got here a bit early so we can have a chat before I have to take on guest-of-honor duties."

"Are we putting coats in Mom and Dad's room?" Ben asked, removing his.

He was wearing the same suit he'd worn to

the council meeting, with a powder blue shirt this time, and Ella couldn't take her eyes off him. When he helped her out of her coat, his fingers brushed against the nape of her neck and she shivered. "You'll warm up quickly, and you look beautiful," he whispered. "Your hair and…um…especially the dress." His fingers lingered a second longer on her neck.

Grace loudly cleared her throat and grinned. "Yes, Ben. Coats are upstairs. Can you take them, please? Ella and I are going to my room for a few minutes."

"Don't keep her too long," he called out as he dashed up the stairs.

Grace and Ella smiled at one another. Subdued voices and dishes clattering in the kitchen drifted down the hall. "I'm afraid we're unfashionably early," Ella apologized.

"Mom always gives Ben a fifteen-minute leeway 'cause—"

"He's usually late."

"You know my brother. Drew's picking up Henry, and Mom is busy with a couple of catering staff. We have a few minutes before the others come."

As she followed Grace up the grand staircase, Ella thought how beautiful the old home looked at Christmastime. Strings of white fairy lights were draped over the large gilt-framed mirror above the antique console near the front door. A giant red poinsettia plant stood at the base of the stairs and another at the second-floor landing. Garlands of fresh spruce boughs wound in and out of the stair railing, filling the entire area with the fragrance of a forest, and LED candles in red-and-green glass holders flickered prettily around the entire entry hall.

The house was magnificent in an old-world way, and she'd always been awestruck visiting here as a kid. But as an adult, she couldn't picture herself living in such an overwhelming home. Even now at Christmas, the glow of LED candles and fairy lights barely managed to overcome the dark wood paneling and dim lighting. From the stories Grace had told Ella when they roamed the place as kids and then teens, both the house and hotel had been built by Grace's grandfather. Recalling her brief stay at the hotel, Ella decided the house had been loved and cared for more attentively. Of course, it had always been a family home.

Grace's room was almost as Ella remembered, except for some minor changes. The bunkbeds had been deconstructed into two singles and painted white, and the cork bulletin board above the matching desk had been cleared of rock-star posters and celebrity photographs. But Grace's favorite Raggedy Ann doll still perched on top of her bookshelf along with other childhood treasures that Ella recognized.

"I feel like I'm in a time warp."

"I know. It's both comforting and creepy at the same time."

They both laughed.

"You look lovely, by the way. Red is your color."

"Thanks, Ella. And your dress is stunning. Black works for you. I remember that last summer when you favored black T-shirts and cutoff jeans."

"Yeah. That was because my mother decided I could do my own laundry while we were here."

"Or maybe you were going for the dramatic effect."

Ella smiled again. "You could always see through me." The silence that fell between them felt natural. Two old friends reminiscing without delving too deeply into painful memories. "So is Drew staying here, too?"

"Yep. He's in the guest room on the second floor."

Ella grinned at Grace's wink. "Too bad."

"And Ben is just across the landing, in his own turret."

"Like old times."

"What did you think of his new house?"

"It's lovely. He must be eager to move in." She ran a finger along the edge of the desk between the two beds, avoiding Grace's eyes.

"Soon, I think. Now that things are settled between him and Dad."

"Settled?"

"You know, the company."

"What about it?" Ella saw a flush of pink rising up from the neck of Grace's dress.

"Uh-oh. I assumed he'd told you. I better not say." The color rose higher into her cheeks. "He's probably waiting for the right moment. You know, when you can be alone together to talk about future plans."

What future plans? Ella wanted to ask. Her shrug and the dismissive sound she attempted sounded lame.

"I know he's hoping to keep in touch."

Now Grace looked embarrassed. "He's been through a lot, Ella, and you have, too. But I haven't seen him smile so much in years. He's almost like the old Ben. The one you..."

She didn't have to finish. Ella knew exactly where she was going with that, and she also knew she wasn't prepared for a discussion about the past with Grace. Not here and not tonight. She stood up. "Speaking of Ben... He's probably wondering what's taking us so long." As Ella headed for the bedroom door, Grace suddenly clutched her arm.

"Don't hurt him, Ella."

Ella was speechless. Her mind instantly flew back to that summer weekend, and she was tempted to say "Shouldn't that be the other way around?" but this was not the night for opening up old wounds. She decided not to dwell on Grace's plea about Ben. She'd meant well and probably thought she was protecting her brother. *But from what?*

People were clustered in the entryway, removing coats and boots and chatting. Grace rushed ahead as Drew assisted Henry. Ella waited at the foot of the stairs for Ben, a smile fixed resolutely on her face. He soon emerged from the knot of people, a pile of coats layered over one arm.

He flashed a smile as he came her way. "More coat duty." Then he paused. "Everything okay? I see you've been abandoned by my sister."

Ella lightly touched his cheek. "Do your duty, Ben. I'll be fine."

"I'll be back in a sec, and then I'm yours for the rest of the night."

She watched him head up to the master bedroom, and as she turned around, Grace and Drew were leading the group into the living room. Ella noticed Henry lagging behind to adjust his tie. "Can I help?"

"You sure can. It's kinda hard doing this without a mirror. Not that I could anyway. Ties have never been my thing."

His smile was heartening. *As long as Henry Jenkins is around, I won't feel too much like an outsider.* "You look very dashing, though, Henry. I don't think I've ever seen you in a suit."

"Humph. Took me a while to find the darn thing. It hasn't been out of the closet since..." His face scrunched up. "Ben's wedding, I think."

Ella was straightening the tie and pulling down on it, so she couldn't see Henry's face, but she felt a surge of heat in hers. When she drew back to say, "There, that's better," Henry clasped one of her hands.

"I suspect this evening might be a tad uncomfortable for you, dear. But remember that there are people who do care a great deal for you. Ben is one of them."

Ella didn't know how to interpret this. Was it a reminder, like Grace's, that Ben could be hurt? Or was he simply reassuring her? When he added, "Keep that in mind," she decided it was simply Henry's way of encouraging her.

She handed him the cane leaning against the entry wall and tucked an arm through his free one. "I will, Henry. Now, I bet there are drinks in the living room."

A couple of young women in white shirts and black trousers were passing around trays of champagne as she and Henry entered the room.

Evelyn spotted them. "Henry Jenkins in a suit! I can't believe my eyes."

Ella noted his flush and felt for him but quickly realized Evelyn was teasing as she hugged Henry and kissed him on the cheek.

Then turning to Ella, she said, "Very nice to see you again, Ella, and welcome back to the Cove."

Her greeting was warm, if a bit formal for someone who'd once hosted Ella for sleepovers and baked cookies for her and Grace.

"Thank you, Mrs. Winters. It's wonderful to see you and your beautiful home again."

"I'm happy you could come." Evelyn nodded toward the sofa. "Charles is over there and I'm sure he'd like to say hello. Why don't you take Henry to sit beside him? I'll send over some champagne for you both."

Ella walked arm in arm with Henry, who used his cane, as well. They slowly navigated around a magnificent Christmas tree, resplendent in yards of tiny, twinkling white lights. *A kind of magical ball gown*, Ella was thinking as she helped Henry sit next to Charles. A pretty, silver-haired woman Ella didn't recognize sat on Charles's other side.

"Mr. Winters, nice to see you again." She smiled at Ben's father.

He nodded politely, but his own smile was hesitant. The woman next to him looked with interest at Ella, and Henry made the introductions. "Jane, this is Ella Jacobs. Ella, not sure if you remember Jane Winters, Grace's aunt?"

And Brandon's mother. Ella forced a stiff smile. She peered anxiously around for either Ben or the promised champagne and was about to make some excuse to move away when she saw Ben coming to the rescue, holding two champagne flutes.

Her relief must have been obvious. He handed her a flute and said in a low voice, "Not much longer. We'll be eating soon and you're sitting right next to me, where you'll stay for the rest of the night as I promised." Then he wrapped an arm around her waist as he greeted his father and aunt. "Aunt Jane! Glad you could make it."

Ella guessed from the woman's smile that Ben was a favorite. Replacement for a lost son? The unexpected thought stabbed at her. She turned away to sip the champagne and noticed a late arrival. *Suzanna. Here to complete my misery.*

Suddenly Jane Winters was speaking to her. "Grace has told me you're a reporter, Ella, and a writer with a new book just out. Congratulations!"

"Thank you, Mrs. Winters." Ella clenched

the champagne flute, as if relying on it to keep her standing up.

Suzanna was weaving around people on her way to the sofa, pausing here and there for a quick greeting. Heads and smiles tracked her path across the room and Ella wondered if the woman had calculated her late entry to time with both the champagne and the full attention of all. Still, Ella had to admit—grudgingly—the woman was resplendent in an emerald green sheath dress that set off her chestnut hair as well as full figure.

Ben's hand tightened on Ella's waist as Suzanna breezed up to them. Ella envied her nonchalance as she bent over to kiss her mother, then her uncle. She hugged Henry and, standing up again, said, "Hey, Ben! Glad to see you emerge from your construction lair. I heard your council presentation was great. I hope any resulting increase in the town's population will spill over to more business for the hotel."

"Hope so, Zanna." He looked across the room over Ella's head. "Uh-oh. I see my mother trying to get my attention. She wants to have the toast to Grace and Drew in here with the champagne." He gave Ella an apologetic smile. “And since I’m making the toast, I should scoot over to see what she’s trying to tell me.”

Ella watched him go, wishing she could run after him. She sipped more champagne and was about to casually wander off when Suzanna said, “Got a sec, Ella?”

She couldn’t have escaped if she’d tried. Suzanna was nudging her away from the sofa toward the windows. Once they were off by themselves, she said, “I’m sorry about my friend’s comments yesterday at the mall. I spoke to her after, but the problem is she doesn’t know what really happened here that summer. I mean, the *truth*. Our family does, but no one else, so it was a bit awkward trying to explain why I wasn’t upset about bumping into you and why I was kind of scolding her for what she’d said.”

Ella had girded herself for some uncomfortable looks that night but hadn’t expected this. Especially from the older girl who’d always seemed to treat Ella and Grace with such disdain.

“I wanted you to know. You’ve been through enough.” She gave a quick smile and walked away before Ella could utter a word.

The tinkle of a small bell silenced the room. Heads turned to the front of the room, and there was a bit of laughter as Ben called out, “Sorry, dinner’s not ready yet, but Mom says soon. It’s time for a toast to the soon-to-be-wedded couple, so please make sure you have enough liquid in your glasses.”

The catering staff navigated around the room with opened bottles of champagne and sparkling water. A few seconds later, Ben began his speech, warning that it would be short because everyone was hungry, and besides, his younger sister was the family member known for speaking at length on just about every topic, especially any connected to lighthouses or the Coast Guard. That set the tone for his toast, which Ella barely listened to because her attention was riveted on the engaged couple gazing without inhibition into each other’s eyes, as if they were the only two people in the room.

She had a vivid memory of a long, adoring stare like that, here in this very house, upstairs in his bedroom the day Ben had promised to always be there for her. *The miles will be our only separation*, he’d sworn. *Our hearts will always be together.* He was packing for college, and it was the Friday before the end-of-summer bonfire when Brandon had died.

People were smiling as Ben finished. "To my sometimes-irritating but always-loving sister and her besotted fiancé, Drew. Welcome to the family, brother."

Ella's eyes welled up and she ducked her head, gazing down into her half-empty flute. There was jovial bustling all around her as Evelyn invited everyone into the dining room, but Ella hung back. By the time Ben reached her, she hoped all trace of tears was gone.

"Have I told you how beautiful you are?"

Ella smiled. "I'm all ears if you want to say it again. And I haven't told you that charcoal gray becomes you."

"Even if I was wearing a gray sweatshirt?"

"I haven't seen you in a sweatshirt since we were teenagers. And by the way, Grace mentioned you had some good news."

"I was waiting for a quieter moment to tell you, but yes, I do. Dad's handed complete control of the company over to me. I am now President and CEO of Winters Building Ltd." His face flushed with pride.

"Oh, Ben, that's so wonderful. Congratulations!" Ella flung her arms around him.

He gazed deep into her eyes. "Maybe a private celebration later?"

She felt a blush creep up her neck. Then voices rose in the other room as people took their seats.

"Come on, gorgeous. Let's go eat," he murmured, grabbing her hand.

Ella's spirits lifted. She could get through this dinner party. Even Grace's friend Julie, who constantly avoided looking her way, couldn't dampen her mood. Ben was attentive throughout dinner, and when Henry and Drew joined Charles in the den to watch the end of a hockey game on TV, he chose to sit with Ella by the fire in the living room. Evelyn and Jane Winters were sitting near some bookshelves at the other end of the room.

When Ella's cell phone pinged from inside her purse, Ben asked, "Work messages already?"

She must have looked startled, because he quickly added, "Just teasing, of course. Go ahead and answer if you want."

"No, I hate when people do that in social gatherings."

"Then, you're an anomaly." He reached for her hand, weaving his fingers through hers. "But you always were, even as a sixteen-year-old." He leaned a bit closer. "Let me know when you're ready to leave. We don't have to stay till the end."

There was something suggestive in his tone, and Ella felt like that teenager all over again until she reminded herself that she was as far from that girl as the earth was to the moon. "Maybe now? I'm sure your parents and Henry must be tired, and I bet Grace and Drew are anxious to have some time alone."

"Sure." He helped her to her feet, his hand still wrapped around hers.

"Are you leaving already?" Grace asked, rising up from the sofa where she'd been sitting with Suzanna and Julie.

"Busy day tomorrow." Ben hugged his sister. "Congrats again, sis. You made a good choice."

She arched an eyebrow. "Shouldn't it be *Drew* who made a good choice?"

He laughed, hugging her tighter. "Ah, but did he *have* a choice? That's the real question here." He uttered an "ouch" as she lightly punched his shoulder.

"You're coming to the ice sculpture judging at Town Hall tomorrow, aren't you?"

"Wouldn't miss it for the world," he quipped.

He really is a golden boy here, Ella was thinking, noting the fond smiles from the three women. But as she and Ben passed them, Julie deliberately turned her face aside so she wouldn't have to acknowledge Ella. Ben paused to make some joking comment to Suzanna, completely oblivious to the slight. Ella was about to continue into the hallway when a surge of frustrated anger stopped her cold.

Incidences like these are just going to keep happening, she told herself. *No one outside the family is going to know the truth until someone decides to make that happen, and since Grace hasn't stepped forward, that someone will have to be you.* She wheeled around.

"Forgive this interruption, but I have to get this off my mind once and for all." She was staring at Julie, but everyone turned her way. Ella saw Ben step toward her but didn't dare look at him for fear of losing her nerve. "Since I've come back to the Cove, I've had people treating me as if I've committed a crime and gotten away with it." She saw surprise in some faces but pushed on, her voice losing its quaver as she continued. "I couldn't even go to a mall in Portland without being accosted by a complete stranger—a woman I'd never met—telling me I had no right to come back to the Cove. Ask Suzanna, if you don't believe me. She was there." Now they were looking at Suzanna, who nodded.

"And at the town meeting, some people were whispering and pointing at me, including you, Julie. Even tonight, you've been acting as if I don't belong here, as if I've crashed the party honoring your best friend. But Grace is my friend, too—at one time my very best—which is why I've kept quiet all these years about what really happened the night Brandon Winters died."

Ella hesitated at the shock wave she felt rolling through the room. Ben inched closer, gently pressing a hand on her shoulder. But she couldn't—*wouldn't*—stop now. "And finally, after seventeen years, Grace has told the truth—that she and Cassie Fielding came up with a stupid and thoughtless joke on me and Brandon, sending us notes to make me think I was meeting Ben and to make poor Brandon think he was meeting me. That I was interested in him."

Someone in the room was sniffling and blowing a nose, but Ella was afraid to pause any longer than it took for her to catch her breath. "That Labor Day weekend didn't only affect me, but my family, too—my parents and my younger brother. They had to put up with the whispers and rumors, as well, along with the stress of being questioned by the police, and even though everyone knew Brandon's death was an accident, I was blamed. My family carried that burden, too, you know. They loved their summers here, but I refused to come back. Their marriage fell apart—maybe not only because of all that, but there were arguments between them for weeks after. Arguments about whether to believe me or not." Ella's voice rasped against the lump in her throat. She scanned the room, taking in their still faces and Grace, staring down at her hands twisting in her lap. Ella felt a surge of regret for her friend, knowing she'd ruined her engagement party.

"Grace didn't trust that people would forgive her for what she did, so she was afraid to tell the truth. I get that." Ella focused on her friend. "And I'm so sorry, Grace, that I've spoiled your special night. I just...I just couldn't take any more." She swiped the back of her hand against her eyes. "I apologize, Mrs. Winters, for ruining your party, but I have to ask why you and the rest of the family failed to clear my name. You've all known for months now, and yet no one has spoken up. Not even you, Ben." She craned her neck to see him behind her, his ashen face saying far more than words possibly could.

She couldn't go on. She left the room, tears blurring the way along the hall to the front door, where she stood, perplexed, as if she'd run out of ideas about what to do next.

"Wait here. I'll get our coats." Ben stood grim-faced at the foot of the stairs, and then he was gone, taking them two at a time.

Her adrenaline surge eased, and Ella sagged against the door. She didn't know what was happening in the living room or how the women were reacting, and she didn't care. Her relief at finally shedding the pent-up emotions of the past several days—*seventeen years*—was immense. Then she heard heels clicking along the hallway and Evelyn Winters appeared. She stopped a few feet away from Ella, who stiffened, waiting for an outburst of anger.

But Evelyn surprised her. "You haven't ruined our evening, Ella. Not mine and not Grace's. She's feeling a bit…startled…right now, but I've come to tell you that we needed to hear what you so bravely revealed. Please try to forgive all of us. Especially Ben."

Too stunned to speak, Ella watched her walk back to the living room. Ben was descending the stairs as his mother disappeared down the hall. He didn't say a word as he helped Ella into her coat, but when he closed the front door behind them, he clutched her elbow.

"Would you like to go back to my place? To talk?"

His voice was quiet and warm. Whatever he was feeling right then, it wasn't anger.

Ella shook her head. "Thanks for that, Ben, but I'm all talked out. I'd just like to be alone."

He didn't argue, and by the time he dropped her at Grace's apartment, Ella was too exhausted for more than a muttered good-night. Just before she climbed into bed, she checked her cell phone and found a text from her editor.

Liked your piece. Nice take on a small-town controversy. Gone to press. Merry Christmas!

CHAPTER SEVENTEEN

BEN WOKE EARLY Saturday morning and decided he needed to go for a run. His head was still spinning from last night. He wished he'd noticed the slights Ella had mentioned but guessed he'd been too wrapped up in his own problems with the company fraud and the town-council pitch. He didn't blame her for saying what she had, though he wished she'd chosen a different time and place. Maybe she'd waited long enough to get all that off her chest.

Still, why hadn't she told *him* what she'd been going through? The teenage Ella he remembered wouldn't have tolerated all that stuff, but then the adult Ella was someone he'd only begun to know. He'd gone up to his room right after driving her back. Later in the night, he'd heard the murmur of voices on the third-floor landing and guessed Grace and Drew were talking. He felt some sympathy for Grace, but at the same time, his sister had had many opportunities to tell her friends the truth. He just hoped she'd do the right thing now.

The house was dead quiet when he left. After a short warm-up in the driveway, he jogged toward the harbor. He'd gotten out of the habit of a daily run since coming back home. Too many duties had called for his attention, especially his new responsibilities for the family company and the people who worked there. Ben realized he'd slipped so deeply into a trough of apathy and self-pity since moving back home that he'd been unable to pull himself up enough to see over the top of it. But now he could, knowing he was actually in charge of the company and, most of all, that Ella was here. The boardwalk along the marina had been cleared for the recent winter-carnival events in town and the forecast predicted more snow over the next few days. Clouds were already forming in the sky above the highway and to the west.

When he reached the end of the boardwalk, he loped up to the road, following it along to where it ended at the beach. The terrain was rougher there, and icy. He tackled it gingerly, remembering Ella's tumble last week, and stopping at the junction of dune and beach to catch his breath, he looked up. He wondered if she'd be able to dispel the memories that she'd mentioned last night. Similar memories had kept him awake for hours.

As he was about to head back toward town, he glimpsed movement on top of the dune. He craned his head to see a woman in a long black coat, peering down at him. When she realized she'd been spotted, she quickly drew back and disappeared. He recalled Ella's remark the night of the tree lighting about the flowers she'd found up there, and he wondered if they were connected to the woman he'd just seen. He had a feeling Grace knew—or guessed—something about that she hadn't yet revealed, in typical Grace fashion. After last summer, he'd thought there'd be no more surprises from his little sister...until she came up with the one that had the most impact on him: Ella's return to the Cove. He waited a few seconds longer, but when the woman failed to reappear, he continued on his way.

The enticing aroma of coffee was the first thing Ben noticed upon opening his parents' front door. The family was stirring, and he looked forward to breakfast before any serious talk with his parents and Grace about last night. He especially needed a calorie boost for his inevitable meeting with Ella later. He ran upstairs and headed for a shower in the bathroom he and Grace shared. The door to her turret room was still closed, so he moved about as quietly as possible, but by the time he emerged, shaved and showered, the door was wide open. No sign of her, other than the usual pile of blankets mounded in the center of her bed. Ben had to smile, thinking that the orderliness of a Coast Guard officer might inevitably clash with Grace's more—well, to be kind—free nature where domestic duties were involved.

The first clue that the day wasn't rolling out in typical fashion was that, except for coffee, there was no evidence of breakfast. His mother and father were sitting at the small table in front of the sliding doors leading to the terrace, and Grace was perched on a bar stool at the island. He guessed Drew was still asleep in the guest room. As he entered the kitchen, they all looked his way.

"Did you know anything about this, Ben?" Evelyn waved a newspaper at him.

While others throughout the Christian world may be singing that familiar carol this Christmas holiday, the voices of residents here in Lighthouse Cove, a former fishing village and now small town northeast of Portland, Maine, are raised in ire these days over the town's expansion and current building projects.

Full disclosure, my family rented a cottage in this seaside village for several years, and for the most part, my memories of the Cove, as it's affectionately called, are wonderful. I know something of its history and community, both of which are at the forefront of the current debate over a proposed condominium development.

A recent public forum on the permit application for the project in Lighthouse Cove was a textbook example of how a community can be split by insufficient or misleading information. The proposed condo design from Winters Building Ltd., a family company based in Portland and Lighthouse Cove, ticks all the boxes for affordable yet eco-friendly "green" living. The town is divided between the old-timers resisting change and the newcomers eager for the economic perks of growth—

chain stores, increased property values, improved social services and so on.

But some residents in town, suspicious of new and innovative ideas that outsiders might bring with them, would prefer to keep the Cove exactly how it's always been.

Community loyalty has clearly been shaken by the angry voices of those who feel that newcomers will bring problems rather than prosperity. Yet as one resident attending the public forum pointed out, "If people from beyond our town limits want to find a better life here, raising families and doing business with us or the folks in Portland, I say welcome. Bring us your new ideas and plans. We need them."

Environmentally sound housing, new income and investments boosting business and local initiatives cannot be a bad thing for the Cove. Approving the Winters Building Ltd. proposal will ensure the town's growth while preserving its pride in community—a pride that could be shared by newcomers and old-timers alike.

Isn't the Christmas season meant to shine on all of our better selves? Welcoming others from a new community surely reflects that promise. People in the Cove would do well to heed that message and be open to change.

Ben stared at the paper a moment longer, waiting for his blurred vision to clear. When he finally set it on the island counter, he looked at his family. "I knew she was writing something for the *Globe*, but…" The words barely squeezed past the lump in his throat.

"It's a nice piece," his mother said. "Fair and gracious, considering how she's been treated here recently, not to mention years ago."

Ben glanced at his sister, who was peering into the coffee mug at her elbow. "Grace? What do you think?" When she raised her head, he saw tears in her eyes and thought how last night had ended for both of them—Ella's confrontation and the knowledge that he and Grace had let her down, not just years ago but even these past several days. In spite of his natural impulse to protect Grace, he knew she didn't need his defense anymore.

"Ella was right," she said, her voice rising in volume as she continued, "I should have told people the truth long ago. I owed that to her, after what she did for me."

"What do you mean?" Ben's father asked,

suddenly rousing himself from wherever his thoughts had taken him.

"That day when the police were talking to the kids who'd been at the bonfire, she could have told them right away that Cassie and I sent the notes, but she didn't."

"Maybe she didn't know," Charles pointed out.

"She guessed. I saw it in the look she gave us when she threw her note in the fire. But she never said a word. And I could have cleared everything up way back then, but I didn't. I was afraid of the consequences." She sighed. "Look where that got me—where it got all of us." The bitterness in her voice lingered in the silence that followed.

"I need to go see her," Ben finally said.

He was about to leave when his father spoke again. "Please apologize for us. For taking so long to acknowledge what we've known since July. And tell her thank you from me for what she wrote about our town."

Our town. Ben resisted a smile at the hint of pride in his father's voice—it brought back all the stories about the founding Winterses and all that lore he'd heard his whole life. He understood what it might have taken

Charles—always the fierce defender of family honor and pride—to admit the family's mistakes. "I will, Dad," he said, patting his father's shoulder on his way out.

ELLA DIDN'T KNOW if it was the insistent peal of her cell phone lying on the night table or the pounding below that had awakened her, as both seemed to occur simultaneously. Groggy with sleep, she sat on the side of the bed, waiting for her mind to catch up with her body. She'd lain awake most of the night, finally drifting off as the first gray fingers of daylight poked around the edges of the blinds covering the window in Grace's bedroom. For a minute, she'd thought she was waking up in her own condo bedroom but then despair hit her. She was still here, in Grace's apartment in the Cove, and she didn't need to check her cell phone or look out the window to see who was banging on the door downstairs. Pulling her hoodie over her pajama top, she slowly negotiated the stairs. The knocking stopped as soon as she unlocked the front door, and Ben walked inside when she opened it.

Ella braced herself for whatever he might

have to say after last night, but he placed a gentle hand on her arm. "We need to talk."

"Come up. I'll make coffee."

He followed her up the stairs and into Grace's small living room off the kitchen. Ella held up a hand when it seemed he was about to speak. "I need coffee first. Sit down. I won't be long."

She decided to use Grace's fancy machine, found two pods and was carrying two mugs of coffee to him in less than five minutes. He was perched on the edge of the sofa, staring at his cell phone. "I just got a text from a reporter for the *Portland Press Herald* wanting to set up an interview about your article and my presentation at council the other night."

"You've seen my column?" She continued to stand, mugs in hands, staring at him.

"This morning. It was picked up by the *Press Herald*."

"Ah, well, I guess that makes sense. Those key words—*Lighthouse Cove*—got the attention of some editor. Local story and all that." Her voice drifted off. She put the mugs down on the coffee table and sat beside him, waiting for his response to the piece.

"I liked it," he finally said. "We all liked

it. I thought it was fair and appreciated the shout-out for the company's proposal."

"We?"

"My parents—all of us. Dad said to say thank you for the support, by the way. And most of all, to say sorry for how he and Mom continued to blame you when they've known the truth for months."

Ella wasn't sure why, but that pleased her. Maybe Charles Winters wasn't as scary in his old age as he'd seemed when she was a kid. She was also relieved that she hadn't included the angry thoughts about the Cove's community that had been in her head while writing. Had her piece compensated a bit for her behavior last night? she wondered. She hoped so.

But right then she realized Ben had more to say, as he ran an index finger back and forth across his forehead. She hid a smile, recognizing his adolescent tic, and felt her heart soften. She ought to start the conversation and give him a few minutes to get whatever he needed to off his chest.

"When I came here for the book signing, I wanted apologies—from Grace, for doing what she and Cassie did, and from you, for not having enough faith in me to stand up against what everyone in town believed about me after Brandon drowned, that I'd led him on, enticing him to the lighthouse at night to say goodbye to him." She took a deep breath. "And you could have learned the truth back then, if you'd come to talk to me."

He seemed about to interrupt, so she held up a finger. "I got the apologies and although I thought yours was a bit weak, I accepted your explanation about how confused and hurt you were at the time, thinking the note was real. I wanted to believe that you'd never really abandon me—not in your heart—and I began to think we might have a chance to put things right between us. I'm still hoping for that. The thing is, last night I realized apologies weren't enough. They didn't make up for what my family and I went through that Labor Day weekend." She stopped to let her voice settle.

"I know you mentioned the whispering and snubs, but I guess I really wasn't listening. I didn't think about what you were feeling and I'm sorry for that, Ella." He placed a hand on her cheek, drawing her close, and she closed her eyes, soaking in the warmth of his hands and arms, the worries and regrets of last night on the verge of disappearing, until she realized she needed to say more.

"I would have, Ben, but something held me back. I'm not sure how to explain it, just that every time I've referred to what happened that summer, I've sensed some kind of barrier between us. As if you didn't want to talk about it. I should have pressed the issue with you, but maybe I didn't trust that you'd understand how I felt then and now. Trust is what all of this is about, isn't it?

"You didn't trust in me when you let yourself be guided by rumors and gossip," she went on. "Grace didn't trust that people would forgive what she did, so she was afraid to tell the truth. That's why I had to tell them how I felt, because I didn't trust that Grace or your parents would speak up, even though I'm sure they've heard comments about me." She stopped to catch her breath and, when she thought he might interrupt, pushed on. "And I didn't trust either. That's the problem with distrust. It's contagious."

After a long moment, Ben pulled apart from her. He tilted her face up to his and whispered, "So, how do we fix this, Ella?"

She gave a half smile at the anxiety in his eyes. "One day at a time?" was all she could think to say. Not that it mattered, because his kiss ruled out any further discussion.

He'd promised to see her later and after he'd gone, Ella wandered about the apartment, debating her next steps. Her plan had been to return to Boston the next day unless there was a compelling reason to stay in the Cove longer. Grace needed to move back into her place, and in spite of Ben's reassurances that his parents would welcome her, she knew staying with them as a guest would be awkward.

But the simple truth was, that although she and Ben had talked about the turmoil and doubts of the past couple weeks, Ella couldn't shake the suspicion that he was holding something back. When he'd kissed her goodbye, a flicker of worry had flashed so quickly in his face and eyes that Ella had decided seconds later she'd misinterpreted it. The problem wasn't just Ben. She knew she herself hadn't revealed everything from that night years ago—her treatment of Brandon when she realized she'd been tricked.

Although she hoped to see Ben later, Ella

decided to pack for the inevitable return to Boston and was tidying the apartment when the thud of footsteps echoed up the stairs. She doubted Ben was coming back and had been mentally rehearsing another apology to Grace the whole hour since he'd left. She ought to have phoned Grace first thing that morning, avoiding the face-to-face confrontation that was about to happen.

The knock on the door was timid, boosting Ella's anxiety slightly as she opened it.

Grace's face was bright red, seemingly more from emotion than the cold. Before she said a word, she noticed Ella's suitcase lying opened on the sofa. "Were you going to leave without saying anything? Not even a goodbye?" Her voice trembled with disbelief.

"Grace, sit down and we'll talk." Ella sat on one of the kitchen chairs while Grace removed her boots. Once her friend was sitting opposite, her winter coat unzipped and big eyes fixed on Ella's, she said, "I'm sorry, Grace. I should have picked a better time and place for my big speech last night. I shouldn't have ruined your party, but I just…I felt that I couldn't continue to let things go. I needed to tell people what was happening. What *had* happened."

"You said what needed to be said, Ella, and no one in my family faults you for that. If we'd still been close, the way we were before—"

"Cassie."

"Yeah, before Cassie." Grace's sigh bounced around the small kitchen. "But I'm not here to blame Cassie. I took responsibility for my part last summer when I told my family the truth, but I didn't go far enough. I should have told my friends and…I don't know…asked them to spread the word. Make the rumors disappear. I see now that I took the easy way out."

"It couldn't have been easy for you at all, Grace. Confessing all these years later when you could have kept your secret for the rest of your life. No one would have been the wiser."

Grace was shaking her head. "No, Ella. After I met Drew…when I knew I loved him and wanted to spend the rest of my life with him, I realized that couldn't happen unless I spoke up. I had no choice. I didn't realize things were that bad for you these past couple of weeks, Ella. I'm sorry you had to endure all that. But you could have talked to Ben and me."

Ella gave a loud sigh of irritation. "But we *didn't* talk. None of us did. Not back then and not recently. There's no point in rehashing all these 'could haves' or 'should haves,' Grace. We didn't. Let's stop beating ourselves up about it. Let's just go from here. Start all over."

"Can you do that, Ella?"

"I can. What about you? How do you feel about the town finally knowing your story?"

"I can handle that. I'm made of much stronger fiber than my family thinks, you know. The Grace Winters I am today isn't at all like the one seventeen years ago."

Ella felt a surge of affection for her old friend. "I disagree." She smiled at Grace's puzzled face. "Except for a few days that summer, you've always been a strong and compassionate person. Don't ever think otherwise."

Grace took a minute to dab her eyes. "So, what now?"

Ella instantly recalled Ben's similar question. "Well, as I told Ben, maybe we can take things one day at a time."

"I'll do whatever it takes to make sure people know the truth, Ella. I promise."

"Thanks, Grace."

After a moment, she asked, "Are you leaving tomorrow as planned?"

That question had been in Ella's head since last night, and now she knew what to do. "Maybe today instead, Grace. The three of us need to take some time to process everything. But I'd like to come back soon. If you and Ben—and your parents, especially—will have me?"

Grace gave a shaky laugh. "Come on, Ella! You already know the answer to that. Don't be so coy."

"Yeah." She shrugged, smiling. "You were always pretty good at reading me. Sometimes Ben was, too."

"Are things cool with you both now?"

Were they? Ella thought of his solemn face when he'd left. "I think so."

"Good. I was hoping to hear that." She glanced around the room. "Drew isn't going back to Portland until tomorrow, if you change your mind about staying."

"Thanks, Grace, and it's tempting, but

there are things I need to do in Boston. Presents to send off to my family and so on."

"Okay." Grace stood up and went to Ella, clasping her in a hug.

Ella closed her eyes and let the memories of all her summer goodbyes with Grace flow through her.

CHAPTER EIGHTEEN

AS ELLA ROLLED her suitcase up the side street to her car, snow was falling so thickly that she could barely see the pavement in front of her. When she reached the lot, her car was covered by a couple inches, which she whisked away with her gloved hands because she didn't have a scraper. She sat behind the wheel for a few minutes, waiting for the heater and defroster to kick in while the windshield wipers swished hypnotically back and forth. Ella watched them, her mind a blank…until the doubts popped up.

Should she take Ben and Grace up on their invites to stay? She was tempted, suddenly craving the ambience of family, even though that family was the Winterses. There was no way she could recapture the sense of belonging she'd felt with them when she was a child and a teen. Too much life had intervened for all of them. A wave of exhaustion flowed through her. First the talk with Ben, and then Grace. What she needed was an antidote, something to cheer her up before the long drive home. Henry Jenkins came to mind and Ella smiled.

Ella texted him after she parked outside his house. He replied immediately.

Door's open. Come on in but watch out for my cat.

She brushed off her coat and stomped most of the snow off her boots before stepping inside. The house was warm—too warm, she thought, removing her coat and her boots.

"I'm in here," he called out from the living room.

Henry was ensconced in his recliner chair with a stack of books and magazines on the table next to him and his cat, Felix, on his lap. When Ella bent over to kiss his cheek, she saw his empty coffee mug. "Would you like more coffee? Or tea?"

"Tea, please." His smile was even warmer than the house.

The pile of dirty dishes in the sink indicated Henry was either not as mobile as everyone had thought or that he was taking a vacation from household chores. She didn't notice a dishwasher so, while she waited for the kettle, Ella ran hot water into the sink to soak the dishes.

On her way into the living room with two mugs of tea, Felix darted past her toward the kitchen.

"I apologize for the mess in there. Wasn't expecting company."

"Is your hip still bothering you?" She set his mug down beside him and sat on the love seat opposite.

"Not the new one, the other one." He grimaced. "Getting old sucks."

"Better than dying young," she quipped and instantly realized what she'd just said. Her face heated up and she stared into her mug, afraid to meet Henry's eyes.

"You can't keep doing that, Ella. Reliving the past over and over is a bad idea and won't help you get on with the future. I'm still trying to get that into Gracie's head, months after she found the courage to confess."

"That's the problem, Henry. People here won't let me forget."

"Is that why you blew up last night?" Then

he winked. "Sorry I missed the drama. Would have been more exciting than the game I was watching in the den."

Ella knew from his face he was teasing, which was exactly what she needed after the drama with Ben and Grace earlier. "I couldn't help it. I didn't plan it, Henry. It just all spewed out." She aimed for a grin but tears threatened.

"Regrets this morning?" His voice softened.

"Not really regret about telling the truth, but I feel bad about hurting Grace. Maybe embarrassing Evelyn. Plus, Brandon's mother and sister were there, too."

He nodded thoughtfully, keeping his gaze on her. Thinking before speaking. That was Henry's gift, Ella decided. She sipped her tea and waited.

"They have their own cross to bear over all that, Ella. Especially Gracie. Don't assume because she's confessed and her family has forgiven her that everything that happened has been laid to rest for her. It hasn't. Might never be."

Ella's eyes welled up again and she dug into

her sweatshirt pocket for a tissue, finally resorting to a sleeve.

"Gracie will struggle with that for the rest of her life. Fortunately for her, she's found someone who loves her enough to help her fight those inner battles. I hope you do, too." His thoughtful eyes rested on her. "Maybe you have already."

Ella bit down hard on her lip. "I hope so, but…I have some doubts, to be honest."

"Don't give up, Ella Mae. That's when regret really happens."

She smiled at his use of her second name, remembering the first time she'd met him in his bookstore when she was six, formally introducing herself—*I'm Ella Mae Jacobs*—and offering her right hand to shake. He'd taken it and replied without a trace of amusement, *Pleased to meet you, Ella Mae Jacobs.*

"How did you get so wise?" she asked.

"Seventy years of life has helped, though I'm still learning." Then he added, "The storm's already started. Maybe you ought to get going or whatever you've decided to do."

"You're right, Henry. I know I have choices." She picked up their tea mugs and headed for the kitchen, ignoring his shout to forget the dishes. That task was completed quickly, and soon she was kissing him goodbye.

"Don't be a stranger," he called from his chair as she was putting her coat and boots on at the front door.

"Never, Henry." She closed the door behind her and paused on the steps outside. The sky was darker now. Common sense argued that she ought to get onto the highway as soon as possible. But Ben had mentioned seeing her before she left town. Did she want to risk the consequence of leaving without seeing him? What would he think? That she'd changed her mind about everything, like wanting a future with him?

No. While she waited for the car to heat up, she texted Ben.

Ella must be a mind reader. Ben had been thinking about calling her to arrange a meetup and was disappointed to hear she'd decided to go back to Boston today, rather than tomorrow. But she did want to stop by to see him before she left. He stared at her text long enough for Glen to pipe up, "Problem, boss?"

"Um, no." He looked over at Glen, who'd

offered to come in on a Saturday to search through some old invoices. "But why don't you head home now? The weather's starting to get bad out there." He peered through the frosted window, but visibility was so poor, he could barely make out their cars parked in the lot next to the trailer.

"You sure?"

Ben pursed his lips at the hesitation in Glen's voice and felt bad that he was still shaken about the fraud scheme. He hadn't been involved at all, but perhaps he'd initially thought he was a suspect. Ben pictured Ella's face last night when she confronted Julie, and he had a sudden revelation. *The whole tragedy and everything that followed it has been about assumptions.* Yeah, he could see that now. He personally had made a regrettable assumption about Ella seventeen years ago.

"I'm sure, Glen. Get going, and I'll see you Monday if the storm lets up." He lifted a slat of the window blind to check again.

He watched Glen clean off his car and get inside, then lost sight of the car before it even left the yard. Maybe Ella's visit right now wasn't such a good idea, but on the other hand, he didn't want to miss saying goodbye because of some snowstorm. When he heard the tap on the office door, he flung it open. A funnel of snow and wind whirled into the office ahead of her.

"Whoo!" Her burst of laughter died as soon as she saw Ben. "It's already bad out there."

They stared at one another a long moment. "I'm glad you came."

She smiled and unzipped her jacket. "So this is where the magic happens."

"Magic?"

"Your work. Designing and building."

Ben rubbed the back of his neck. "I guess so, if that's what you can call it."

"Creating things is magic, don't you think?"

He didn't want to get sidetracked from his intention to continue their talk from the morning and maybe also to make plans for Christmas. "You didn't come here for a philosophical discussion, did you?"

"No. Just delaying a serious one." Her grin was sheepish.

"Take your coat off and don't worry about the boots." He pushed a couple chairs close to the electric heating panel. "Want a coffee or tea?"

"No thanks. I had tea with Henry."

Ben decided he needed more caffeine and made a mug of instant coffee as she spoke, heating it up in the microwave. "How is the old man?"

"Okay, though he said his hip is bothering him."

"Again?"

"The other one now."

He stirred powdered creamer into his mug of coffee and hesitantly sipped some, then grimaced.

"That bad?"

"Worse than bad. You made the right call there. I suppose Henry might need a second hip replacement."

"Perhaps."

"Look—"

"I—"

Ben smiled with her. He didn't know who ought to go first, but he definitely knew that he wanted to pull her off the chair and into his arms.

"I need to say this," she started again. She swept back a strand of hair that fell across her face as she leaned forward on her chair. "This morning we talked about trust, and when Grace came—"

"Grace came to see you?"

"Shortly after you left."

His sister had been quiet that morning, but she hadn't seemed upset about the dinner party, though he had to admit he'd been mainly focused on Ella's article.

"How was she? Upset?" He sighed with relief when Ella shook her head.

"No, we had a good talk. I…I think we'll be fine now."

She ducked her head, and Ben had a feeling another revelation was about to happen. He tried not to show his disappointment that the few minutes of cuddling he'd been hoping for were not about to happen. He got up to move around, to prepare for whatever she was about to spill. He suddenly stopped pacing to listen. "Hear that?"

She looked up. "The wind?"

"I think so." He lifted up a window slat, but all he could see was a ghostly swirl of snow. "I think we'd better stay put for a bit. Looks kind of bad out there. Are you warm enough?" he suddenly thought to ask.

"Yes…but will we be okay here?"

"Sure. We had the electric heating installed

when we figured this office was going to be more permanent than we'd planned."

"Do you think it's too late, Ben?" she suddenly asked.

"Too late? For us to stay here a bit longer?"

"No, I mean for *us*?"

The appeal in her piercing blue eyes was gut-wrenching. He wanted to embrace her, tell her again how much he loved her—had *always* loved her—and how she'd been in his head practically every day of the last seventeen years. The hours he'd fantasized about this very moment—not here in the office—but with her, in the flesh and not in a dream. To have the bad memories just gone.

Was it too late? He didn't know. And he was saved from answering when the lights went out.

It wasn't completely dark. An eerie light filtered through the window blinds and Ella guessed it was only about four or five o'clock. She'd left her cell phone in her car. Ben was typing on his phone, his back to her while he stood staring out the window. She got up and walked over to him just as he finished texting.

"Thought I'd better let my folks know I'll be here for a while."

"How long do you think this will go on?"

"No idea. I can't see beyond a few feet out there. I'll check the weather networks." After a few seconds of searching, he said, "Um, well, Portland area weather predicts storm activity—high winds, drifting snow and poor visibility—for the next twelve hours." He looked up from his phone. "Or until the morning."

"Well, we can't stay *here*."

This time he managed a real smile. "Would that be so bad? The place is insulated, though now we won't have heating, and those chairs aren't very comfy, but—"

"I think we should try to get into town. We could both go in one car and—"

"That's not a good idea, Ella. You've never been through a Maine winter, much less a storm. People have died trying to get somewhere when they should have stayed in a car or house or wherever."

That emphatic tone was new to her. She went back to her chair, slumping down with a slight huff.

"Is that frustration at not having any control over the situation?"

It took her a second to realize he was teasing. "Guess we have lots of time to talk, then."

She couldn't tell from his expression if that appealed to him or not.

"So, back to where we left off a minute ago? When you asked if it was too late for us?" His serious eyes probed hers. He walked over to sit in the chair next to hers and reached for her hand. "I'll do whatever it takes to make sure that it's not too late, Ella. Starting right now and, as you said before, taking it one day at a time."

She squeezed his hand. "I needed to hear that, Ben. I feel the same, but—"

"But?"

"I'm worried about Grace and what will happen when more people learn the truth and how she and your parents might be treated afterward." *Because I'm the one who insisted she tell everyone.* That irony wasn't lost on her.

"That's a lot of worrying, Ella."

Despite his smile, she bet those thoughts had occurred to him, too.

"The people that matter to my family—our friends, work colleagues and even Grace's loyal customers—may be startled or shocked at first, but eventually they'll forgive and accept. That's part of belonging in a community, isn't it?"

"I don't know. Except for our summers here when I was a kid, I've never felt attached to a community, really. I mean, I have the community of my workplace, which is great, but…"

"But?"

Ella shrugged. How to explain? "I know if I left it, I'd be quickly replaced, and after a few days, I'd be forgotten."

"Yeah, I guess I know what you mean. I felt a bit like that when I was with the architectural firm in Augusta. Even though I was born and raised here in the Cove, my sense of being part of this community disappeared when I left for college. But lately, I've been feeling more reconnected to the town."

Ella imagined his life after the prank. All of them had been affected. She was about to mention this, but then a strong gust of wind shook the building. "Oh!" she gasped.

Ben pushed his chair up against hers and

drew her close. "We'll be fine, don't worry. This unit is structurally sound."

"Tornado-proof?"

He laughed. "Uh, well, there's not much danger of a tornado or a hurricane here in winter. It's just a storm."

She wished she had as much confidence in that small word *just.*

Ben's cell phone pinged, and he pulled out of their hug to reach for it on the desk.

"A text from Grace." After he replied to it, he said, "She asked if you were here with me. Apparently, she'd texted Henry to see if he was okay, and he told her you might be coming to see me."

Henry should take up mind reading, Ella was thinking.

The phone pinged again. Ben sighed. "There's never a complete end to Grace's texts, I'm afraid." He read the message and set the phone down without a reply. "She said she was glad you were here. She'd been worrying about you driving back to Boston in the storm and told us to stay safe."

Ben was right. His sister didn't hold grudges. *But what about me?* Ella realized for the first time that she'd held on to grudges for most of her life, blaming the prank for every bad thing that happened. Like her parents' divorce and even her own divorce, despite knowing months into the marriage that Jake was never going to morph into Ben Winters. Ella bit her lip hard. She'd shed enough tears.

"Let's see if we can make ourselves more comfortable. It's getting pretty dark now." Ben went over to the counter with the microwave to rummage through the cupboards below. "Okay, this will be handy." He held up a large flashlight.

"Anything to eat in that cupboard? Is that a minifridge under there?"

"Um, yes, but I don't want to raise your hopes." He peered into the fridge. "Well, I see a piece of cheese and an unopened little tub of yogurt. Plus— Whoa! A couple of granola bars."

"Water?"

"No, but good thinking. The power's been off long enough to shut down the system's pump in town, but we might still get whatever's left in the pipes."

She watched him run the faucet at the sink and begin filling mugs. After two had been filled, the water trickled off. "That should be enough anyway. We won't go hungry between now and morning, nor will we suffer from dehydration."

"And there's always snow," she piped up. "Not that we could use the microwave to melt it." She smiled at his laugh but continued to look anxiously at the dark windows.

"Come here." He pulled her gently into his arms. His heart beat steadily beneath her cheek and she nestled into him, warmed by his thick, wool sweater and the reassuring arms that tightened around her.

"I think we should get ready for what could be a long night." He relaxed his hold and went to the hooks on the wall next to the door, where the work crew hung their gear. He yanked down his jacket and a bulky, waterproof coat emblazoned with yellow safety bands. He lay the canvas coat on the floor, then he peered around the room. "Not sure if we have anything to use as a pillow."

She couldn't believe they were really going to be spending the night there and watched with mounting dread while he opened drawers and cupboard doors. Eventually he extracted some tea towels along with what looked like a teapot cozy.

"Not sure how this got here," he said, frowning. "But it'll do." He placed the small cloth bundle at the top of the coat and then proceeded to lie down. He smiled encouragingly, patting the space next to him. "Come on. Put your jacket on and we can use mine as a blanket."

Ella stared, mute with disbelief.

CHAPTER NINETEEN

BEN WOKE WITH a numb left arm. It was under Ella's head, and he hated to disturb her, but at the same time, he couldn't tolerate another second of pins and needles. She was lying curled up next to him, facing the other way. He didn't know when they'd fallen asleep or how long they'd been sleeping. Sometime in the hours between setting up their "nests," as Ella insisted on dubbing the makeshift beds, and the memory games—favorite songs from their teens, worst summer job, best movie—their competitive spirits flagged. He couldn't even recall drifting off to sleep but suspected it had happened midsentence. The one topic neither had raised had been any memory linked to their last summer together in the Cove.

Ben slowly extracted his arm out from under her and gently laid her head back onto the balled-up bundle of tea towels they'd used as pillows. Not a good substitute, he decided, sitting up and massaging the back of his neck.

He had no idea what time it was. The bit of light filtering through the slats was a tad brighter than the interior of the room, so he was guessing daybreak at least. He got to his feet, a bit clumsily due to stiff joints, and stretched. Then he raised the blinds. The storm had vamoosed but had left behind a huge reminder of its presence. Snow, as far as Ben could see, blending with the cloudy sky to form a vast landscape of grays and whites. He could barely make out the roofs of their two vehicles. They'd have to dig their way out. Thank goodness the office had a shovel, purchased after the season's first snowfall weeks ago.

Ella was stirring behind him, so he moved back to the blanket and sat down next to her. Her drowsy eyes and cheeks flushed from sleep tugged at his heart, and her smile, shy from the novelty of awakening with him, prompted him to lean over and kiss her cheek.

"Is it over?" She sat up, rubbing her eyes.

"It is. But we'll have to dig our way out."

"With a shovel, I hope, and not our hands."

He chuckled. “Yeah, fortunately I have one here.”

Her stretch was slow and languorous, almost seductive, and Ben had to stand up, afraid to trust himself with even another kiss.

“I can’t believe I slept so well! Did you?”

“Surprisingly, I did.” He picked up his cell phone from the desk. It was dead and he didn’t have his charger with him. “Have you got your phone with you?”

“I left it in my car.”

“Oh well. Once we’ve cleared a path out of the lot, we should be able to get into town.”

“No breakfast?”

Ben smiled at the fake pout on her face. *This is the Ella I remember. Her sense of humor.* He knew more than ever that he wanted a future with her, but could he have one as long as he held on to his own secret? Once they were out in the snowbound real world, he figured other immediate tasks and issues would hamper their chances of being alone together in the days ahead. There was still no power, and people in town, like his parents and Henry, would need help.

He stared longingly at her, reluctant to break the sweetness of this moment.

She was standing up now, flexing joints and stiff muscles. “Hungry?” she asked. Then without waiting for his reply, she wandered over to the counter. “Hey, there’s still a granola bar here. Dibs on it!”

“Be my guest. I regretted the one I ate last night.” He pulled a face and she laughed.

She came toward him, unwrapping the granola bar, and he said, “Ella, I need to tell you something.”

She heard the tone in his voice, and her grin disappeared. “What is it?”

“Come and sit.”

She sat down next to him and began munching on the granola bar, though Ben saw that her enthusiasm for it was waning.

“You were brave to tell people your story Friday night about how my family and I—heck, the whole town—didn’t question the rumors. Even after Grace told my parents the truth months ago, they continued to cling to the illusion that their beloved daughter couldn’t be part of such a scheme. I know we kind of touched on all this yesterday. The thing is…” He had to stop to take a breath. “Grace wasn’t the only person who should have come clean.”

Ben didn't let the growing apprehension in her eyes stop him. "The night of the bonfire, one of my buddies told me he heard you had a rendezvous with Brandon on the beach. At first I laughed, thinking how ridiculous the idea was, but then my insecurity got the better of me. I recalled how you sometimes defended Brandon when Grace or Cassie were making jokes about him, and I began to wonder if the rumor was true." He stopped, taking in how much bigger her eyes looked in a face that was suddenly very pale. She was about to speak, and he held up his hand. "I need to finish this, Ella. It's been a long time coming.

"I went looking for you, but on my way to the bonfire, I met Brandon. It must have been right after he found out he'd been tricked, because he was running away from where I think you'd seen him, on the lighthouse path. I grabbed hold of his arm and saw he was crying, but…see?…all I was thinking was that my friend must have been right, that you *had* been meeting Brandon. I was angry and accused him of going behind my back with my girlfriend. He laughed, but in a horribly bitter way, and shouted something about a note. He flashed this paper in front of me, kind of taunting me, and I tried to take it from him." Ben had to pause.

"Go on."

Her cold voice frightened him, but he had to finish. "We had a scuffle and I pushed him. After he ran off, I saw that he'd dropped the note. I was confused, Ella, and not thinking straight. I read the note, saw your name on it and believed the rumor was true. I'd planned to confront you with it the next day, but then the police came in the night to tell us Brandon was missing and asked if we had any information. I didn't know what to do. We were all shocked. I immediately thought of my encounter with Brandon and wondered if that had had something to do with his disappearance. To tell the truth, I can't remember if I gave the note to my parents or to the police. I told them I'd found it. When we heard early the next morning that he'd drowned, I was more afraid than ever to come clean about meeting him, because I thought his death was on me. That he'd run to the lighthouse after our scuffle. Later the same day, we heard the gossip about what had happened." He waited, controlling the emotions that flooded through him. "And that's when I believed the rumors, too."

He reached for her, but she abruptly stood up and began to walk in circles, forking her fingers through her hair, as if to exorcise everything she'd heard.

"I'm sorry, Ella. I should have said something right then. And last week, I should have told you the whole story when I apologized for not going to see you before you left the Cove." He lowered his face into his palms, unable to look at her, afraid of what he might see in her eyes.

She stopped pacing. "Let me get this right. If you hadn't given that note to the police, they wouldn't have come to question me about Brandon's drowning. The people in town wouldn't have been blaming me for setting Brandon up. *Blaming me for seventeen years, Ben!*"

The fury and pain in her voice confirmed his worst fears. There was no going back, and now, maybe no going ahead.

ELLA WATCHED BEN shovel a path from the cars to the road into town. She'd finished sweeping off the cars, using the broom that he'd found in a closet, and was about to start hers to warm it up. She sat in the driver's seat, keeping her eyes on the rearview mirror and Ben. The physical work of the last half hour had been good for both of them. She'd had a chance to vent some of her anger following his confession, though she knew the hurt would take days to fade, if at all. As for Ben, she figured all that shoveling was a kind of penance for him. Not that it would be enough, of course.

She tried not to dwell on how her life could have been different if Ben had shown her the note first, rather than his parents. She wasn't sure she believed him when he said he couldn't remember if he'd given it to the police or if his parents had. Did that even matter? The point was, if he'd shown her the note as he said he'd planned to, she'd have told him about the prank right away.

She switched on the front and rear windshield wipers, clearing off the rest of the snow and the areas that had melted from the defroster. She didn't know whose car they were taking into town yet. They'd decided to just use one, as the roads would be bad and it was better for them to be together rather than separate. Although Ella was beginning to think *separate* was going to be a permanent state where she and Ben were concerned.

Another glance behind confirmed Ben was finished and heading toward her. She rolled down her window. "Yours or mine?"

He avoided looking at her, angling his face slightly to the right. Ella was annoyed. She was the wronged person here. Why was he giving her the silent treatment? Then she thought of her outburst minutes ago and the way he'd sat quietly through it, his face buried in his hands.

When she'd started sweeping off the cars, she'd decided to take the high road. She'd expressed her feelings, and now the ball was back to him. There was nothing to be gained by going back over what he'd done. *Even though he'd altered the course of my whole life!* She sensed she might be exaggerating about that but also knew so much had been affected by Ben's action. He'd have followed through on his promise to visit her during his freshman year. Her family would have returned to the Cove the next summer. She wouldn't have missed out on more summers—years—of being with Ben Winters.

Ella was so wrapped up in all the what-ifs

that she gave him a blank stare after he spoke before she blurted, "What?"

"Uh, I suggested we take mine. It's a four-wheel drive and the highway probably hasn't been cleared yet." He was frowning.

Without a word she rolled up her window again and turned off the engine. Ben was inside his SUV already, heating it up. She pulled her suitcase and handbag from her car, not knowing how long she'd have to stay in town. Judging from her limited view of the road ahead, she guessed she wouldn't be leaving the Cove anytime soon. Once they left the office parking area, Ella understood why he'd suggested the SUV. Fortunately, the wind direction had drifted snow onto one side of the road, leaving the other fairly navigable. Ben drove slowly and carefully, bypassing occasional mounds of snow that encroached on the other half of the road. By the time they reached the turnoff from the highway, they'd encountered only one other vehicle, a snowplow heading in the opposite direction.

"The town will be the last place to get cleared," Ben said. "Limited resources. The council will probably have already asked for assistance from Portland, but who knows when it'll reach the Cove." He didn't speak again until they reached Main Street. "What are your plans, Ella? I doubt you'll be able to go to Boston today—maybe not even tomorrow. I should check on my folks and Grace and Drew. Then I'll see how we can help people in town."

She stared blankly at him. What *were* her plans? The last hour, her head had been either completely empty or teeming with confusing and angry thoughts. "I don't know."

He turned away to focus on driving, and after plowing for what seemed like hours through rutted side streets, they pulled into his parents' driveway. Grace and Drew were standing by the front stoop, leaning against their shovels, and waved as Ben parked behind Drew's SUV.

When Ben killed the engine, he looked at Ella. "Do you want to get out or wait here? I can take you wherever you like after I let my parents know my plans."

Ella was on the verge of telling him to drive her to the hotel *right away*, but as she watched Grace's hesitant wave, she knew if she left again, as she and her family had years ago, nothing would ever be fixed. "I'll get out, too. Maybe there's something I can help with before, um, before I leave."

He nodded but kept his eyes on hers, as if he were waiting for her to say something more. Not that the time was right for that, Ella was thinking, as she opened the car door.

"We were so worried about you two," Grace called out. "I guess your phones died?"

"Mine did, but I've been charging it on the car battery," Ben said. "Mom and Dad okay?"

"They'll be better now that you're here. Mom's cooking breakfast. You're just in time."

Breakfast. Ella's stomach rumbled at the very word but churned at the thought of sitting down to it with Ben's parents.

"You okay with that?" he asked in a low voice.

She nodded and followed him up to the front door. As she passed Drew on the way in, he murmured, "Glad you stayed in town. And don't worry about Friday. They understand."

Ella smiled, thinking Grace was lucky to have such an intuitive partner. The mouthwatering aroma of bacon wafted from the kitchen as they removed coats, hats and boots. She lagged behind as the others headed for the kitchen, getting up her nerve to face his parents. Passing the dining room, she noticed that the table had been laid and Grace was coming her way with two more plates and sets of cutlery. She smiled at Ella, brushing by her to place the additional settings on the table, and Ella's tension eased somewhat. At least she had Ben and Grace on her side.

Evelyn was lifting rashers of bacon from a frying pan onto a platter lined with paper towels. "Charles and I are relieved you two are okay. Breakfast is set to go." She smiled at Ella and turned to Ben. "Will you get your father, dear? He's in the solarium. And, Drew, the pancakes and eggs are under that foil-wrapped platter on the counter." She looked back at Ella. "I'll let you take the bacon into the dining room, Ella, and the orange juice, if you can manage that, too. I'll bring the coffee. Fortunately, I kept my old percolator, because we all need some caffeine." As she handed Ella the bacon, she lowered her voice to say, "Don't worry about Friday night. We'll talk later."

Ella would have hugged her but figured that might be rushing the reconciliation a bit. She was placing the bacon and juice on the table when Ben came in with his father, who gave a quick nod her way. Ben helped Charles get seated at the head of the table and pointed to a chair on the window side of the table. “Come and sit here next to me, Ella.”

She sat down, grateful for the gesture that made her feel this brunch—her first at the Winters home in seventeen years—was no big deal. Grace and Drew sat opposite, murmuring to one another as the food was passed around.

“I apologize that the eggs and pancakes aren’t as hot as they would have been if I’d kept them warm in the oven,” Evelyn said as she set the pot of coffee on the table.

“I don’t think anyone’s complaining, Mom. But why doesn’t the oven work and the stove top does?” Grace asked.

“Gas,” Drew put in, munching on a piece of bacon. He swallowed and explained at her puzzled frown. “The oven has an electric ignition, so useless in a power outage. But I lit the stove burners with a match.”

“And frightened the devil out of me when he did it!” Charles exclaimed.

Everyone laughed, and the tension in Ella’s shoulders loosened a bit more. Everyone ate quickly from hunger and perhaps, Ella thought, from wanting to find out what was happening in town. While Ben and Drew stacked dishes in the sink to be washed when water was available, Ella retrieved the empty platters from the dining room.

Grace was alone in the room, scrolling through her cell phone. "Lots more information now, thank goodness. The town website is asking people to help their neighbors shovel out, especially seniors. I texted Henry to tell him one of us is going to shovel his walk, and Mom has wrapped up leftover brekkie for him. People are setting up soup kitchens for those who can't cook or who need provisions. One's in the church off Town Square and the other's at the hotel. There's also a volunteer center set up at Town Hall. I was thinking of going to the hotel 'cause it's closer. Are you interested in coming with me?"

"Um..." Ella hesitated.

"I know we went over this yesterday morning, Ella, but seriously, let's try to forget about Friday night. You forgave me for what I did that summer, and maybe we're even now. We both still have some angst about everything that's happened, but I figure that will go away in time...if we let it."

Ella pursed her lips. Grace was right. "I'll go to the hotel with you."

"Good."

BEN WATCHED HIS sister and Ella heading down the drive to the road. They'd insisted on walking rather than risking taking a vehicle.

"I don't want to get stuck somewhere. Besides, you and Drew might need both cars to go help with shoveling," Grace had said as she was getting into her boots.

"Sure you're okay with this?" Ben had whispered to Ella. He'd been afraid that Grace might have railroaded her into going to the hotel, where volunteers were gathering. Although her quick nod wasn't exactly reassuring, he didn't push. She was definitely going to be in the Cove for another day or so, and he guessed helping out was preferable to sitting in the solarium with his parents.

He closed the front door behind them. Drew was taking his jacket out of the closet, getting ready to drive to Henry's with the package of breakfast leftovers. Ben's plan was to drive to Town Hall, where a volunteer table had also been set up, and then patrol some streets, looking for houses and businesses that needed to be shoveled out. But first, he wanted to talk to his parents.

"Guess we'll meet up somewhere during the day," he said as Drew made for the front door.

"Yep. I'm sure I'll be here at least until tomorrow, maybe the next day. Depending on how the cleanup goes in Portland."

That reminded Ben to get an email chain going for his employees. None of them would be able to venture into work tomorrow and, perhaps, even the day after. Then he noticed Drew was still standing by the door.

"One thing I've learned since getting to know all of you Winterses, you're pretty resilient. Speaking from experience, troubled times settle down eventually." Drew grinned. "My wisdom for the day. See you." He closed the door behind him.

Yeah, Ben was thinking. *He's right. And my sister's lucky.* He headed along the hall toward the solarium. His parents looked up from their books as he sat down. He decided to bypass small talk and get right to the point. "I've told Ella what I did that morning when the police came to tell us about Brandon. About giving you the note Brandon had. Or maybe it was the police. I can't remember which happened first."

"You gave it to me," his father put in. "And I handed it over to the police."

"Yeah?" Ben frowned. He didn't know if that detail was important or if it even mattered anymore.

"Why, Ben?"

"What do you mean, Mom?"

"I mean why did you bring this up with Ella *now*?"

"Because I knew there was no way I could have a life with her if I kept what I did a secret. She has a right to know all of it."

His mother was shaking her head, clearly upset. But then she said, "Ella does have a right to know everything, Ben. I think the Winters family has caused her enough damage in this whole sad affair."

"Is that what you want, Ben? A life with Ella Jacobs?"

This unexpected question from his father, asked in a softer voice than he'd ever heard from him, brought tears to Ben's eyes. He stared out the solarium windows until his eyes cleared, knowing that the worry in their faces stemmed from love and concern for him. “It is what I want, Dad. I don’t want to lose her again. Though right now, I’m not sure if she’ll have me. She’s still processing what I’ve just told her. That note had a profound impact on her life.”

“If she loves you enough, she’ll eventually understand that what you did was the spontaneous act of a confused and grieving teenager.” After a moment of silence, Evelyn added, “And be sure to tell her we’d like her to spend the night here, with us.”

Ben hoped his mother was right about the understanding part. “I’ll see you both later.” He leaned down to kiss them on their cheeks. As he put on his jacket and boots, he realized he’d kissed his parents more in the past few days than he had since he was a kid. *Maybe showing your love for family—for Ella—has been long overdue*, he told himself, stepping out into the cold, snowy day.

CHAPTER TWENTY

GRACE DIDN'T SPEAK all the way to the hotel, except for a few warnings to watch out for a patch of ice or a slippery spot. The streets and sidewalks were treacherous, and they were forced to slow down to a fast waddle, like penguins. Ella smiled at the image and would have mentioned it to Grace but for the awkwardness that seemed to pop up whenever they were alone. She'd noticed at breakfast how easily they all chatted while eating, as if Ella's outburst at the engagement party had never happened.

Although Evelyn had said they'd speak later, the opportunity never arose. For that, Ella was grateful. She needed more time to absorb Ben's confession. He'd seemed let down when she'd told him she was going with Grace to help at the hotel. Perhaps he'd expected her to shovel with him or, worse, wait with his parents until he was finished.

They didn't encounter many people on the way, but once they reached the hotel, clusters of adults, some in family groups, were going in and out the hotel doors. Some carried large aluminum food containers and others carried boxes or plastic bins. A van was parked right in front, and two men were unloading cases of bottled water. Grace and Ella stomped the snow off their boots before stepping onto the long strips of cardboard running down the center of the lobby's marble floor. The makeshift path led to wide-open doors tucked into a corner near the elevator.

She came to a dead stop on the threshold. "Is this a ballroom?"

Grace smiled. "It is. Who knew, eh? I have a fuzzy memory of coming here to someone's wedding when I was about eleven or twelve."

"Was there also a restaurant in the hotel then?"

"I don't remember a restaurant, but downstairs, there's a huge kitchen."

The hotel certainly had undergone some transformations, Ella thought as they walked into the large room filled with long conference-style tables and throngs of people setting out food, drinks and supplies. Ella figured the hotel had generators, because the old-fashioned sconces along the walls were dimly lit, as were the chandeliers along the whole length of the ceiling.

A few people greeted Grace warmly, their gazes skimming briefly over Ella. She braced herself for questions or whispers, but none came. While Grace was chatting to an older woman, Ella wandered around the tables to see where she could help. Grace caught up to her as she stood by a table of nonperishable and hygienic items.

"If the power isn't on soon, people will need a lot more than what's here." Ella's broad gesture took in the whole room.

"For sure, but this is a start. Let's hope the utility crews from Portland arrive by tomorrow."

"True." Ella looked around, noting every table had at least two people handing out supplies or dishing food into containers. "Where do you think we should help?"

"I don't know." Grace scanned the crowd. "Wait. I see Zanna over there." She pointed across the room, where Suzanna was speaking to an attractive man.

Grace marched ahead and Ella followed,

feeling oddly like a child with her mother. She hung back, letting Grace take the lead.

"Zanna? Are you in charge? It's just that we want to help wherever we're needed most."

Suzanna's hazel-green eyes flicked over Ella and back to Grace. Ella couldn't tell from her impassive expression whether she was surprised to see her or not. There'd been that moment at the party when Suzanna had apologized for her rude friend, which Ella interpreted as a sign of acceptance. Still, she was sorry Suzanna and her mother had to hear about that night again. Even though they already knew the real story, listening to her version of events must have been painful.

"Sam and I were just talking about how to get help where it's needed most. You remember Sam Hargrave, Grace? And, Sam, this is Ella Jacobs, a friend of Grace's."

Ella nodded. Was this the Sam from Mabel's Diner?

"Thanks for coming to help, ladies. Word is gradually getting out, so we think the place will fill up quickly. Our intention was to have people eat at the tables and chairs, but obviously some will want to take food home." He pointed to the far end of the room, and Ella saw that people were carrying plastic plates of food to the seating area as well as heading for the exit.

"Do you want us to help serve?" Grace asked. "Though I see there are people already doing that."

"Yes, and many are helping themselves. I've got volunteers replenishing the paper plates, cutlery and serving utensils. We're still getting food brought in, but that might taper off as the day goes on. What're your thoughts?"

"What about people who can't get here? Is there a way to deliver food or other stuff to them?" Ella put in, thinking of Henry and other seniors.

"Good thinking!" Sam smiled. "Would you like to be in charge of that?"

Suzanna gave her a thoughtful look. "I think Ella would be the perfect person to organize it, and, Grace, why don't you help her?"

Ella laughed. "I see you two have good management skills."

"Helps when you're running a bakery and a hotel." Sam grinned.

"You're Mabel, then."

His grin broadened. "In another incarnation."

"I've become addicted to your scones and hot chocolate. I just hope I can find a place as good when I'm back in Boston."

"You're from Boston? What's brought you to Lighthouse Cove?"

Ella recalled the server at Mabel's saying the owner was new to town, and he might not have heard the old story. She was thinking of a simple explanation when Suzanna interjected, "Ella's my cousin Ben's girlfriend. You know Ben Winters?"

"Hey, for sure. He's a regular customer, too. Cool. Very nice to officially meet you." He stuck out his right hand.

Ella felt her face heat up as she shook hands with him. It was refreshing to have a normal encounter with someone from the Cove. "Guess we got ourselves a job," she quipped, turning to Grace. "Want to find a quiet corner to come up with a plan?"

"Sounds good. Thanks, Sam and Zanna. Maybe see you later."

As Ella started to follow Grace, Suzanna said, "Ella? I meant to call you yesterday morning, but I was helping Mom get ready for her trip back to Bangor and things got a bit hectic here with checkouts and so on."

Ella tensed, although Suzanna didn't seem upset and was hardly going to make a scene.

"I wanted to tell you that I admired your speaking up Friday night."

"I'm sorry you and your mother had to hear all that, Suzanna."

"She was okay, Ella. We had a long talk about what you said when we got back to the hotel. There are many sides to what happened that weekend. It's good that some of them are beginning to emerge." She paused and added, "I hope to see you around in the days ahead."

Ella barely managed a "Thanks" over the lump in her throat. An elderly couple took Suzanna aside in conversation then, and Ella went in search of Grace. She soon found her sitting at a table with about half a dozen men and women of varying ages. As Grace breezed through introductions, Ella caught the reference to her as "my friend." In spite of all that had happened between them, they *were* still friends, and the realization filled Ella with new hope. Perhaps it wasn't too late to mend things with Ben.

One of the volunteers dug out a piece of

paper and a pen and they quickly allotted sections of the town. An older couple stated they were from the *new town*, referring to the subdivision near the highway. Ella liked the term. It was a good way to bridge the gap between newcomer and old-timer.

As the group dispersed, the couple approached her and the man said, “We appreciated your piece in the *Portland Press*. Those of us in the subdivision need to hear that not everyone is against us. Some of us plan to write or email the town council supporting that new proposal the young fella from Winters Building pitched at the meeting a few days ago.”

Ella was amused at the reference to Ben as a *young fella*. She caught Grace’s eye and winked. “Thanks so much. I’m sure Mr. Winters will be pleased.”

The group split up, with Grace and Ella opting to canvass the area beyond the marina in Henry’s neighborhood. As they left the hotel, Grace sighed. “I was hoping to work inside.”

“This is where we’re needed, I guess.”

“You *guess*? It was your idea!”

Ella realized Grace’s wide-eyed reproach

was in jest and smiled. "Well, the exercise will be good."

"Too true, especially after that pancake breakfast. By the way, I heard some of what that couple from the subdivision said. I think that's how most people will feel, even here in—"

"Old town?"

Grace smiled. "Yeah. It was interesting to hear them call themselves *new town* up there."

"That's a good thing, isn't it? For the future of the Cove?"

"It sure is. And what you wrote has obviously kept the momentum from the council meeting going." She patted Ella's arm. "Thanks for that."

After the last two days, this is exactly what I needed to hear, Ella thought. She wrapped her arms around Grace in a tight hug and, when they drew apart, said, "Ben will be happy to hear what they said."

"Maybe not so pleased at the *young fella* part, which I plan to pass on to him."

Their laughter took Ella back to the days when she and Grace had giggled and joked constantly, teasing one another but knowing at the same time their friendship was unbreakable. *Until that summer.* Yet broken didn't mean a friendship couldn't be mended. The last couple weeks were proof of that. She had the chance to repair what she and Ben once had—if she could forgive him keeping secret what he'd done back then.

When they reached the end of the marina boardwalk, Grace suggested they start at the farthest end of the road and work back toward town.

"Are many people living at that end of the beach area?"

"A few seniors and some others who might not be able to get to the hotel or Town Hall."

The depth of the snow forced them to use the middle of the road. As they neared the beach, the lighthouse was barely visible through the haze of fine snow blown up by the wind off the water. As treacherous as the area below the lighthouse was at high tide, Ella bet it was deadly in winter. She shivered and was about to suggest they turn around to knock on doors when she noticed a car idling in the middle of the road ahead. She motioned to Grace and they plodded toward it, walking in its tire tracks. As they got closer, Grace grabbed her arm, gesturing to the left, and Ella saw that the car was parked right in front of the Fielding place.

She made for the car door, tapping on the fogged-up window, which silently rolled down. The woman sitting behind the steering wheel, cell phone in hand, gaped at them.

"Hi, Cassie," Ella said. Grace came up beside her, breathing hard.

The car's engine switched off, and Cassie Fielding climbed out. Ella's first impression was that Cassie hadn't changed much. There was the same thick red hair, fashionably trimmed now, and the same scatter of freckles across her cheeks, although they were paler. She'd always been a bit shorter than Ella and taller than Grace, and Ella suddenly thought how ironically their heights reflected their status with one another that summer years ago—Cassie wedged between her and Grace.

"It's been a while," she said, straightening out her winter coat.

Cassie Fielding was the last person Ella had expected to encounter in the Cove, especially in a snowstorm, though she found it slightly fitting that the instigator of the summer prank ending in Brandon's drowning should blow into town this way. She couldn't think of a thing to say at first, and Grace was unusually speechless, too.

"Have you just arrived or...?"

"Got here yesterday, before the storm hit, thank heavens. Though I'm not sure of my chances leaving." She peered up at the sky.

How odd to lapse into small talk after all these years, after everything that had happened. Ella had sometimes imagined this very scene, coming unexpectedly upon Cassie Fielding somewhere, and even pictured what they might say to one another. Now here was her chance, but for some reason, she was as tongue-tied as Grace. But not for long.

"I heard your mother passed away. I'm sorry," Grace said.

Cassie stared down at her boots, then raised her head and said, "Thanks. That's partly why I'm here. Had to collect some stuff from the house. It's been sold, so no more reason to come back this way."

"Where are you living now, Cass?" Ella asked.

"Near Bar Harbor."

"Has it been you leaving the flowers up

there?" Grace suddenly asked, tilting her chin toward the lighthouse.

Ella stiffened, remembering the frozen roses she'd seen a few days ago. Brought by Cassie?

"You saw them, I guess."

"Last summer, when I was helping Henry at the lighthouse."

"You've been leaving flowers up there? For *Brandon*?" Ella's voice pitched higher as she put it all together.

"Mom was in a nursing home in Portland for the last few years, and I visited her once a month or so. When she started to decline last spring, I went every couple of weeks, depending on my work schedule."

"So you would stop here on your way with flowers," Ella said.

"Most of the time. Not always. And yes, they were for Brandon." Her voice trailed off and she looked away for a second. "I read about the memorial you're establishing up there for him. In *The Beacon*. I keep a subscription to find out what's going on in town. Just out of curiosity, not from any desire to come back here."

That was a small glimpse of the old Cassie—

on the defensive when she didn't need to be. Yet now Ella saw something beneath Cassie's seemingly dismissive personality that she'd missed as a teenager. Maybe a lack of self-confidence that Cassie might have worked hard at concealing.

"I'm sorry, though, that you were blamed all these years," she unexpectedly murmured, looking directly at Ella. "I wouldn't have wished that on you, despite my jealousy over you and Ben that summer." Her mouth twisted. "I'm guessing everything worked out for you and Grace anyway. Maybe with Ben, too. I saw him on my way to Portland. From up there." She gestured to the dunes behind them.

The three women stared at one another until Cassie mumbled, "Guess I should head out. I just saw on my phone that part of the highway is open." She placed her hand on the car door.

"Wait! Tell us how you've been and what you're doing. We could…we could talk a bit more."

"I really ought to go, but thanks for asking, Grace."

"Are you sure? The hotel here is open," Ella suggested.

Cassie smiled. “Always liked that place. I appreciate that both of you are asking me to stay longer, considering the damage I brought you. Not that I’ve kept track of either of you, but from the way life turned out for me after—at school and even when I went to college—I’m thinking your lives must have been affected, as well. Am I right?”

Ella nodded and heard Grace murmur a faint “Yes.”

“What I thought. I’m sorry about that. It was all my fault and I never said a word when I could have. I wish I had, but—”

“I didn’t speak up when I should have either, Cassie. You weren’t alone in that.”

“You always were sweet, Grace. I’m sorry I pulled you into it.”

“Let’s stop blaming ourselves and each other,” Ella cried. “I was jealous of the connection between you two, your high school friendship that was a new thing for me that summer. Grace was ticked off because Ben was getting more of my attention than she was. As for Ben, he was the attraction for both of us, wasn’t he, Cassie? All three of us were on this roller coaster of insecurity that we couldn’t have controlled even if we’d wanted. Until everything crashed that Labor Day weekend." She took a deep breath, adding in a calmer voice, "We were teenagers with adolescent behaviors."

"And undeveloped prefrontal cortexes to boot. I'm a social worker, mainly dealing with teenagers," Cassie explained.

Ella heard Grace say, "Oh my," and added, "That's awesome, Cassie."

"Thanks. Took me a while to get there, mind you. Anyway—" she opened the car door "—I really need to leave. If either of you are ever up Bar Harbor way..." She climbed inside and shut the door, then rolled the window down. "And I know I can get in touch with you, Grace, through *The Beacon.* I saw Ben's name on the masthead in this last issue. Also saw your article in the *Press Herald*, Ella. Nice piece. Thanks, you two, for...for this talk. I'm guessing we all needed it." The window rolled up.

Grace and Ella stood back as the car inched forward, then picked up momentum, heading toward Main Street and the road out of town.

"A social worker dealing with teens!"

"Makes sense, though." Ella stared at the car until it disappeared from view.

"How?"

"That's Cassie's way of making up. Atoning. Like you and the memorial."

"And you and your novel."

Ella couldn't help wondering if any of their atonements would ever bring them peace of mind. Yet what could possibly be gained from continually fanning the fires of blame? Suddenly Ben's face from that morning appeared in her mind. Her response to his confession about the note had been to blame him. He'd been a teenager then, too. She took a deep breath. Maybe it was time she fixed things.

"Come on, Grace. We have doors to knock on." She tucked her arm through her friend's as they left the Fielding cottage behind.

CHAPTER TWENTY-ONE

HIS BACK WAS killing him. Ben didn't know how many sidewalks and porches he'd cleared, but he did know his body felt years older. Midafternoon he texted Drew to ask about Henry and to see if Drew wanted to meet him at the hotel to look for Grace and Ella. Maybe they could grab a bite to eat at the soup kitchen they'd been telling some of the snowbound people about, those who could walk to the hotel for food. Drew had texted that Henry was okay, happy to subsist on cheese and crackers until the power returned. It was late afternoon by the time Ben met Drew inside the ballroom of the hotel. They scanned the room for Ella and Grace but found Suzanna instead.

"Haven't seen them for a while. Ella suggested they go through the residential areas to check on people. Seniors or others who may not know the assistance locations."

"Ella said that?"

"Yep, and I bet she and Grace are still canvassing. Some of the volunteers they enlisted have gone home, but not those two. I've seen them coming and going all day, delivering items to people who can't make it to the hotel. A lot of people who managed to get here did so because Grace and Ella told them what we were doing. Some of them had no cell phone connection and were very appreciative of the information. When you see Grace and Ella, pass on my thanks, too, will you?"

"For sure." Ben found Drew talking to someone from the historical society, a man whose name Ben couldn't remember. "Sorry to interrupt," he said with a nod to the man before focusing on Drew. "Zanna says Ella and Grace are out spreading the word about where to get help. I'm going to text Ella and see if she's ready for a break. Maybe we'll go back home for a bit since it's pretty crowded in here."

"Sounds like a plan. Leonard says parts of the highway have opened up but no word yet on utility crews."

Ben immediately wondered if Ella had heard the same news about the highway.

What if she went back to Boston without seeing him? An irrational sense of urgency swept through him until he remembered her car was still at the worksite. This was his chance, and he wasn't going to let a snowstorm ruin it. He turned his back on the two men while he texted her.

Are you and Grace finished yet? Meet up back at the house? Please!!

ELLA'S FATIGUE WAS the good kind—the physical euphoria after a strenuous workout. Her mental state was another matter—a mind in turmoil that needed rest more than her body. She and Grace had traveled more streets in the Cove than she'd known existed, and her head was full of all the smiles, thanks and best wishes heaped upon her throughout the long day. Although they'd split up, they'd kept in touch by text and had seen one another on the trips back and forth to the hotel, collecting things for people. Fortunately, those items were fairly small, like batteries for flashlights, candles, matches and bottled water. Two of the volunteers had brought sleds to ferry bulkier items.

When she got Ben's text, relief seeped through her. The urgency of that last word was oddly touching, as if he seriously needed to see her as soon as possible. Her phone died before she could reply, and Grace was nowhere in sight, so she decided to walk back to the Winters home. Trudging up the snow-covered hill leading to the highway, she heard the rev of an engine behind and moved to the shoulder. Craning her neck around, she waved when she recognized the car.

"Want a lift?" Ben called through the open passenger-side window.

"You bet." She opened the door, letting a blast of icy air into the car and exhaling loudly as she plunked onto the passenger seat. "Good timing!"

He took his foot off the brake and pulled back onto the road. "Do you know where Grace is?"

"She got a text from Drew just before you sent yours and has gone to meet him at the hotel. She thinks he'll probably go back to Portland if the highway's open."

"And what about you?"

"What do you mean?" She hated to play

coy, because she knew exactly what he meant but wanted him to say it.

"I mean, will *you* have to leave?"

"Well, I can't stay forever, can I?" She regretted her tone, but seriously, why didn't he simply ask her to stay, if that's what he was hinting at?

"Why not, Ella? Why *can't* you stay? Here in Lighthouse Cove, with me? I know you haven't had time to accept what I told you this morning, and it's way too early to expect you to forgive me, but I'm hoping you can at least let me know if I have a chance of being forgiven. I…uh…I need that to be able to get through the days ahead." He took a deep breath. "The thing is, I can't lose you again. A life without you will have no meaning at all for me."

Ella looked out the car window, struggling to control herself. The car slowed as he pulled it over to the side of the road again. She heard Ben shift gears and then his soft voice. "Hey, are you crying?"

She knew if she tried to speak, the emotions from the past two weeks would spill out into loud, embarrassing sobs. But she couldn't keep it inside a moment longer.

She had to tell him how she'd treated Brandon that night, laughing in his face and humiliating him. What did her silence say about their chances of being together in an honest, trusting relationship like the one Grace obviously had with Drew?

"This morning you took the brave step of confessing about the note and I let my hurt and anger get control of me, but I also had a secret shame. When I realized Brandon and I had been set up, I was embarrassed and took it out on him. I was mean, even though he'd been duped, too. If I'd been nicer, he might not have run away. We could have had a laugh about the whole thing and our lives would have turned out so differently." She had to stop, overcome with tears.

He pulled her away from the window into an awkward embrace over the car's console. She laid her head against the damp fabric of his down jacket and closed her eyes, her whole body soaking up the warmth of the car, his arms and the low shushing sound he was making, as if she were a baby needing to be rocked to sleep. Ella nestled farther into his arms, ignoring the gear shift digging into her thigh, her mind lulled into a kind of hypnotic state that she wished she could float in forever. But eventually she could no longer ignore the hard metal of the gear shift, and she moved away.

"This morning—no, maybe it was last night—you asked me if I thought it was too late for us. Do you remember?" Ben asked, keeping his eyes on hers.

"Yes," she whispered. She reined in the questions and thoughts that had been racing through her mind since he'd told her what he'd done with the note. She knew she'd been mean to him afterward, but now she could see his admission as courageous. He could have kept quiet about it, and she'd never have known.

"My answer is still no, I don't think it's too late, *but*—"

He stopped, and Ella stiffened at that conditional last word. "I have to pass that question back to you, Ella. After what I told you this morning, do *you* think it's too late for us?"

She pivoted around, reaching for his hand. "No! Oh no, Ben. I...I don't want it to be too late and I'll do whatever needs to be done to make it *not* be too late."

He drew her to him. "I may hold you to that

promise," he whispered, his lips brushing the strands of hair across her ear.

Ella kissed his neck and the underside of his chin until he got the message, lowering his mouth onto hers, and she knew she wanted to be like this—in his arms with his lips on hers—for the rest of her life.

Then the rumble of a stomach echoed in the car, and they broke apart, laughing. "Yours or mine?" she asked.

His grin was the answer. "Can we take a lunch check for the rest of this conversation?"

"Is that a promise?" she teased.

"Definitely." His eyes lingered on hers a moment longer, then he shifted the car into gear and they headed home.

MUCH LATER, AS THEY were finishing lentil soup at the island counter in his mother's kitchen while his parents napped upstairs, Ben watched Ella scrape her spoon around her empty bowl, transfixed by the concentration in her face and the way she ran her tongue along her lower lip after every lick of the spoon. He recalled the night they'd sipped hot chocolate down by the harbor her first weekend back in Lighthouse Cove and the way she'd enjoyed it, uninhibited by him sitting next to her.

This Ella Jacobs was a contradiction in many ways, he now realized, and far more complex than the sixteen-year-old girl he'd fallen for that summer. She could be coolly aloof, her emotions tightly held in check until a simple word or gesture shattered the icy calm, exposing the vulnerable woman inside. That was the woman he wanted to shelter, but at the same time, he knew Ella could stand very well on her own. She didn't need his protection.

But Ben also knew in his heart that his desire to keep her from harm was linked to the past and what they'd both experienced. She'd been brave to expose her pain from that summer, and he'd been hiding his own behavior. All through lunch, he'd been thinking about that and wondering what he could do to compensate. An idea didn't actually take shape until after she set her spoon down and said, "Grace and I met Cassie Fielding today, near her old house."

The comment, delivered in such a matter-of-fact tone, left him speechless.

"I'll tell you the whole story later," she

went on, "but I think she's suffered as much as Grace and I have. Maybe more. I realized after talking to her that her suffering wasn't caused so much by whispers and innuendo, because she's been away from here. It was caused by guilt and shame. Maybe even by the choices she made later, too. All of us have made some questionable choices since then, haven't we?"

He nodded in spite of the small stab of regret that the talk was turning serious. He'd been hoping for a return to that moment in the car when his lips had been on hers.

"I can't speak for you or Grace," Ella said, "but I think I can live with my choices, knowing—"

"Knowing what?" he asked, every nerve in his body on full alert. When she glanced quickly away, as if afraid to continue, he said, "What *I* know is that I'll do whatever it takes to convince you to stay."

"Here in the Cove?"

He saw the apprehension in her face. "I know it'll be a challenge, but you've got my whole family on your side now, and I'll be with you. *Always.* Like the title of your book."

Her laugh filled the kitchen and his anxiety

eased enough for him to add, "I have a feeling in a very short time you'll be a townie, like the rest of us."

"You mean I won't always be *summer people*?"

"Nope. Never again."

"My job—"

"You can have a job here if you want one." The offer was impulsive, but he liked the idea at once. "My friend Paul, who's part owner with me at *The Beacon,* wants a year off to travel with his wife. I'll be looking for a temporary manager-editor. Someone with established newspaper experience."

"Wouldn't that be a conflict of interest?" She arched an eyebrow.

He pretended to seriously mull over her question. "Not if we set up a ground rule or two."

"Such as?" She was grinning now.

"What happens at the paper stays at the paper and what happens at home—"

"Stays at home. I think I can live with that."

It was all coming together now. A way for her to be in the Cove and hopefully not have to put up with the stress of being misjudged.

Another, more important thought took shape.

"There's something else. A challenge, if you're willing to take it on." She looked so serious he rushed on, "Why not tell your story to the town? I mean, I know Grace plans to let her circle of friends in on what happened to you, but the community that judged you then and now needs to hear the truth—from you." The sudden flash of interest in her eyes told him he was on the right track. "I think your first task as managing editor of *The Beacon* should be an editorial on community loyalty and solidarity—focusing on how those very values failed a sixteen-year-old girl one summer. Write your story for the Cove to read."

She didn't speak for such a long time he began to have second thoughts about the idea. Then she said, "I'd like that, Ben. Very much. It would give me hope about staying here with you and feeling like a part of the town. A real part, as a resident."

He reached across the counter to clasp her hand. "I love you. I have always loved you and I will always love you."

"I love you, Ben."

When he trusted himself to speak, he asked, "Then I suppose you'll agree to spending the night here, at home with us? And will you come for Christmas? I can round up some borrowed furniture for my place."

That brought a smile. "I'm all yours, Ben. Always have been and always will be."

He stood up and rounded the counter to pull her into his arms. "That's what I've been waiting to hear," he whispered as he kissed her.

THE TOWN SQUARE Christmas tree wasn't as pretty as it had been a couple weeks ago. The crane was back and workmen were restringing the tree with lights. Other than losing lights, some decorations and a few broken branches from the weight of the snow, the tree had managed to withstand the brunt of the storm. Ben watched them for a few minutes after leaving Town Hall from his meeting with the mayor and a few councilors.

Hard to believe that four days ago the square was hidden beneath a massive blanket of snow, and even more incredible that less than two weeks ago, he and Ella had stood here as the tree was officially lit. Ben was beginning to understand what his parents meant when they lamented the rapid passage of time. Except in his case, the sense of fleeting time wasn't due to aging—though he did feel years older—but to the turmoil and upheaval of the last fourteen or so days.

But he wasn't about to waste the day before Christmas ruminating about all that had occurred since Ella's return to Lighthouse Cove. Finding out his condo project had been given the green light from town council was a big step toward healing from all the recent "bad vibes," as Gracie would say.

Yesterday he'd met with Harold and the execs from Harbor Lights Supply. As Ben had guessed, neither company wanted the publicity or hassle of laying criminal charges against their employees. Their lawyers assured them a resolution of dismissal without references was not uncommon in the corporate world. The losses had proven to be relatively minor but obviously could have mounted if not for Glen's scrutiny and, especially, that of the Harbor Lights temp employee, who most likely now had a permanent position.

When he opened the front door of his family home, he was immediately assailed by the familiar aromas of childhood Christmases: the sharp tang of pine from the Christmas tree and branches on the stairway banisters, and the heady smells of his mother's baking—shortbread, he hoped, his mouth watering. He hung up his coat, removed his boots and paused in the entryway, sniffing a spicier fragrance. Hints of cinnamon, clove and nutmeg led him into the kitchen, where he found Ella hovering over a steaming pot. She swung round, her face flushed from the kitchen's heat, her smile the best part of an already magnificent day.

"Is that what I think it is?" He pointed to the pot on the burner behind her. "Plum pudding?"

Dropping the pot holder in her hand, Ella moved into his arms. "It is. I was just checking the water level in the bottom section of the steamer. How did the meeting go?"

"It's a done deal." He grinned, wrapping his arms around her.

"Oh, Ben, that's wonderful. You must be so happy. Congratulations!"

"Well, still awaiting confirmation from Portland National Bank for the loan, but I think that'll be a yes, too."

She tightened her hold on him. "Yay!"

"Good news?"

Ben turned to see his mother in the kitchen doorway. “The condo project is a go.”

“Wonderful! Go tell your father. He’s been on tenterhooks all morning. I need to take the shortbread out of the oven, and then Ella is making lunch for us.” She smiled at Ella.

“She is?” Ben grinned as Ella slipped out of his arms and headed for the island counter, where he suddenly noticed an array of vegetables and seafood.

“Don’t get too excited. It’s my first attempt at a Nakamura recipe. From The Daily Catch cookbook you gave me,” she prompted at his puzzled expression. “I brought it back from Boston.”

“Seafood chowder?” His stomach rumbled.

“Yep. Evelyn had a stock of frozen clams and shrimp in the freezer.”

“Butter biscuits, too?”

Both women laughed at the excitement in his voice.

“That’s your mother’s territory, though I’m hoping she’ll share the recipe,” Ella teased, smiling at Evelyn.

Ben didn’t know when or how this new relationship between his mother and Ella had blossomed, but over the past few days since the storm, he'd felt the tension easing. There was some hesitation at physical contact, he'd noticed. Their hugs were quick but warm, and smiles were frequent. The changes weren't only between the two women but with his whole family. He'd also seen more evidence of the teenage Ella he'd fallen for as she began to shed the layers she'd been building up around herself for years. She was beginning to trust others, accepting comments or remarks at face value rather than searching for hidden meanings. It was as if that storm had blown right through the Winters home, shaking loose all its secrets and buried pain.

"Please don't make me have to say whose biscuits are better," he pleaded teasingly.

Evelyn smiled. "I'd never ask that of you, Ben, because I know Ella's biscuits will be made from the heart and only for you."

"Aw," Ben teased, giving his mother a quick hug before folding Ella into his arms. Seconds later he was being shooed from the kitchen.

"We have work to do, Ben," Ella protested.

"Okay, okay. I have to see Dad anyway." Ben followed the blare of the television toward the den, still in disbelief at how much had changed in such a short time.

Ella had taken him up on his suggestion to write her story for *The Beacon*'s special Christmas edition, which had been published yesterday. She'd also submitted it to her own paper—her last op-ed piece. Ben had liked it, finding it balanced and without reproach or finger-pointing. She'd struck exactly the right tone, focusing on the importance of a community working together in challenging situations, like the debate over the new development, the aftermath of the storm and, especially, the response to a tragedy striking one of its children. Rather than revealing the true perpetrators of the trick that led to Brandon's death, she'd talked about the pitfalls of making baseless assumptions and how a person's life can be affected by a community's failure to listen and learn before judging. All good lessons, Ben knew. The family had not only accepted her need to write the story but also admired her for doing so.

As for himself? Was she trusting him more now, too? All he knew was that they were inching their way toward trust and forgiveness. It was a start, and he had high hopes.

He hesitated at the door to the den, bracing himself for the TV's volume, then went in to tell his father the good news about the council approval.

LONG AFTER THE chowder was enjoyed and the kitchen readied for Evelyn's traditional Christmas Eve fondue supper, Ben drove Ella to the bookstore. She'd promised to give Grace a break for what was turning out to be one of her busiest days of the year, and Ben was heading to Henry's to help him pack and get moved to the Winterses for the next two days.

No one should be alone at Christmas, Evelyn had insisted.

Ben had caught Ella's eye and given her an encouraging smile. She'd phoned her mother from Boston and emailed holiday greetings to her brother and his family, who were on a cruise. He knew she envied his family's togetherness, but she didn't fully understand the emotional journey all of them had traveled to get there. He kept telling her it took time and persistence to hurdle the misunderstandings and the hurts families sometimes suffered, but love was in that mix, too.

You can't overcome pain or bad memories if you don't love or feel loved. That was his personal mantra these days. He refused to give up on gaining back Ella's unconditional trust.

ELLA HAD NEVER been to a Christmas Eve candlelight service. She'd expected real candles, not plastic LED tea lights at the bottom of gaily decorated glass jam jars. Otherwise she'd had no preconceived ideas, other than people would gather in worship. The church near Town Square was full, with latecomers standing at the rear. The ends of each row of pews were festooned with large red bows and stands of poinsettia plants flanked the altar.

The choir paraded into the aisles of seats on either side of the altar, and everyone stood as the reverend began to pray. When he finished, the congregation sat while the choir sang "O Holy Night," and Ella teared up at her childhood memory of that beautiful carol. Ben nudged her partway through the hymn when Grace left the choir and walked to the mic. She had a lovely voice, something Ella had forgotten, and had been asked to sing a solo verse.

Ella suspected the invitation to sing wasn't only because of her voice. She thought the request could be a sign that the community had forgiven Grace, whose role in the tragedy that had struck the town years ago had gradually spread. Ella guessed Grace herself was responsible for that, because Ella's column in *The Beacon* had just been published and she'd been discreet about names. She'd decided to center the piece on the importance of standing together, even in troubled times, of grasping all the facts before judging.

While Grace was singing, Ella glanced at Drew across the aisle and saw the gleam of pride and love in his eyes. They were flying to Iowa the day after Christmas to meet his family. Ella envied her friend the chance to be with people who knew nothing—and would never need to know—about what had happened in Lighthouse Cove years ago. She worried a bit about her future here, in spite of publishing her story. There would always be people who'd remain skeptical, but she vowed not to let those people govern her anymore.

Last night Ben had asked her to marry him and spend the rest of her life in the Cove. His proposal made her happier than she'd been in years, but she'd had moments of doubt. Sure, many people in town had thanked her for helping after the storm, but appreciation and acceptance were very different things. Ben's parents had been nothing but kind to her and Ella guessed they'd be happy about the engagement when she and Ben told them.

Ella and Evelyn were more comfortable in each other's company, even able to tease and joke with one another, but it was Ben's father who had been the surprise. Ella discovered she and Charles shared an interest in watching the news on TV, and they enjoyed debating the merits or weaknesses of the various pundits analyzing current politics. Their discussions were sometimes heated but always ended with a laugh and sometimes even a pat on the hand—this from a man she knew had seldom been physically demonstrative to his own children.

As the chorus of the last Christmas hymn ended and a loud "Amen" resonated in the church, Ella was filled with the hope that her welcome into the Winters family—and in the Cove—would continue to grow every day.

The congregation began to disperse, many

people filing down to the basement hall for treats brought by the congregation and hot beverages provided by Mabel's. She was separated from Ben on the way and couldn't see him as she entered the large hall. At the far end, she spotted Evelyn and a couple other women setting out baked goods onto plastic platters, and Ella wound through the crowd to help. On the way, a hand emerged from the crowd to clasp her shoulder. She spun around.

"Ella!" It was Suzanna with Sam. "I was hoping to bump into you. I wanted to talk to you before we see each other at dinner tomorrow."

The last time Ella had spoken to Suzanna was at the hotel days ago, when she and Grace were volunteering after the storm. Despite the woman's gradual warming to her, Ella's uncertainty about Ben's cousin persisted. She was Brandon's sister, a hard fact that would always exist between them. Suzanna knew the truth, but was she still questioning it?

"I need to tell you something," Suzanna clarified as she pulled Ella aside.

Ella braced herself.

Suzanna leaned closer, speaking in Ella's ear over the noise. "I read your piece in *The*

Beacon yesterday and I admired it very much. Your honesty about blaming without having facts was right on. There's been too much speculating and not enough soul-searching in this town, and not only about what happened to my brother. Some of that denial, even after learning the truth, has come from me, and I'm sorry for that. I respect what it must have taken you to publicly talk about what you endured. That took guts."

Ella was speechless.

"Merry Christmas, and see you tomorrow," Suzanna cried as the crowd drifted between them.

By the time she reached Evelyn, most of the baked goods had been laid out. "Sorry," Ella said. "The crowd—"

"No need to explain." She stretched to see over the people milling around the table. "Have you seen Ben?"

"Nope, lost him. But I'm sure he'll show up for one of your shortbreads." She eyed the platter closest to her. "Did you bring them all?"

"Heavens no! Charles and Henry would have a fit."

Ella laughed with her. The two men had opted to have a quieter evening at home.

"When you find Ben, can you tell him I'm going home with Grace and Drew now? I know they'd planned to give you two a ride as well, but I'm tired and tomorrow will be a long day."

"Of course." Ella patted her hand. "Are you feeling okay?" She knew Evelyn's rheumatoid arthritis sometimes flared up when she was fatigued or stressed.

"I'm fine, but if I'm in bed when you and Ben get home, Merry Christmas!" She stretched up to kiss Ella's cheek. "And thank you for forgiving my family and, most of all, for making Ben so happy." Then she reached for her coat on a chair behind her. "I'm meeting Grace and Drew at the front door. Good night, dear."

Ella watched the small woman negotiate the crowd, pausing now and then for a quick greeting. Evelyn would be a good mother-in-law, she decided. She picked up a couple cookies and worked her way around the tables and chairs set up for the older members of the congregation, searching for Ben.

On her way, one white-haired woman sitting with three other seniors stopped her. "I think you must be Ella Jacobs, am I right?"

The woman was smiling, so Ella's tension ebbed momentarily until she went on to say, "I still remember all of that sadness from years ago. Many people here, myself included, misjudged you at the time. I'm sorry for that. But I'm happy the Winters family has welcomed you back. We do, too. Welcome back to the Cove." She and her friends beamed at Ella.

Ella nodded through the sudden blur of tears and headed back into the crowd. She needed fresh air and Ben's comforting arms. A few minutes later she found Ben at the top of the stairs talking to a young couple with a toddler and a baby. Ben's smile enveloped her, vanquishing every person in the room.

"Ella, I'd like you to meet Glen Kowalski and his wife, Maggie. And this is Mary and her baby sister, Angie." His big smile shone on the baby in particular.

Ella was struck by the revelation that Ben might like children, even tiny ones. Having children with him hadn't been even a thought in their new relationship, much less a discussion point. Yet as she studied him beaming at the infant, she saw for the first time a future father in Ben Winters. The four of them chatted a few seconds longer until the baby began to fuss, and the family made a hasty retreat. "Glen is one of my employees," Ben explained as he helped Ella with her coat. "An important and trusted one."

His tone caught her attention. Although he hadn't told her the full story of the situation at work—a fraud scheme—Ella knew Glen and another employee had supported Ben in the challenging aftermath of the discovery.

"Your mother asked me to tell you she's gone home with Grace and Drew."

"Oh? Weren't we supposed to go with them, too?"

"She's tired and didn't want to wait."

"I guess she has a lot to do tomorrow, and despite the help from the rest of us, she'll want to—"

"Supervise."

He laughed. "You've already got Mom figured out. That bodes well for the future." He held the church door open for some people to pass, then placed his hand at the small of her back as they followed. "I don't mind a slow walk home, do you?"

"Not at all." She buttoned up her red cashmere coat and, reaching for his hand, thought about what he'd just said about the future. Days ago, she'd had mixed feelings about one with Ben. Her worries weren't about Ben—she knew he was the man she wanted to spend the rest of her life with. But the dilemma about living in the Cove for perhaps the rest of her life had been chipping away at her peace of mind. Now, after those words from Suzanna plus some from a complete stranger, she felt confident she could find a peaceful, contented life there after all.

When they reached the top of the street leading down to the harbor, Ben exclaimed, "Look!" The Christmas lights had been rehung after the storm, and their multicolored rainbows arced across the black water in the marina and beyond to Casco Bay. Except for occasional ribbons of smoke drifting from the chimneys of the homes below, the night sky was clear and starlit.

"Beautiful, isn't it?"

Ben's voice was as soft as the sea breeze and for a split second, Ella heard the voice she recalled from that summer when a future with Ben Winters was still an unbroken dream.

She snuggled against him. *You can do this, Ella Mae Jacobs, with him right here like this. Forever.*

* * * * *